A CHRISTMAS CARCASSING

by Corwyn Matthew

FOREWORD

Good tidings, my dudes! First off, thanks for snatching up the book! I had loads of fun concocting this morbid mishap of a story and am stoked to get to share it with anyone bored enough to dive in. I really feel like this is a good niche for me and am hoping to get to write more of the same, but it *is* a bit of an anomaly (as is its creator). The prose is a strange mix between contemporary "dudisms" and literary artistry that makes the market for a target audience pretty much none-existent... But I have faith! I have faith that not all stoners are too brain-drained to follow along, and not all fans of well-crafted literature are too uptight to let their hair down a little. So feel free to enjoy the *shit* out of this comedic horror and prove me right. And if you're lucky, there may be a few extra pages loitering at the end of the book you could roll up in a crunch. I'm looking out for you dudes, bro! Fuck yeah!

-CM

CHRISTMAS EVE

Crimson stalactites of frosted what-the-twisted-fuck-is-*happening-right-now* chillingly maturated from the corners of the truck-bed's gate like demonic slushie fingers bent on being noticeably villainous. One tail light busted, the two thoroughly baked teens in the truck's cab were lucky to be navigating Winterset, Iowa's version of the river Styx on a dreadfully snowy night that harbored the dreary and barren air of the planetoid Pluto in a K hole. Not a creature was stirring…other than *these* two hungover hamburglers, carting around several near-frozen carcasses five hours before midnight.

The delicate flakes of a white Christmas swirled in their pickup's wake. They'd coursed this path before. Maneuvering the bumpy backroad with close to pitch-black looming at their periphery was becoming old hat. Hardly a word was exchanged between them on the drive.

Four boots crunched against the frozen, wet annoyance at their feet before two heavy doors slammed shut, both sets of galoshes aiming their clumsy paths toward the truck's gate. One screeching of angry old hinges later – like the howling of a sickly, injured beast – and two hands reached to heave while one mouth hooted—

"Ho…ho…*ho*… Waitaminute…"

Marvin, the taller of the two youths, angling for the bit of the tarp that burritoed a sizeable head, paused, discernibly numb to the moment. He was the darker of the two teens. Where Shawn could compare the shade of his melanin to that of Ice Cube's, Marvin would more closely blend in to a scene with Chris Tucker. *Either*, consequently, could match bowls in a bong-off with Smokey and Craig despite being just short of legal age. In their senior year at Benjamin Bakem High, at this point in the semester they both wondered if they'd ever get the chance to throw up the "deuces" at their graduation and doobie the fuck on out; blunts tucked under beanies, boastfully rebellious stroll carrying them off the podium…

"What?" Slightly sticky with stupor from the hold up, Marvin's bloodshot eyes told the tale of a young man who'd been heavily over-medicated.

"*You* get the legs, man. I got the legs the last time." Shawn, just as spent in the tanked-bank as his best dude, hung slothfully in the moment, waiting for their mutual agreement. Facial hair like lint on his chin, if the town were to put it to a vote it's likely they'd motion for him to just shave it all off and stop pretending his scruff was dignified.

"The fuck difference does it make?" The afore-described "sticky with stupor" escalated to a gooey, mystified squint.

"The legs is heavier. Dude's got big ass feet – fucking boots on an' shit."

"You seen this fucker's belly? All the weight's in the *middle*, bruh." Marvin found the strength to fail at a gesture toward the cadaver-burrito's bottom half. "Dude's short, anyways – legs are like…I dunno… Fuckin' corndogs or some shit."

"Fuck, man… Just get the legs, a'ight? Damn… We in this shit *together*."

A sigh moved Marvin's light green, alien-beanied forehead to meet the tarped torso before he discovered more of that strength he waisted gesturing and used it to lift his chin and nod. "A'ight, man, chill… Here, get on this side."

Boots depressed snow, positions exchanged, and Shawn grabbed just enough head to *lose* his half the minute the weight slid over the other two tarped bodies and off the pickup.

A *thump* preceded Marvin's drowsy concern.

"Dude…f'real?"

Shawn attempted to recover his fumble but found his ass in the snow sooner than he found redemption.

Marvin's shoulders slumped; beanied, alien antennae appropriately lackluster over his skullie. It was one of those uber hip, pop-culture snow caps that looked like no male over the age of four should own but somehow found their way into men's sizes. Reflective, elliptical alien eyes adorning his forehead with two moveable antennae, green-balled tips, braided green rope dangling shoulder-length from the earflaps…

"Hurry, man, shit…"

Battling gravity and his weather-weary gear, Shawn made his way to his feet and found a stable grip under the twine that kept the tarp closed. He lifted at the neck – six inches shorter than Marvin in eight inches of snow – just barely getting the cadaver's caboose up high enough to lug it toward its unlikely place of final respite, several miles into the woods and an hour north of the mall where the trio had first been acquainted. The path they tromped was another familiar one, blood and what was likely a small intestine dripping from the center of the tarp. By the time they made it to their destination – a quarry they figured would soon fill with snow – seventeen feet of some sad sap's colon lazily laid behind.

"On three."

Shawn nodded, and the sendoff proceeded as planned. Three counts and a release sent a two hundred and thirty-five-pound body over a steep ravine with serpent-like sinew whipping behind. Shawn's fingers had loosened the twine around the tarp so that it unraveled in its fall, unveiling the barely-hanging-together carcass under it in jolly red velvet with white trim. The bloody and matted flag of a once proud, long white beard waved in the gully's wind…until the elastic keeping it attached slipped from his head along with his Christmas hat and fluttered the rest of the way down. The body splattered into several pieces when it landed and joined the unthinkable carnival of gore that presided there before it.

Seven other jolly dead sons of the Happiest Time of Year already decorated the snowy floor, spread in fragments over a hundred feet; bits of red and green fabric and pink flesh scattered about like yuletide sprinkles over vanilla frosting.

"C'mon, man…"

Marvin led the way back for the next two flavors to add to their very troubled snowy desert while Shawn dragged behind. Santa's little helpers were easily half the big man's size, so they grabbed a tarped-elf apiece and proceeded to top off their evening's burdens after both stumbling to their rumps three or four times, trails left behind as glairing as neon signs reading, "Murder Depository in 100ft". The two elves' tarps came apart like Santa's before them, and if there was ever a greater waste of a sexier pair of candy cane thighs under holiday green skirts, it was not only a crime against Christmas, but against all of mankind.

Afterward, Shawn – brow and ears hidden under his red, black and white Star-Wars-themed Christmas beanie – shuffled back over their path, kicking up snow to hide the trail of death they left behind. But Marvin stayed fixed, manifesting a moment of clarity (or a resemblance of something thereabouts). His eyes cut through the icy winter breeze into the vicinity of an unspoken decree, and there, for the first time in his near-adult life he discovered something most weed-heads thought to be a myth:

Resolve.

His plod back to the passenger side of the truck and into the cab was an assiduous one.

"Grandad Santa."

"Wha?" Shawn was exhausted when he got in the truck: a lump of snot stuck on the seat. Not in any kind of condition for purposive conversation.

"That's who's next. That's where we gotta go."

"Fuck you mean, man? We can't—"

"This shit ain't over, man." He looked to his one and only true friend, eyes never more unfaltering than now. "Not until it's over."

"What... You mean like right now?"

Shawn knew what he meant. An answer wasn't required. Truth be told, as exhausted as he was, he was just as ready as Marvin was for this to be over... He'd just prefer to handle it after a few bong loads and a month-long nap.

He sighed.

The key in the engine turned, the emergency break went the way of the killer whales, wet boot met pedal, warm grill sucked cold snow...

The "day of" was nearly here...and only one man was left in town who was down on his luck enough this season to have agreed to take the velvet reins – and all for a beggarly wage of ten-eighty-five an hour...

Merry-corporate-fucking-Christmas, chump...

But for the sorry son of a bitch known as Grandad Santa, it may be too much to hope for a happy New Year.

DECEMBER 19TH

1:10 PM

Six days before Christmas:

"Yoooo!"

Shawn clutched Marvin's hand with an elaborate slip-of-the-grip to some snap, slap, pop or other that led to a pound. His candy cane Christmas hat with the elf-green puff on top was mesmerizingly festive. Marvin's head-warmer was more classic but tipped with a jingle bell as opposed to a cotton ball.

"Sup, man." He sat down in class next to his main bud-buddy, both a little restless seeing as how it was the last hour of school before Christmas break.

"Drop a deuce or what? You missed the beginning of the flick, man."

"Nah... I was talkin' to Shandra – said she wants to chill later."

"F'real? What, like with us?"

"Nah, nigga... Like, wit' *me*."

Pierced by the prickly needle of selfishness, Shawn groaned, "Aw, *c'mon*, dude. How you ain't gon' look out for yo' boy?" He insistently slapped his chest to be sure Marvin knew to whom he'd been referring.

Marvin reassured him with a grin and a swat from the back of his hand. "I'm just playin', bruh. She gon' bring Yvonne – said they got dabs—"

"*Gentlemen.*" Painfully Texan in his inflections, tall, thin, and decorated in all the silver and leather trimmings allowed a teacher-slash-cowboy during office hours, Mr. Greggerson decided on putting their conversation on pause with a little reminder. "I know break's right

5

around the bend, but yer still stuck with *my* pasty hide fer another hour. And some of us here wanna watch the picture." A few kids laughed. The rangy, fifty-seven-yer-old teacher was one of the more laid back and likeable educators on school grounds. His brimmed cowboy hat was never far from his reach, his mustache like groomed tumbleweed.

Marvin looked around as if to quietly challenge the assumption, wondering who might actually be into some overly wordy, dated comedy about Shakespeare in love, but kept his mouth sealed. Despite the boys' perpetually illegal pastimes, they were generally agreeable teens. Plus, Mr. Greggerson had been considerate enough to hire him over the break at his and his wife's ice cream parlor in the mall. And as far as middle-age MILFs went, Marvin would take a mallet to his PS4 *and* the twenty-six fantasy and horror games he'd amassed for a shot at being at the whims of her slender, pale, late-thirty-something's thighs...

"Sorry, Teach."

He decided on offering a diplomatic apology as opposed to a snarky remark. Greggerson seemed to have accepted his offer but with a side note Marvin almost missed. As the young man's eyes shifted away, the heavily mustached Texan cultivated the beginnings of a sneer that looked like he smelled horse shit on his desk while glimpsing upward at Marvin's headdress. The sneer was so twisted it seemed akin to revolt; malcontent, even. When Marvin's eyes reverted to what he wasn't sure he saw, the regularly good-natured Texan shook his head rapidly and rubbed his nose with a sleeve, fighting off a sneeze.

Attention floating back toward the old flick they'd been assigned to sit through, Shawn snapped a few fingers down low to slyly recapture his friend's notice. He was holding his phone so that Marvin could see the screen displaying a Snapchat image of Shandra and Yvonne; Shandra's tongue laid out like she could melt the North Pole with a single lick, and Yvonne's puckered lips provocatively close to her bestie's nearly visible tonsils. Marvin's eyes lit up while Shawn mouthed the popular exclamation "*daayyuumm*" before a fifty-something's throat cleared intrusively and both boys jumped right into coverup-mode like they'd just got caught with their hands down their pants.

After stowing the mobile and straightening out in their chairs, the remaining period was one laced with romantically adventurous, quiet contemplation over the rhythmic soliloquy of classic Shakespearean dialog. The clock ticked off seconds and minutes while Marvin and Shawn were lucky to not tick off the one man left standing who could set back their winter break an hour.

"Mr. Jones!" The bell had sounded, and Christmas break was in full, wintery effect, but Mr. Greggerson caught Marvin just on his way out. "Five-O-clock sharp, now, ya here?" His "O" was accented excessively, being sure no one could mistake him for anything *but* a southerner. "The misses'll be countin' on ya to be more punctual than you were this afternoon." He winked, hands gripping his belt as if preparing his jeans to mount a steed.

Marvin turned back to address him with Shawn a few steps ahead. "Cool, Teach, I'll be there" —he jingled the tip of his Christmas hat with a flick and caught a twitch in Greggerson's eye— "with...bells on." Chary for an instant, Marvin's gears slowed to a crawl until the professor twitched again and then sneezed a ferocious *ahchew* that threw his somewhat stylish, short hair awry, his glasses landing crooked across the bridge of his nose. "...Gesundheit."

"Much obliged," came a muffled reply under his hand while he reached toward his desk for tissue. "Allergies..."

"Yo, c'mon, man." Shawn swiped at his friend's elbow, prying him away from kissing up to his future source of holiday income. Then he looked back over his shoulder to be sure their teacher was out of earshot, both teens weaving through the hyped-up crowd of Freshly Released who were eager to be out of school. "Bruh...is it me or does Mr. G look jus' like that Lord Jessex cat in that flick?"

"You f'real right now, fool?" A wry smile teased his friend at the comparison to the character in the movie. "You were actually payin' attention to that shit?"

"I'm jus' *sayin'*... Turn back the clock an' slip ol' boy in some frilly lace an' them dudes is fuckin' Bizarro copies of each other, man..."

"*Pshh...*" Marvin chuckled with a shake of his head. "You high, bruh."

"Shit was trippin' me out right now, though... Swear dude was eyeballin' me through the whole flick, too – like tryin'a decide if his cover was blown. ...Bugged-out shit." He shivered.

Marvin took a second to actually look into his friend's eyes. "I take that shit back... You *really* fuckin' high." He pushed a stuttered laugh through his teeth like letting gas out of a tire. The droopy, bloodshot glaze coating his friend's lenses was so thick he was surprised Shawn wasn't outside hiding under a rock somewhere. "Yooo... The fuck you *on*, man?"

Shawn looked up, looked back, checked over both shoulders, then, when the coast was clear, said, "Bud brownie, bruh. *Here...*" Unzipping his backpack, he pulled out a Ziploc baggie with a single chocolate square and enough crumbs to suspect at least three more were recently behind the seal.

"*Damn*, nigga... How many you eat?!"

Shawn examined the bag closely, inspecting the crumbs, mystified by the lumpy clumps of gooey darkness and their almost organic consistency. Marvin gave up on an answer after a few seconds and just swiped the bag to grub on the leftovers. Shawn found his thought process sometime after.

"So, when we hookin' up wit' these *hoes*, man?"

Marvin, enjoying the flavor, chuckled a little at his friend's sudden moment of enthusiastic clarity.

Neither of the two teens were what the kids would call "pimpin' it on the daily". Their vaunting exchanges were mostly in playful jest. Generally, they were more well known for their prominent thumb-eye coordination – high kill-scores and blunt rolling techniques that surpassed...well...no one in particular. If there was an annual award handed out for being especially average, these two would probably smoke and gamer their way into being amongst the runner ups for nominees...

Maybe next year, fellas.

"She said to roll through tonight after I get off. Meet me behind the mall at, like, 9:30. We'll burn one real quick, then dip."

"A'ight." He extended his hand for their personalized departing maneuvers. "Have fun suckin' up to Mrs. Texas tonight. Write her a play or some shit, Shakespeare. White bitches love that shit." He laughed with a pestering posture while Marvin kicked him in the butt of his sagging backpack.

"Fuck out of here, man..." He shook his head while Shawn jogged off. "And don't be late tonight, nigga! You leave me in backa that mall for long you'll be drivin' a black ass *snowman* back to chill wit' them hoes!" He chuckled a little, emptying the crumbs from the bag into his willing maw. "Damn... Thick as fuck. There's like...a pounda *butter* in these fuckin' things."

He had a solid two-and-a-half hours before his first day on the job. He figured it was plenty of time to catch a light high, freshen up for his age-inappropriate lady crush, pound a Monster to get in gear and earn his keep while getting his flirt on with the sexiest white woman in the whole damn—

"Them *what* now, nigga?"

Eyes maneuvering through the obstructions of his tilt-back head and pouring-hand holding the emptied bag, he may've taken a bite out of his own *heart* when it jumped into his throat at the sight of Shandra and Yvonne behind him, just exiting the school; both young, well-curved ladies fashionably festive in skeevy, holiday elf outfits. Short green dresses; candy cane knee-highs; gold buttons and hoops...

"Shit..." Think quick, jackass. They heard you shouting that "hoe" bit. "Damn... You two look lit as *fuck* standing there in them outfits."

"Uh-huh..." Hips cocked, and eyes set to incinerate—

"Seriously, though..." They're not buying it, man, bullshit harder! "I don't even know what to say... Got me all stuck on stupid right now..." He flashed them the classic hungry eyes, hoping to distract them from his untimely, bumbling brownie-hole.

"Yeah, you *stupid*, alright..." Shandra turned her head with her arms crossed.

"An' we ain't no hoes." Yvonne wasn't going to let him off as easy has he'd like. She was the lighter of the two, half Irish with soft freckles across her nose and reddish, crimped hair.

"Nah, girl, you know how guys talk. S'like when you call your girl 'yo' bitch', you know? Or when I call my boy 'my nigga'. Same thing."

"Yeah, yeah... See if *you* get laid tonight."

"Or like, *ever*," Yvonne had to add, and both ladies stomped off with an extra measure of sway in their stride to be sure their departure pained him that much more.

His posture deflated, Santa hat and jingle bell flaccid and sad, crumb-speckled brownie bag hung low. Then a thought occurred, and he perked up to inquire toward their marching posteriors,

"Wait… You sayin' we was gon' bone down?!"
Two middle fingers simultaneously flew up to give him his reply.

An hour turned into two, submersed in the 3D digital RPG world of The Call of Cthulhu for PS4, and Marvin realized his "light high" was a runaway train car going off its tracks and into some dark, unsanctioned tunnel without periphery, steering or breaks…

He got up from the gamer-throne he contrived from pillows on his bedroom/basement floor and reached for the sixteen-ounce can of Monster he was sure would straighten him right out.

Empty.

…the fuck?

He checked the floor and counter top, rubbing surfaces to inspect their texture for moistness and found none.

He didn't spill his drink. He must've drank the damn thing and not noticed…

Conjuring up some urgency, but being too numb and estranged to find panic, he started fumbling through drawers for work appropriate attire, putting a leg into a pair of khakis before even removing the jeans he had on. After a few thrusts he discovered the fulcrum of his struggles and chuckled at the dilemma

"Goddamn, nigga… High as fuck, right now…"

It had been a while since he'd eaten a pot brownie. He'd forgotten they usually take a little longer to fully work their way into your system and hit pretty hard if baked right with potent ingredients – it was a good thing he *always* looked stoned… This shouldn't be too hard to pull off if he stayed on top of his game. It would probably help, he thought, as he looked down at his kicks after conquering the bottom half of his wardrobe, if he were wearing a matching pair of shoes…

He laughed again, kicked off the gray Timberland and slipped on the khaki one to complete the set.

"I'ma need to seriously Monster-up for this shit." He tucked the pink Tasty Creams polo into his pants, slipped on a pink visor with a three-scoop Neapolitan logo embroidered, somehow found his eyeballs with a few drops of red-eye relief, then made his way to his fridge, calling out to his mom for a ride. "Ma! Gotta go! Firs' day on the job!"

Whether he would make it there on time would be left to the whims of the mighty Bud Gods and the punctuality of their chosen consorts—

O Wise Ones be merciful.

"You doin' alright, Marvin?"

Humming yellow-striped walls dripped honey and vanilla extract until the top half of the parlor's decor met the solid bottom portion that wrapped the whole place in a frictionless sheet of icy white.

He could see her breath when she spoke – it smelled like pralines and cream...

The buckets of ice cream flavors he was meant to wrangle into some sort of order were limitless grottos of mysteries with radiating warmth and color, which was strange since their contents were frozen. He'd managed to keep it together in the stock room and follow along with procedure, but as soon as those yellow, dripping walls and sun-bright, ceiling lights saturated his retinas in some sugary reality that was in total contrast to a man of his...*hue*, it was like he was utterly exposed; denuded...laid bare...

Pupils like the dark side of the moon, he tried focusing on Mrs. Greggerson's frosted, rouge lips.

"I, uh..." He found, as he gazed cautiously, she looked about fifteen years younger on his current high. "Jus'...think'm a'lil sick... Stomach's buggin'..."

"Oh, you poor thing..." her hand to his head, she pouted a bit in sympathy. "Yer burnin' up!" Holly Greggerson's accent may've been even thicker than her husband's but sounded immeasurably more charming coming off her tongue. "C'mon, now..." She put an arm around him and walked him into the back to her office. "I'll get ya some water, and if yer up for it, some ice cream. I get the feeling this kinda sick will pass in about twenty or thirty minutes."

He plopped behind her desk and melted into the chair, somehow finding the fortitude to scope out her ass in the heather-gray yoga pants she was wearing under her apron as she turned away.

"Thank-thanks, Mrs...." His murmur of gratitude trailed off as she left the tiny office.

He'd chowed down on bud brownies before... This wilted experience felt more akin to a *shroom* trip – and not an especially clean one... Shawn's older brother had a batch of boomers a few weeks back he was pushing to all the stoner kids. He probably gave the leftover shake to Shawn to add to his brownie batter: Potent, but also unpleasant on the guts. He got a hint of a chuckle from the thought of how hard Shawn would be tripping off the three squares he engulfed earlier. He probably turned as green as a Christmas tree, vomited something that looked like Rudolph flew into a wood chipper, then balled up into a little lump of unbaked chocolate cookie dough, gnawing on his thumb-knuckle and counting the non-existent sleigh bells.

This'll pass, he thought. Cool water, ice cream, white-woman gym-booty... As far as trips at work went, this one wouldn't likely be so bad considering how well the boss-lady seemed to be taking it. He just hoped the daunting dipshit who slipped him the "mickey" would be coherent enough to pick him up later. If he had to catch the last public buss out in that winter chill, shit just might get downright *fugly* between gamer bros the next time they were going head-to-head.

A half-hour gone, three extra-large waters and a double scoop of raspberry vanilla with white chocolate chunks artfully stuffed into a waffle cone, and Marvin was beginning to see the benefits of working under his new management. Nearly as tall as him with wavy brown hair pulled into a working woman's ponytail, she truly was a joy to observe digging into buckets of Tasty Cream flavors for customers with a bright smile and a gleaming row of icy whites. It was remarkable this woman was peddling treats in an ice cream parlor and not posing in some studio where her natural talents could have easily set her up for life... With her level of charm and good looks, she could've married a celebrity or even been one herself – the star of her own story, the Texas princess turned Queen of the Manor.

"Feelin' better, darlin'?"

Eyes lifting from her athletic curves, he wondered how many times she'd already caught them wandering below the surface of the counter tops...

"Yeah...damn..." he drew attention to the last few bites of his waffle cone. "*This* thing jus' changed my life."

She smiled, a little embarrassed by the compliment since she picked it out herself. "It's mah favorite."

"That cherry on top, though... I mean... I'm not jus' sayin' this cuz you my boss now, but... That...was...*insane*... I'm jus' glad you weren't there when I was eatin' it. The noises I was makin' was straight up *raunchy*... I was like...lost in this...this land of cherries and vanilla...and like, when the cherry was gone, it was like there was this moment of deep *depression* for me. I...I'm not afraid to admit I got a lil choked up..."

She lowered her head and laughed as he went on.

"But I jus' kept goin', you know? I knew I had to get through it. Then there were these, like...explosions of...of raspberry in my mouth. Then this smooth, opposing force of white chocolate – like some kinda religious war bein' fought inna vanilla snow..." He shook his head.

"And then what happened?"

He was surprised she seemed into it. He was sure she was just being cool since she knew he was entirely whacked out of his skull but figured he may as well ride this tide all the way ashore and see where it landed it him.

"Then that's when shit got *really* crazy, ok? I'm talkin' buildin's crumblin', the ground breakin' open and swallowin' up both sides – innocents and soldiers alike. Pure, waffle cone *chaos*—"

"Aahaa!" A high-pitched, surprise explosion of laughter burst from her throat.

"No, f'real... It was Armageddon for all. Not even the cold vanilla winter survived."

A bright smile tried to hide under her shaking head. "That's so sad..."

"But from the crunchy chaos, a new kinda peace emerged!" He spread his arms wide. "Like I said: I feel like a new man."

She walked toward him, eyes never leaving his goofy smile, took off her latex gloves and playfully used them to smack him on the shoulder as she passed. "Yer adorable." He turned his head to watch her walk by. "Now let's see how this 'new man' handles his first customers. Next one's yers, honey."

"Yes, ma'am."

A new man, indeed. He never felt better. Hell... He'd never had a woman smile at him like that before. Usually when he'd let loose and start spilling his fantasy gamer, alien freak-boy mind, the teeny-bopper's brains would just shut down with boredom, change the subject and/or call him "weird". Apparently, older women were "where it's at".

The next few customers that came in were a breeze. Most of the people strolling through malls were there to have a pleasant time, especially those looking to get ice cream. Unlike the drama-filled TV shows and movies, generally everyone was pretty patient and were able to pick up on it being his first day with Holly walking him through the register and giving him tips on scooping and how to not crush cones and such. Aside from that detour into Sicksville he took at the start, considering he was working so close to one of his favorite crushes he could feel the heat from her body (among other tips of perky things), this night was quickly turning into one of the best he's had in a very long time. So when Shawn walked in two hours before closing wearing scuba goggles over his beanie with a snorkel and a flashlight, he braced himself for the topple down the mountain of good vibes he'd spent the evening conquering.

Sketched-out and sweaty under heavy extra gear, Shawn's echo of a voice struggled to reach Marvin through the snorkel in his mouth.

"Ooooob!!"

"What?" He could hardly believe what he was looking at. Thick winter coat with a fur-lined hood zipped up to the blue snorkel, he hoped Holly would skip coming out from the back on this particular chime and allow him the opportunity to rid them of this nuisance before things got awkward. "Nigga… Take the damn *snorkel* out yo' mouth!"

As luck would have it, Holly joined the party just in time to partake in the ensuing conversation. Marvin internally cursed his *ex*-best friend's healthiest vital organs.

Hesitating to remove his protective breathing apparatus, Shawn eventually took the risk for the greater benefit of clear communication, unplugged his mouth piece and said, "Doooood—"

"What, man?" Flustered, Marvin partly feared what brand of Silly Shit might unintentionally spill from his tripped-out friend's yap.

Holly could hardly tell what to make of him before Shawn went on.

"…I…" He swallowed hard. "…I barely even made it here alive!" His pupils were two vats of motionless oil; mouth wide and starving for ears of sympathy…

Marvin was so taken by the intensity sewn into every fiber of Shawn's character it reignited his own high to the point where he couldn't contain himself. After several frozen moments of utter disbelief, he exploded with a "BAAAHAHAHAHAHA!!" that entirely melted Shawn's world. The poor kid went from looking like he'd just made it safe ashore to like he'd been tricked into stepping foot onto the surface of Hell, and as soon as Holly's shrill, gleeful laugh followed suit, Shawn took off sprinting out the door for the safety of mall elevator-music and the open space of the distant food court.

"Holy jumpin' *Jesus*, you two're sumthin' else!" She wiped tears of jubilant hysteria from her eyes while Marvin tried catching his breath.

"Oh, god..." Head thrown back, he let out an exhausted sigh of amusement. "That was too much... F'real... We ain't usually this much of a hot mess."

"Don't fuss, hun." Another light touch across his shoulder and the butterflies fluttered in droves. "Clint said y'all're good kids and I can see ya are. I was a teen once too, ya know." She turned back to look into her reflection over the sink, checking her eyes. "Winter break comes 'round an' all bets're off, I know." He tried not to watch and went to the opposite sink instead to rinse off a perfectly clean scooper. "Look, as long as you show up an' help out, we won't have any problems. I'm having a lot of fun tonight. I don't see any reason why you kids can't stick around."

He was probably blushing... Good thing that sort of flushed response couldn't get past the badassedness off his tinted pigment.

"Wow... You are...like...*seriously*...the coolest chick I ever met..." He wondered if she caught his eyes shifting in hesitation after hoping it wasn't inappropriate to call her a "chick" but knew enough, at least, to do his best to feign confidence in his words.

"Marvin, my man... I'd be lyin' if I said you weren't the coolest teen I'd ever met."

"F'real?"

"God's honest." She smiled.

"Wait... How many teens you met? Am I like, the third one or what?"

A little laugh preceded a playful punch to his shoulder as she headed back to her office.

"Aw, c'mon... The fifth? Ya gotta give me a number..." With two arms up to his sides, he offered, "Is it less than ten?"

"Hey, hey, *heyyyy*… Lookit who it is!" Mr. Greggerson showed up right at closing time as Marvin and Holly were locking up, mustached-smile wide with a palm coming in for a fatherly pat on the arm. "How'd the kid do on his first day, sugar? Did he set the ice cream on fire?"

Marvin tried to smile, a little disappointed to have to share his crush with her man so soon. He hoped him showing up after work wasn't an everyday thing… "Sup, Teach."

"Oh, this kid is a riot!" Her hand found Marvin's shoulder with a reassuring wink as if to say, "Don't you worry, honey. I didn't go and forget about you the minute my old man showed up". And she went on to insist, "He worked hard, learned fast, and is as *sweet* as can be. You were right about this one, daddy. He's a keeper."

Probably blushing again (on the inside), Marvin let out a stream of compressed air through his teeth with a smile.

"You gotta ride home, kid?"

"Yeah, Teach, I'm cool."

"Alright, then." He threw an arm around his special lady and tipped his hat. "See ya around, Keeper."

And Holly added, "Night, darlin'."

"G'night."

He partially waved while directing an arm into his bomber jacket, balancing a steaming cup of creamy joe in the other, preparing for his walk outside toward the back of the mall.

Shawn had found the courage to make a reappearance inside the parlor (after slithering by four or five times, scoping the place out through the sides of his eyes) and verified he'd be where he said he would when he was meant to. He'd mentioned something about meeting up with some folks in back to smoke when the place shut down. Marvin, of course, didn't have him clarify considering he was alluding to loitering, among other illegal pastimes near-to, or possibly still on, company property, but Holly wasn't hovering over their every word. He was pretty sure she was cool with his stoner way of going about his teen years as long as it wasn't hurting anyone. And it never was. Marvin and Shawn weren't the type of kids to go around shaking down runts for drug money or getting waisted and diving into brawls. *Their* trips generally consisted of voyages into netherrealms inside an imagination fueled by sugar, caffeine and video games. Either that or just utter vegetation – asses growing roots in rugs, mothers pouring glasses of water on their heads every few days so they wouldn't shrivel up and die...

Hot coffee in hand, he took a timely sip while approaching the security officer at the door, trying to hide his face out of habit, knowing he'd rather not be easily recognized from afar with a blunt in his lips through a cloud of smoke—

"Oh, shit... What up, man?!" He laughed a little when he saw who it was. "Bro... You *security?*"

Big, brawny and ginger-bearded, Marvin used to buy weed off this guy a few years back. *Shitty* weed, if any one was so inclined to know, but he was a pretty decent human being, all things considered. He always loaded bowls gratis and wanted to hang with his patrons when they swung by.

"Heyyyy... Sup, Melvin?!"

"S'Marvin, man."

"Marvin! Yeah, yeah, my bad. Been a while, bro! You work here now?"

"Heh. Yeah, man, firs' day. Tasty Creams. Sweet deal."

It took him a minute, but... "Ah, ah hah, ah hah... Nice. Nice. Cool, man, cool. Yo, you still blaze, bro?"

Marvin took a quick peak over his shoulder. "You know this, man. Had a fuckin' *wild* one today, bruh..."

"Oh shit... That was your *boy*, right?! Scott or somethin'!"

"Who, Shawn?"

"Shawn, dude! He was tripping fucking balls, bro! Oh shit!"

Marvin laughed. "Damn... He get into some shit or what?"

"Ah hah! Nah, nah it was cool... Just some complaints about 'suspicious behavior' is all. We talked to him and just chilled with him for a bit; had him hanging with Santa at the tree. Got him on some good vibes, you know?"

"*Pshhh*... Silly ass nigga..." He shook his head with a smile and took a sip of his roasted beverage.

"But, yo, I'm *holdin'* if you dudes *need*, man. You still got my number?"

"Uh, yeah, bro, probly. My boy's brother got us, though. But, you know... He runs dry, you my man, Bry."

"Yeeeah." He swung his beefy hand out for some love. "Right on, man. You have a good night, alright? Take care of your boy. Kid was *on* one, ah hah."

"Yeah, man, probly see you tomorrow, though. Later."

Cool guy. The quality of his merch was wanting, and he was a little strapped for creative conversational skills but was basically as mellow as any mega weed-head. He was a large enough specimen that he could sell his sacks without anyone trying to do him wrong – no need to be a dick when no one pushed your buttons. Not that pot-heads generally broke into houses or beat people's skulls in for a fix, but Big Bryan was known to push some ecstasy pills from time to time. It was likely he delved in a few other flavors of recreational indulgences that might attract some sketchier types. But, like most burly and bearded small-town twenty-somethings, Big Bry was not without an assortment of barrels that went boom, and likely stoned enough to let off a round at an unwanted intruder without giving the consequences much thought.

"*Woooo*...shit!" A gush of howling, polar wind bit Marvin in the face and he quickly wrapped his Five Nights at Freddy's scarf tighter around his neck and chin. Fur-lined hood hugging the circumference of his face, he was Han Solo searching the blizzards of Hoth for a warm animal carcass to cut open and jump into. "There you are..." He spotted young Skywalker on the horizon – injured – hardly able to— "Ha! No fuckin' way..." The enfeebled, last of the Jedi Knights had company, it seemed...

Truck backed into a spot so that the bed opened into the vast, shadowy wilderness behind the mall, Shawn sat nearest to Marvin, facing away with his back obstructing all but the cotton-balled tip of what was likely—

"Ho-muthuhfuckin'-ho! Freeze, scumbags! Cough up the doobie!"

Shawn, at this point, was too exhausted to bother being startled, and Old St. Nick was just too damn old to care.

"Yo." Shawn puffed, puffed, restrained a cough, released, then passed. "This is—"

"Aw, c'mon, man... Don't ruin the moment. Lemme just burn one wit' Mr. Clause for a minute, shit." He laughed. "Oh shit—" And when good old St. Nick turned his head: "—*And* you black?! This is like my child hood dreams come true!"

Santa chuckled. "What's good, young blood?"

"Aw, *man*, Santa…" he took an inspired puff with a cheery grin, "…had a *wild* one today."

The jolly hatted icon nodded with a jubilant quake of his admirable belly. "If it was any 'one' like what yo' *boy* here was on, I don't doubt it…"

"Damn…" Marvin shook his head. "*This* nigga…" He passed the finely rolled blunt to Mr. Clause, smacking his lips, noticing the flavor. "Peppermint?"

"Uh-huh." Santa grabbed the torch as Marvin went on.

"Nice one," he had to say, then, "But, nah. This dude went to Never *Ever* Land." They both chuckled at his pun. "I just hada lil body fry. Firs' day on the job, though."

"Where at?"

"Tasty Creams, man." A goofy grin smeared across his face, reminiscing over the company he kept.

"Sheeeit, lil nigga… I seen *that* look a thousand times…" His voice was a bit hoarse, but soothing; his eyes yellowed.

"What look?"

"Yeah… 'What look'." He *hmphed* and shook his head. "Like I ain't know when a young nigga caught 'the fever'."

"Aw, c'mon, man… This shit ain't nineteen-fifty-two, Grandad!"

"Oh, I know… I know… An' she fine, boy. I seen her."

"You ain't never been wit' a white woman?" Shawn wondered, ashing the cherry.

"I wuz young once, lil nigga, shit." He shot him a raised brow like the kid should know better than to doubt He Who Commanded the North Pole. "I've felt the sway of them pale blue eyes—"

"She got brown eyes."

"The temptation of that blazin' red hair—"

"Brown hair."

"Whatever color *hair*, nigga, damn! Point is: yeah, I got mine. And yeah, I felt like I conquered the goddamned world; like I surpassed the limits of my very bein'." Puff, hold, exhale, quiet reflection… "Back then shit wuz a lot diff'rent… White women di'n't just go throwin' 'emselves at niggas so's to check a box off their list like they do now. Only the rare few would risk travelin' down that road. Nowadays, pretty much alla'em wanna try a nigga on fo' size at least once. Like we some kinda option off the rack at Nieman's'r some shit."

The boys were entranced with the conversation, not sure if they should just let him go on or jump on in while the water was warm. After a few moments of silence, Marvin got curious.

"So, you think it's jus' more'a the same? Like, we were slaves before; now we jus' the fresh meat on the menu?"

The aged velveteer took a sip from his flask, offered it to the boys who declined, then responded. "I can't speak much on bein' a slave – it was before my time. But if bein' *meat* means you boys get yo' choice'a pussy without gettin' jumped by a bunch of socs or greasers for bustin' a nut in a horny white woman? ...I'm all in, baby." He raised his flask and the boys laughed. "So, yo' *man* here says you two got yo' self somethin' *nice* lined up fo' tonight."

The blunt found its way back to Marvin and he shook his head, staring into the cherry as if he'd find some form of redemption in its glow. "Shit... I'on't even know, man..." Puff, puff, hold, then pass. He went on afterward with his words encrypted under a cloud of smoke. "Think I kinda fucked that up earlier."

"What happened?" Shawn couldn't even fake disappointment. He was just too spent at this point to really care.

"*I* happened. Opened my damn mouth and wasn't payin' attention. They caught me slippin', man. Heard me call 'em hoes. *Told* 'em I was jus' playin'... Think Shandra wan'ed to fuck too."

"Fuck it." Shawn flicked the roach into the frosted shrubbery. "They boujee, anyways. They ain't *gamers*, dawg!" The back of his hand found Marvin's chest with a swat to instill some brotherly pep into his man.

"...*Fine*, though."

"Fuckin' ass for hours, bruh..."

Marvin laughed.

Right around then the cavalry could be heard on approach. A choir of footfalls belonging to a gaggle of arctic bodies marched across the glacial asphalt, chattering festively over the subtle jingling of bells trailing a foreboding perfume of tobacco and pine. Marvin looked back to see three more jolly St. Nicks and six elves, two of them genuine little people.

"Oh, shit..."

"We been gettin' together afterhours all this week. Tryin'a keep it goin' till Christmas. ...You boys in?"

Shawn looked up at Marvin, almost pleading for mercy, but saw in his eyes his friend's excitement and made the call. "Fuck it. Let's do this. Where we goin'?"

Grandad Santa sapped on his flask with a knowing little smirk. What he had in mind would be better offered as a surprise.

DECEMBER 23ᴿᴰ

Four days later:

When his phone rang, Shawn laid awake staring at it, eyes wired open at 7:00am after a nearly sleepless night. He knew it was Marvin calling. And he could only imagine one reason why he *would* at this hour and on a morning like this.

Still, he didn't answer. If he didn't answer, maybe the reality of it would go away. Maybe if the phone would stop ringing he could fall asleep for a few days and when he'd wake up it'd be Christmas, and—

No.

No, he was pretty goddamn sure he never wanted to see another Christmas tree, ornament, elf, Santa suit, or red bow again…

….

……

………

When it rang the third time, he knew *Marvin* knew he wasn't asleep, and that this thing wouldn't just go away… So he reached for the damned cell and allowed the weight of the real world to reach his ears. Marvin's languid and lethargic tone haunted him even before he managed to utter the words,

"It's not over."

When Shawn made it to Marvin's, he'd came prepared. Bleach, gloves, tarps, spray bottles, masks, nausea pills, a jug of water, and a monstrous blunt for after the cleanup on aisle fuck-this-sucks. He slipped alongside the house and on toward the back of the property to where he found his friend already hard at work…smoking a bong load from Marvin the Martian's nose at the foot of a tangled assortment of corpses arranged in a type of giant wreathe, intertwined in gore and pine – a holiday horror comprised of Santa and some helpers, a reindeer or two, and what was very likely at least half of Mrs. Clause.

"Holy fuckin' *fuck*..." His hand covered his mouth and nose, instinctively trying to dull his senses to the horror.

Marvin blew out his hit over the ten-foot wreathe laid flat on his single-mother's neglected, open backyard covered in a fresh sheet of fallen snow.

"Hope you brought an ax..."

"Fuck, man... *This* shit..." Shawn dropped his gear in a slump and collapsed onto his ass next to his partner in crime on the backdoor steps. "This is too much, man... We can't keep doin' this shit..."

Marvin, green alien beanie pulled tight over his ears, wiped his runny nose with a sleeve and shivered at the chill of the morning wind. "The fuck else we gon' do? Too late to go back now... We already in too deep."

"But... Fuck, man... Choppin' up bodies? ...Tha's some *white* people, shit, bruh! The fuck we know about choppin' up bodies?"

"Shit," he assured him. "...But we gotta do it quick." He almost saw the artistry in it, the creativity in its brutal intricacies... But wouldn't let himself look at this disgusting display of sick and twisted barbarism as anything other than what it was: evil. "If my moms sees this shit..."

"Fuck..." Shawn put his head between his knees. If he hadn't already vomited twelve times in the past two days he may have tossed his guts again, if for nothing else, out of respect for the dead, but he was all out of bile to offer his sympathies. All he had left was a sense of self preservation. "Maaaan..." he drew the word out in an exhausted whine, "what the fuck is going on?!"

"Wish I knew, bruh..." Again, the arrangement sparked some level of intrigue in his mind, like there had to be some significance to what he was seeing. But the sight of it – arms twisted, broken around legs; branches through the base of skulls and out eyes and mouths; necks broken and torsos contorted; spines and antlers snapped to run the course of the curve – was just too revolting to let fester long enough to divulge any reasoning from.

Shawn grabbed the Looney Tunes bong, ripped a heavy load from the bowl, exhaled, then got up to leave.

"Yo, where you goin', man?"

"To get an *ax*, nigga." He shook his head. "The fuck... You want some egg mcmuffins while I'm out, too?"

"What in the name of the *Lawd* are you two boys doin' up at 8:30 in the mo'nin'?" Pink fleece robe with matching curlers and a knee-high baby brother in a Rug Ratz onesie, both mother and son stood in awe of the two teens on the back steps a solid four hours before they'd usually see daylight during winter break.

Egg mcmuffins halfway gone, the two youths turned to look up toward Marvin's mom and little brother, mouths full of breakfast, eyes deprived of sleep... Marvin figured the only reasonable answer would be,

"We just got home," which was actually code for: "we just finished drudging four tarp-loads of chopped up corpse-sacks through the snow and into Shawn's truck, so don't go 'round the side of the house till after we're gone".

His mom *tsked*. "Boy... You *best* not go losin' that job... You know we need the cash."

"I know, ma, it's cool. I won't."

She shook her head, cinched trash-bag now visible in hand, and started making her way down the steps.

"Whoa, whoa! Ma, *chill*, I got it." Marvin jumped up and Shawn almost dropped his mcmuffin in the haste.

"You volunteerin' to take out the trash at 8:30 in the mo'nin'? Boy, you *must* be high..."

"Quit playin', ma. You in a pink-ass robe and it's cold as hell out here. I got this."

"Uh-huh..." She looked skeptical handing him the bag. "I best not come back later and find that damn thing layin' there at the bottom of them steps..." She started to turn away before something caught her eye. "Marvin... What'n the hell are those?"

Trash-bag in one hand, mangled mcmuffin in the other, he followed her eyes to the pile of bloodied, broken antlers on the cement next to Shawn. They didn't put them in tarps for fear of them busting through but weren't sure whose blood stained them so thought they'd better take them somewhere they could be burned.

"Oh, Shit… That's, uh…" Shawn got caught off guard, giving Marvin a second to think.

"Shawn hit a reindeer."

Immediately, Marvin's little brother started to cry, pacifier slipping from his mouth.

"Dude… Why's it gotta be a reindeer?" He turned toward the baby. "It wasn't no reindeer, baby Chris. It was just a, uh, a *regular* ol' deer."

Baby Chris wasn't convinced, waterworks escalating exponentially.

"Well, what *happened* to it?"

"Ma, seriously?" Marvin's eyes eluded to his little brother, and Shawn filled in the blanks in consideration of the leaky-eyed tyke.

"Oh, he was cool. We helped him up, dusted off his coat."

"Yeah, yeah… Took him, took him to the Christmas store and got him some new antlers. Good as new, lil bro. I promise."

"Oh, c'mere, baby boy." Momma picked up the sniveling cutie and gave him a kiss, tending to his tears while turning inside.

Afterward, both teens regained their exhausted postures, Marvin losing his appetite, letting his mcmuffin hang low, Shawn finding it in him to try another bite on for size that didn't quite fit.

"Let's go, man."

"Yeah…"

They'd tied down the four tarp-sacks in the back with one large one over-top. Luckily, (and it was probably all sorts of wrong to think it, but…) two of the bodies were those of Miguel and Xavier; the little fellas they'd met on Marvin's first night on the job at the mall, so they didn't take up much room in the tarps. They had to bag up the animal bits and all since they weren't clever enough to know which parts were which when it came down to the gory details and didn't want to go leaving some Christmas Gnome's severely saturated liver lying on top of a deer's split open intestine. Who knew *who* might be trudging through the woods, studying animal leftovers for some freakish veterinarian fetish they called a hobby. They figured it better to hide it all where they'd stashed the rest – keep it as far away from them as they could get it.

There was already a thin layer of ice forming on the windshield when Shawn flipped on the wipers, both their breaths visible inside the cab.

"We can't keep doin' this shit, man…"

"You think I don't know that?" Marvin turned to look at his best friend. "You think I ain't heard you the first ten times you said it?"

"I know, I know… Just…" He started the car and shook his head.

"My bad, man… This shit got me as stressed as you."

"Does it, though?" He pulled into the street, trying to adjust the heat on the dash.

"Whatchoo mean, man?"

"I'on't know, man… I'm jus'…trippin' right now…"

Marvin watched him fondle the dash, avoiding the question. Was Shawn contemplating what he *thought* he was? …How could he even think…?

"Bruh…seriously?"

Shawn looked over, trying to play off what he probably shouldn't have hinted at.

Marvin just stared, almost rupturing in betrayal, barely keeping it together, so Shawn manned up and addressed it.

"Look, man, I'm jus' trippin', a'ight? I mean…what the fuck *is* this shit, man? An' why the fuck it keeps happnin' 'round you?"

"Like you weren't there the first two times?!"

"Yeah, but…I was passed the fuck out—"

"SO THE FUCK WAS I!!"

Shawn shook his head, trying to wrap his brain around it all, so Marvin helped him along.

"Bro, you *saw* that shit! You saw what I saw, all *three* times! How the *fuck* you think I could pull somethin' like that off?!"

"Well, not alone—"

"Man, *fuck* you, nigga, seriously?! Fuckin' seriously?!" He punched the dash. It wasn't like Marvin to act out in violence. Shawn knew that. "Man… We was together all them times like, the whole fuckin' *night*… Think, man! *Fuckin' think!"* He looked over, eyes watery, desperate not to lose the last bit of strength he had in the only man he could trust.

Shawn began to see the truth in his words and to remember the facts despite that he felt the need to place blame. He remembered that at the start of it all, it never once crossed his mind that Marvin could've been responsible, and he wasn't sure why it had now…

"Shit, man…" He sighed. "You, right, a'ight? I'm sorry. There's no fuckin' way – no fuckin' way…" He shook his head again, voice trailing off.

Marvin leaned back, angst-switch nearly set on meltdown, and rubbed his eyes dry. "Nah, man." His voice was shaky. He took a deep breath and reached down for their jug of water. "I don't even know *how* a person could do that shit… I mean, *physically*… 'Specially in a single *night*…" Two gulps made it down before his throat swelled closed. He wiped his mouth, shook his head and went on. "We seen, uh…What's dude's name…? *Joe* and Mrs. Clause at the Mall *yesterday*…"

"Yeah… So, there's gotta be, what, like a cult or some shit, right? Some fuckin' Christmas hatin', Satan worshippin', Santa slayin' cultist fuckers, bruh. And they straight up huntin' right outta the mall."

"Yeah…"

"But why the fuck they tryin'a set *you* up?"

He gazed through the fresh sleet outside his window. Shawn knew he didn't have an answer to give. How could he? He'd never been around anything remotely *like* a cult… As from the start of this all, their only real option was to clean up the mess and try not to get caught. At least not until another option jumped up, hissed in their face and bit them on the ass—

"Shit…"

"What happened?" Marvin snapped out of his daze at the swear.

"Shit!"

"What?!"

"Fuck!" Shawn's eyes told the story, blue and red glare reflecting from the rearview mirror.

"What the hell, man?!"

"Think I ran that light!"

"Oh, fuck, no…"

"Just be cool, man, be cool!" Shawn pulled over and Marvin checked his eyes in the visor.

"Fuck, I look high as *hell*…"

"You always look high, man, *chill*."

Marvin tried leaning back and sitting inconspicuously, looking suspiciously stiff as a rail with fidgety specs darting around the cab. "Shitshitshit… Where they at, man, what they doin'?"

"He pullin' up, man, chill, just *ch-ch-ch!*" He made a shushing noise with a low wave signaling for him to back off while the Land Rover approached.

"Boys." The deputy sheriff in the beat-up County Police dad-hat nodded at the two teens. "In some kinda hurry?"

"Oh, nah, sorry, Dep. Ma's got us up early as hell, is all. We was just talkin' and I didn't see when it turned yellow."

"Huh-huh…" He eyeballed them a bit, like any cop would. "You two been smokin' the ganj?"

"Uh, no sir." He looked to Marvin whose eyes were still trying to find a place to settle.

"Nope," Marvin confirmed, never making eye contact.

"Nuh-uh. Not since, what…?" Shawn feigned contemplation. "…Was that *two* months ago you snatched our stash?"

The deputy nodded once, appreciating the balls on the kid. "Yea. Sounds 'bout right."

"It's cool, though. I'll put it on yo' tab." He shrugged. "Give you the Po-po discount. We'll call it forty bones, even."

The officer wore his stare for a solid three seconds that felt like ten minutes until he cracked a smile and laughed. "You two *lucky* it's cold as shit outside this mornin' and I just got my coffee. …Now go on and git 'fore I decide to come over there and empty them pockets an' *add* to that tab."

"Ah ha! Don't gotta tell me twice, Dep! …See ya!"

"Yeah, yeah…"

Shawn took off with a little gusto to play the part of the excited teen but did his best not to lose his mcmuffin through his shorts in the process.

"Oh, my fuckin' god…" Marvin put his hand on the dash to try keeping his heart from breaking through its cage in his chest. "Oh fuck, that was some fucked up shit…"

"We cool, man, we cool." Shawn's was pounding too, but he knew Marvin had already been overly worked up. "Don't forget – like we said at the start: We just kids, man. And we *innocent*. Yeah, it looks bad, but there's still a chance they gon' catch who doin' this and we gon' be clear. Just a couple of young, dumb, scared kids who were afraid they wouldn't get a fair trial."

"Yeah... Easy for *you* to say... All the bodies ain't showin' up in yo' backyard." He leaned back, catching his breath. "Don't run no more lights, a'ight? No fuckin' stop signs, no crosswalks – nothin'." He started pawing at his pockets. "Fuck, man, I gotta smoke..."

"Yeah... I can't roll through no stop signs, but you can blow clouds of doj out the window..."

Marvin pulled out his vaporizer pen that'd been preloaded, hands shaking while clicking it on. "Fuck it... Smoke out the window on a cold ass winter mornin' ain't gon' get us pulled over. Runnin' a fucking stoplight will." One smooth, electronic hit later and he was already starting to find his nerves. "Here..."

Shawn happily (as could be expected, in such a circumstance) accepted the device and partook in the refocusing of their chi. After a few pass-arounds, Marvin could almost be accused of a chuckle.

"What?"

He smiled when Shawn handed him back the pen. "You said, 'call it forty and we even', nigga..."

A goofy stutter of a partial laugh broke the surface at the thought.

Marvin sort of laughed too. "Damn... Thank the fuckin' Bud God's for my lady, Maryjane, man. I'd be fallin' apart without this bitch right now."

"*Mmhmm*," he agreed, taking what was likely the last puff in the chamber. "If Snoop Dogg did one thing right, it was the G Pen."

"Smooth as hell," Marvin agreed.

"Yoooo..."

"What?" Upon retrieval of the highly regarded device, Marvin went through the motions of twisting off the end to autonomously reload without a thought for keeping a somewhat clear head.

"What about that *thing*, man?"

"What thing?"

"That fucking *thing* I saw, bruh? I told you... Behind the club with X."

"Maaan... You were *waisted* that night. You said you saw fuckin' Mad Hatter or some shit—"

"Nah, fool, I said Cheshire... The *cat* from that shit. But it was like, blue and white, insteada purple an', uh, *purple*, or whatever. And fuckin' giant, man. Like bigger than a *bear* giant."

Marvin shook his head and chuckled while he lit up again. "But X di'n't see that shit."

"Nah, man, he was in the car, gettin' those pills for me. I'm sayin' though. Yeah, I was fucked up, but that was earlier. An' it was dark an' all, but that shit was vivid as fuck. The fucking trees were movin', I could hear its breath. And it's fur... Fucking majestic shit. It was, like...*glistening*..."

Marv coughed out a laugh as he passed the electric doobie. " 'Glistening', nigga?"

Shawn partly laughed at the thought too, taking a puff at the wheel.

"Shit..." Abruptly, Marvin squirmed around like he had a mouse in his trousers when he heard his phone go off, digging through a plethora of pockets, each one a crapshoot; who knew what he'd turn out. But when he found it, "...What the hell?"

"What?"

"It's Holly..."

"Who?"

"My boss, nigga... Fuck."

"Don't answer it."

Of *course* he was going to answer it...

"Hello?"

He, of course, then wondered why in holy fuck he *did*, all the same...

"Oh, hey, darlin'! Sorry to be a bother. I know you aren't feelin' well. It's just that I can't make it in tonight, so I had to make sure yer gonna be okay to shut the place down all by yer lonesome."

"Uhhhh..."

"You remember all the procedures, right? You seem to catch on pertty fast..."

"Shit... What-what time?"

" 'Bout five, when Melanie leaves. Everythin' okay, hun?"

"Yeah... Yeah, no, it's cool. Yeah, I got it."

"Got what?" Shawn wondered intrusively, and Marvin swatted aimlessly at the interruption.

"Okay, hun, thanks a bundle. Hey, you feelin' any better?"

"Uhh...shit...not...not much...nah... But don't sweat it. How hard is it to serve up some ice cream?"

"That's mah keeper! Thanks a million, darlin'. I'm gonna make it up to ya, I promise. Tell Shawn I said hey."

"Yeah, cool, I will."

"Bye, now."

"Bye…"

After a stoner's-moment for it to all sink in:

"Fuuuuuck!"

"Bruh… I wouldn't be goin' in to work after a day like today… Fuckin' *no* one would."

Marvin thought about it for a minute, then—

"Fuck it. At least work's another alibi, right? I mean, shit, I called out yesterday so…"

"But we was with them girls, man. They'd vouch for us," he figured, but then thought, "probly…"

"Still, though. You heard my moms… I can't lose this job, yo. She's countin' on that Christmas check. Plus, I'ma try to be more alert while I'm there. You need to shoot through, too – keep watch on who's watchin' *us*. Somebody's gotta fuckin' *thing* for me or somethin'. That prolly means they got their eyes on me; fuckin' gettin' off on watchin' me squirm."

"So, what, like one of the Christmas peeps?"

"I'on't know… Jus' roll with me. S'not like you wanna be alone right now."

"Fuck no… I was probly gon' come through anyways." He handed him back the empty pen and started down that lonely, bumpy road that lead to accessory to multiple murders or worse.

For a pair of dipshit stoner kids who couldn't catch a mouse in a trap because they'd get high and eat the cheese, they weren't horrible at disposing of human bodies. They'd found four plastic snow-gliders in Marvin's garage and had the tarps sitting on top so they could slide them off the cold, wet bed and push them over the snow and into the ravine. The four tarps tied at their tops looked like four, giant, malformed Hershey's Kisses, frosted where their flags would be for wintertime marketing. And although they'd planned ahead, even with the gliders the damned sacks still weighed several hundred pounds apiece – they were a bitch for a couple of scrawny, underdeveloped teens to get moving.

"You even pushin', nigga?!" Shawn wondered with a face full of their second snowy Kiss of mountainous morbidity.

"Fuck you, you short-leg-havin' lil midget—" He almost caught himself but, by then, it was too late.

"Bro..."

"Shit..." They both stopped pushing. "Fuck..." He felt like an ass... "S-sorry, X an' Mig," came his mindful offering toward an anonymous lump in the tarp's face, softly patting it for additional support.

"Dude... Do you even know what bag they in?"

"Man... They prolly in *all* of 'em... Why you tryin'a make this worse for me?"

"Yeah..." he nodded and bowed his head. "Yeah, sorry." And after a breath and a moment of silence: "Ok, on three."

"No, no... I said the Crunchy Christmas Caramel *Deluxe*... The green and red one right there." A spare finger pointed past the toddler in her arms while another little sprog bounced at her feet.

"Oh, my bad..." Marvin dumped the mistaken Caramel Crunch Supreme back in its bin and went for the appropriate receptacle.

It had been a lot busier than he'd expected. He'd forgotten it was almost Christmas... A ridiculous thing to think, considering the heaping piles of Clause he'd been recently wrists deep in, but a lack of sleep, a spirited regimen of intoxicants, and utter psychological exhaustion had him one step away from forgetting his own mother's name.

Shawn was occupying the corner closest to the window looking into the mall, vigorous in his intent, but not so much in his result. He'd caught an hour or two of sleep before making his way to his post but had already dozed off a few times while on the clock. Marvin was late getting in and Melanie was noticeably peeved, but she could see he had been as much "under the weather" as he was rolled over and trampled by it. She quickly sympathized before speeding out of there to leave the parlor in the hands of the noob.

After he'd served up his twelfth frosty treat in succession he pushed through the swinging gate to join Shawn at the corner table and melted into the bench. Shawn hadn't even realized he was there until Marvin's forehead hit the wood in utter defeat, startling him. He jumped, looked back, then got his bloodshot, overworked eyes back on the job.

"Brooo…" Marvin groaned from under his arms, face still planted in a painted tree. "I can't fuckin' do this shit no more…"

Shawn broke his concentration for a minute to look back, then up at the clock on the wall. "Nigga… It's 5:45… You been here thirty minutes…"

"I'm sayin', though… How the fuck I'ma make it through the night?"

"Coffee, bruh."

"Fuck coffee, man. That shit just gon' work for like an hour…"

"Well, what, then?"

"I'on't know… Go hit up Bry for me. See what he's got—"

"Man, I ain't about to go askin 'round the mall for meth or some shit."

"Nah, man… Fuck that. Just see what he's got. Dude might have some of that Adderall shit or somethin'. College kids eat that shit up."

"Damn, man! You serious? We on a mission, right now, fool!"

"And we both about to pass the fuck out in the middle of it."

Shawn thought about it, irritated at the concept, wanting to stay true to his beloved psychedelics, but knew Marvin was right. They were spent. Burnt out. Used up… Something had to be done.

He sucked at his teeth in reluctance with a shake of his head. "A'ight, man, shit. I'll go hit him up." Hand held out with an open palm, he waited.

Marvin took his friend's palm in his and gave him the love he'd earned. Shawn looked baffled.

"I don't want yo' *props*, nigga, I want money!"

"Aww, c'mon, man, my wallets like…a thousand miles away right now…"

"Closer than Bryan is, yo!"

"Damn…" His head met the table again before he found the strength to stand. "A'ight, hold up…"

Five more festively titled multi-scoops on cones and twenty or so minutes later and Shawn skittered back into the parlor while Marvin was finishing up.

"No, no… The vanilla Ol' St. Nick with Twix and Caramel Sleigh Mud Tracks… Yeah, that one. Thanks."

Almost sick at the thought of another customer, he nearly slumped to the floor in relief when he saw his friend sketchily reclaim his front-corner table, eyeing over both shoulders, backside to the mall, waiting for the shop to clear. Marvin dawdled toward him with a gratuitous cup of joe for them both as soon as they found themselves alone.

One more skittish glance to Shawn's rear brought a little baggie up to the table with six, light yellow pills inside. He dumped them on the table and passed three to Marvin.

"The fuck are those?" Marvin swiped his three across the table into his palm.

"Ritalin. He said it's usually five for twenty but he gave me six so we could split 'em—Dude!"

Marvin made all three disappear in a gulp without a second thought, chased down his throat by coffee so thick with cream and sugar it could be counted as a meal.

"What?"

"You ain't 'posed just pound all three!"

"Why the fuck not? They give this shit to grade-schoolers to help 'em pass their math classes." He didn't see the problem.

"Those kids are like, chemically imbalanced, fool! That shit make's 'em normal! You ain't imbalanced, nigga, you just burnt!"

The firm clutch of hesitation shackled his mind, then— "Fuck it. It ain't gon' kill me..."

"Nah, but you gon' be tweaked the fuck out. Probly be all paranoid an' shit..."

"Like I ain't already?" He brushed it off. "Long as this shit gets me alert and keeps me vertical, we cool."

Shawn shook his head and took his twenty-milligram serving. "A'ight, man. Jus' don't start buggin' out an' try goin' off on yo' own. We need to stick together."

"Yeah, man, it's cool. I'm too beat, anyway. An hour from now you gon' wish you took all three, too." Shawn shook his head. "You see anything weird out there?"

"Bry was actin' a lil sketchy. Prolly cuz he was on the clock, though. I'on't know... You remember seeing him at the club?"

"Nah, why?"

"He brought it up. Asked if we had a fun night. Said he saw us chillin' with the Arctic Click..."

"Shit… Didn't even know he was there…" He sighed. "Wild night, though. Had my eyes on other things…"

"Yeah," he chuckled. "Same here…"

"Nothin' else, though? Didn't see no covert, coordinated shit goin' down between suspicious peeps hangin' outside the stores?"

He looked back into the mall. "Shit, man… Way I'm feelin', everybody is lookin' at me shady as fuck. Moms pushin' strollers got me checkin' my back to see if they still eyein' me after I walk by… And half of 'em *are*."

"And you worried about *me* being paranoid…"

"I'm jus' sayin', man: I ain't exactly in the right mind for this shit right now."

"That's why we got the meds. They'll have me closin' this bitch down with the quickness and you with yo' eyes on point, pickin' up all the details on who's watchin' who."

"Yeah, a'ight." He was on board, ready to do his part. They just had to make it through the next three hours or so without burning the place down. Or without anyone else burning it down on *account* of them…

A few customers later brought in a pair neither of them expected and sure as hell weren't prepared for. Shandra and Yvonne strolled in with heels as heavy as planets, fur-lined hoodies pealed back to show off the time and effort they put into their hair and face. If looks could kill, these two young ladies were out to maim first, disembowel second, and devour slowly over the course of several savory meals.

"*Marvin.*" Shandra's sharp tone coming from behind him made him feel like he was six years old getting scolded for using Ma's makeup to draw on walls.

He stopped dead in his tracks for just long enough to look guilty, then shook his head, sighed, and turned to face his dilemma.

His first instinct was to come up with an excuse for why he hadn't answered any of her texts, but that thought hardly lasted as long as a scoop of Candy Cane Cream would on the surface of the sun. She started pouring exaggerated theatrics from her hate-hole and shooting lasers from her eyes while her sidekick reinforced every intensified inflection with a sneer, snarl, or scowl. Shawn sat as still as a doe in crosshairs when it realizes it's being stalked, attempting to blend in to the milieu. He knew this species of beast was drawn to drama and fed off revolt so remained passive; invisible…

Marvin's hand covered his eyes, massaging his temples, leaning back against the sink behind him. Eventually the fireworks ceased, and silence smothered his senses like a hot blanket getting warmer by the second, begging to be ripped away for ventilation. When he tore it off to breathe a word, he was just as shocked as anyone at what came out—

Heat warmed his belly and escalated his heart, rising through his chest and into his throat like fire from a dragon's gullet. He wouldn't be surprised if his eyes were orange embers of coal, beads of sweat on his brow turning to steam. His roar – a voltaic grumble from a pit as hot as Hell that burst from his mouth as a ball of blue flame – cauterized every gushing wound Shandra had laid bare. Two words backed by a release seventeen years and a hell of a holiday season in the making, quieted all others she may've thought she had…

"FUCK……*OFF!!!*"

Veins like worms writhing in boiling water bubbled at his temples, and even the wandering patrons outside, passing by the parlor, all turned at the ferocity of his howl.

Eyes nearly trembling, the practiced pillars of strength the two girls barged in with waned at the weight of real conviction, and a strategic decision was reached to retreat under the guise of indifference. They sassily blew off his attack, whipped around and stomped out; coats, lashes and locks singed from the burn.

Shawn, as aghast as any, eyed his friend closely, concerned he'd gone over the edge.

"Fuck, man… You okay?"

Flushed from his uproar, Marvin spun around and rinsed his face in the sink with cool water.

"Yeah… Just…couldn't deal with that bullshit right now…"

It didn't come as a surprise to anyone that not even a minute passed before the door's chime proceeded a new challenge.

"Howdy, darlin'."

Shawn's eyes lit up at the provocative appeal of Mrs. Greggerson in her long, formal dress and white fur coat. Hair done up for an obviously glitzy event, with ringlets like ribbon decorating a gift and a dark blue, glistening bow to match her dress, Marvin nearly *instantly* was drained of all frustration for the merrier sentiment of adoration.

"Holy..." he started.

"God damn..." Shawn finished, both too stunned to offer a more reasonable response.

She noticed Marvin's fatigue right away. "Hey, how you holdin' up?"

It was a scene from a teen romance novel, where the beautiful older woman floats in on an uplifting breeze of floral *parfum* to cater to the temperamental, pubescent beast and set his mind at ease with a delicate whisk across the floor and a cool hand to his cheek... Until it wasn't...and her hairier half clopped in in tacky, rawhide boots under a matching sapphire-blue suit.

It had almost been perfect...

He feigned a cough and leaned laggardly against the counter, despite the sudden urge he felt to run laps around the mall with his apron like a cape around his neck, blazing in flames against the turbulence of his wake.

"What?Yeah,no,I'mgood...   *cough*   Jusaliltiredan'hot... problyafever...   *cough*   andacough,   Ithink,maybe...*ahem* Throat'salljackedup.Sratchy,itchin'alittle,butI'mgood.   What,uh... Whatchooguysdoin'here?"

"Whoa, sport! Someone got a little caffeine in 'im?" Greggerson smiled under his waxed 'stache twisted upwards at its ends, then slid into the booth with Shawn who had to peal his eyes from Holly's figure, seductive even when just teasing from under her coat.

"*Coffee!*Yeah,coffeeandDayquil.Lotsofboth.Keepin'mekickin',go in'goin'strong." He partially flexed a bicep and growled.

"Well we was just headed to our Christmas ball," she explained. "Figured we had time to stop on by and make sure you were doin' ok—"

"Yeah!" He took a breath, straddling his soaring nerves and rolling his fingers to exercise some tension, then exhaled. "Heh... *Woooo!* It's a... It's been a long few days, but I really wanna be here for you— *Uhhh*, for the *job*, I mean. The money. I...I mean *we* – me and my moms – could really use the cash."

Her heart melted for the kid. "Aww, sweetie, don't you go worryin' about all that." She reached into her bag and pulled out a roll of bills. "Here… Let's just get this out of the way now." She started counting out hundreds and twenties and Marvin hardly knew what to say.

"I, uh… You know, it's cool, I mean… You don't have to just cough it up like that. I can wait till tomorrow after my shift—"

"Oh, stop…" A hand full of money waved away the thought. "I have no problem takin' care of my Keeper a little ahead of schedule." She held out the cash for Marvin to come get. "Tomorrow's pay's in there too, sugar. And an extra day for the one ya missed bein' sick."

He was at a loss. He'd never been handed so much money at once, and never any at all with such perfunctory nonchalance accompanied by a smile…

"Wow… That's…" That loss he was at never seemed to morph into anything oratorically tangible.

After he filled his palm in a daze she pulled him in for a hug—

Pralines and cream…

"You deserve every bit of it, young man."

Arms holding him tightly, the embrace was as magical a thing as any he'd ever experienced. He would've handed her right back the cash and just taken the hug for pay if he didn't know it'd make him look utterly pitiable.

When she let him go – fingers running the course of his back and neck – she took every bit of pent up irritation in him with her and it slid from his muscles into a swirling stream of her scent in the air. He was suddenly so relaxed he had to clench his urethra to avoid pissing into his shoes. And at the door – Mr. G escorting his wife like a man who knew what he had – she turned back to say,

"And, Marvin, honey? Close the shop early. You've been through enough for one day."

It took several seconds of silent awe while the two gracefully drifted away before either of the boys could react. Marvin, basking in his newfound tranquility, finally remembered he had nearly a grand in his hand and distantly placed it in his pocket as Shawn spoke up.

"Holy *shit!* That chick is *definitely* into you…" His shocked smile spoke of a man who could hardly believe his own words.

Marvin shook his head while trying to disguise his grin. "Quit playin', man…"

"Nigga… You didn't just see that shit?!" He proceeded to plead his case while his buddy moved to lock up. "*I* just saw that shit – front row *seats*, bruh. I almost stood up and clapped!" He leaned back, still astonished. "She's definitely feelin' my boy!"

"*Pshhh…*" Embarrassed, Marvin turned off the sign when the door was locked then moved to change the subject. "C'mon, man, help me clean this shit up real quick."

Shawn's expression went from teasing to toilsome in a flash. "Fool, I ain't the one just got handed a wad of Benjies…"

"I'll give you ten beans."

Offended, he sucked his teeth with an expression like he'd just swallowed a bug. "Ten dollars?!" He shook his head. "Nigga, you more stingy than my *brother* with them greenbacks."

"Fine, man, I'll do that shit myself," he shrugged, turning away, calling his little pal's bluff.

"A'ight, a'ight… I'll do it for fifteen."

Marvin drew his knot from his pants and unraveled a twenty. "Ten, nigga. Shit will take like twenty minutes. Tha's thirty dollars an hour – *twice* what I'm makin' doin' this shit."

Shawn stood up and swiped the twenty from his grips. "Oh, you a math whiz now, *huh*, big baller…" Twenty sneakily filling his pocket, he continued to lay it on thick. "Don't think I won't forget how you changed, man."

Eyes like daggers, Marvin remarked, "Oh, but you gon' forget about my *change*, though? That how this shit is?"

He hung his head and shook it with a sigh. "Harsh, bruh. Real harsh…" hands finding his wallet, he dug for the proper difference. "Like I'd do you like that…"

Marvin tried not to laugh. "A'ight, man, let's get the fuck out of here."

Shawn was hardly worth the wages paid, but it was nice to have a friend to work with. They handled the goods, washed the dishes, and cleaned the floor and counters in just over twenty minutes. Marvin took care of the money-drop after closing out the register and the two were out before eight. A few salty onlookers gazed in annoyance through the windows while they closed up, thirsty for their late-night fix, but Shawn was happy to send them on their way. He couldn't wash a dish for shit, but he knew how to turn away a paying customer.

The mall was still buzzing with last-minute gift-getters settling for whatever was left on the shelves. There had to have been half their senior class hanging around the corridors, and somehow, when most wouldn't look their way to say "excuse you" if they sneezed, their prying eyes were on full tilt, necks turned, and whispers shared between all genders of teens in their midst.

"Yo," Shawn was starting to notice the heat. "Am I not wearin' pants? Why's everybody eyeballin' me right now?"

Marvin was relieved to hear Shawn was seeing what he was. He thought he might be taking a turn for the worse, paranoia beginning to peel the paint off the walls in his mind...

"Fuck, man, somethin's up..."

"Nah," Shawn tried to rationalize it. "Probly them girls, bruh. They just burnt us on Snapchat, or some shit."

Suddenly, Marvin could breathe. "Yeah... Yeah, f'real." He rolled his neck to work out the tension, then stopped dead—

"What?" Marvin's sudden panic startled him.

"Shitshitshit..." He turned away while grabbing his accomplice by the jacket. "*Cops*, man, the *cops*," strained from his throat.

Shawn followed his lead so to not draw more attention but was more curious than panicked. He looked back to see two officers questioning some of the Christmas crew. "Whoa, whoa, wait a minute..." It was *his* turn to stop now, pulling Marvin to a halt while a thought stirred.

Every instinct was telling Marvin to make a mad dash for the other end of the mall, no matter how conspicuous it seemed, but the last thing he needed was for more eyes to be plastered to his sketchy ass. So, after nearly breaking free of Shawn's grip, he gathered himself and let him say his piece.

"We need to find out what's goin' on."

Voice as tight a violin strung by Thor, Marvin wheezed, "Fuck that, man! We need to get the fuck outta here!"

"No, man, seriously. *Chill*, a'ight? We *innocent*, remember?" A plan was forming... "I'll go over there and chat up some folks – see what's goin' on." He looked for a nearby shop. "You roll over to Cinnabagel and order somethin'. Look to see if anybody acts funny when I'm walkin' over there. Keep yo' eyes on everybody, man. Maybe somebody'll twitch when they see me getting' close to the cops. ... Shit, I might go talk to one – see if someone jumps."

"*Nigga*… You fuckin' serious right now?!" Voice still strung tighter than piano wire, he could hardly hear himself think over his racing heart.

"Jus'… Jus' chill, man. Get *focused*. 'Member how you felt when Mrs. G gave you that stack?" Marvin nodded strenuously. "Get back in that place, yo. Imagine you with her right now, doin' some James Bond, secret spy shit with her on yo' arm. I'll be back in five."

Shawn started off, bold and determined with Marvin still pawing at his coat, wheezing silent exclamations.

"Nononowait—*Shit!*"

But his breath was waisted; Shawn had found his purpose.

Cinnabagel was a life raft drifting in a turbulent sea, almost too far to reach on such slim hopes as his. Marvin hacked his way across the crowds, splashing up so much notice he may as well have been chumming the waters with his own blood. Pulse like drums beating in his ears, when he found the back of the line he immediately closed his eyes, searching for that calming place in his mind between Holly's lips and eyes; her smile; her voice; the smell of her standing near…

She let her hair down in his thoughts and put her hand on his cheek. His fingers reached to find the curve of her lower back and she stepped into his hold. The warmth of her body against his eased his mind and slowed his heart, and the gentle touch of her lips on his neck was only half as sweet as the taste of her tongue when they finally kissed—

"Excuse me… Are you in line?"

The little Filipino woman's voice behind him snapped him back into the now.

"Huh?" Eyes resistant to open, when he saw he was next up to order he realized he was ill-prepared to make any sort of decision. "Oh…yeah, nah, nah, go ahead… Don't know what I want…" Making room for her to pass, he let another two patrons go ahead while he was at it, allowing him to hang back and observe.

Yet, he couldn't bring himself to look…

Two or three deep breaths later and he still had trouble getting his chin to lead the way. He felt like the minute his eyes found that crowd his guilt would be blinding; any who'd lay their peepers on his would know what he'd done…

Before long he realized he was next in line again and used the distraction as an excuse to think about something else. Roving the menu with his thoughts hardly able to focus on food, when he stepped up to the plate he swung for the fence—

"Large coffee, please."

Knocked it out of the park!

Or at least he *thought* he did, until the gangly dirty blond taking his order spied the cup of joe in his mitts from under her bagel visor and quickly veered her sights, not wanting to make taking this kid's order any more awkward. He'd already made a spectacle of himself by botching up the line. Anyone within eyeshot could guess that the last thing he needed was more caffeine.

After slinking into a corner to wait for his order and tripping over – or bumping into – nearly half the shop's customers in the process, he found he almost felt shielded enough by the crowd and painted windows to take a peek at what was going on. Head repositioning to attempt to penetrate the masses, by the time he got eyes on the cops he wished he'd never tried. Shawn stood face-to-face with two of Winterset's finest, probably asking all the wrong things and putting them *both* on the hot-list for potential interviewees.

"Fuckfuck*shit*fuck..." He oozed back out of sight into his chair like hot slime slipping off the table and landing in a pool of himself on the tile. The staff would need a *mop* to get him out of there at the end of night... And a bucket to squeeze him into that they could roll over to the police for preliminary questioning.

When someone knocked on the window beside him, he knew for certain he was going to prison for life...

Shawn stood bewildered by his friend's lack of contribution to their plan. Both palms up in a peeved gesture that asked, "what the hell?", he couldn't believe what he was looking at.

Marvin looked over Shawn's shoulder through the glass for signs of a setup, expecting to be lured into custody for a repeal in his friend's sentencing. And when he decided he still held hopes of making it out of the mall without a pair of shiny new cuffs, he broke through his paranoia to get up and meet Shawn outside.

He tried not to look – or *look* like he was looking – over at the X-mas crowd while he approached and asked,

"What the hell, man?! You—" He caught the decimals of his voice sailing through the melee.

Shawn yanked him by his jacket's elbow to head for the exit... *toward* the police...so Marvin fought against his grip until Shawn decided not to push his luck.

"You talked to 'em?! Are you fucking strange, nigga?!" he continued in a half-whisper while walking away from a lifelong jail sentence.

"Yeah, man. I *told* you I would—"

"I didn't think you'd actually do it!"

"Just fuckin' chill, a'ight? It's cool. You makin' shit *un*-cool by flippin' out – lookin' guilty as fuck, right now..."

Both hands holding hot, Styrofoam cups, Shawn relieved him of one while Marvin took a breath.

Shawn took a sip and winced. "Damn, nigga... Shit's black as fuck..." he shook off the bitter flavor. "You cool, now? You gotta grip?"

Marvin, several deep breaths into chill-mode, nodded nervously.

"Look: I jus' told 'em somebody stole my bike outta the truck and asked what I should do."

Marvin's face turned sour. "The fuck for?"

Shaking his head at his friend's lack of tact, he replied, "So I could ask 'em what was goin' on without soundin' suspicious."

Sour turned to mildly impressed. He'd never credited Shawn with half the sense that God gave a Gila Monster.

"You with me?" Shawn wondered patronizingly, and Marvin nodded.

"So, what happened? What they say? Who they think done it?"

"Done what, bruh?" He tackled another sip from the cup, just out of morbid curiosity, then shivered at the taste.

"Kilt those *people*, fool! What the *fuck*, 'done what'?!" Voice lifting above the crowd again, they both looked around to see if he'd caught any ears. When they saw they hadn't, Shawn hissed some shushing sound and said,

"Nah, fool, that's what I'm sayin'!" His whisper was intently agitated. "They don't know anything happened to *anybody*... They just realized dudes is missin' *today*."

A warm aura of calm flushed over his muscles, releasing the grip that mania had wrapped around his organs. His next breaths were alleviating. "How many they know about?"

They were nearing the wrong end of the mall, headed out the backside where housekeeping took the trash through a long, pale blue corridor.

"They only knew about four of 'em, but they jus' found out half the staff is gone."

"Shitshitshitshit—"

"That prolly means they gon' start lookin' soon." He braved another taste, wrestling it down while they pushed through the employee doors into the hall. "Knowin' *these* lazy-ass niggas, they probly gon' wait till after Christmas. 'Specially in *this* weather."

"Right… Right… And them bodies will be buried by then…"

"And that shit's sixty miles out, man. They ain't finding that shit till summer."

"Yeah…" It was all good news…accept… "*Fuck…*"

"What?"

They exited the back of the mall into a loading dock with two industrial dumpsters lining either side.

"Then we still don't know shit, *neither*. If they don't even know nobody's dead, they don't got no suspects."

Shawn shook his head. "Yeah. Which means we right back where we started…" He looked up to his friend. "Unless you spotted somethin' with those laser eyes while you was lookin' out."

"Fuck you, man, you know I couldn't watch that shit…"

Shawn stared for a second then laughed. "Scury-ass nigga."

"A'ight… You were right, a'ight? I shouldn'ta took three of them pills… Shit got me buggin'…"

"Told you, man…"

"Yeah, yeah… *You* try wakin' up to dead bodies three days in a row…"

"I *have*, nigga."

He brushed him off. "You know what I'm sayin'…"

Nearing the end of the dock, barring a foray of rotten scents whisking from the cold dumpsters, the refreshing aroma of a peppermint Macabi hit both their noses at once. Marvin's arm reached out to stop Shawn from stepping around the corner, guessing good ol' Grandad Santa was taking a breather around back.

"Shit…" Marvin was still trying to pull himself together, steady his nerves. "Should we say somethin'?"

Shawn pushed Marvin's hand from his chest like his touch was tainted. "Nah, fool, you crazy?!" he whispered frantically.

"I'on't know, man, I feel like we should try an' warn him…"

Shawn shook his head in partial defeat, knowing Marvin had a point. They couldn't just let whoever was doing this keep picking off their friends one-by-one. For all they knew, they were the reason the Christmas crowd was being targeted.

"Jus'…" he sighed, "Jus' let *me*, a'ight? You still strung the fuck out. You gon' say some stupid shit and let him know we *know* somethin'…"

Marvin had no argument.

Close enough now to see the white smoke streaking inside the wind, when they rounded the corner Shawn immediately went to work.

"Oh shit, Grandad… I *thought* I smelt this nigga!" He smiled and held out his palm for some love.

Marvin came in right afterward for a slightly awkward hand-greeting that just felt out of rhythm. "Sup, Grandad."

"Lil niggas!" His strap-on white beard was tucked in the back of his pants, likely trying to avoid it reeking of scented tobacco. Santa hat snug over his ears and forehead, he looked into both their eyes and couldn't miss the lingering distress they held. "You boys look like Satan done made you his bitch in Hell… Prolly should ease up on the hard shit 'fore Christmas, lest you wanna break yo' po' mommas' hearts."

Marvin tried to smile, and Shawn responded.

"Fuck, Grandad… Shit's been wild lately. Prolly havin' a little *too* much fun… You off already?"

"Hell nah… Just takin' a break while they question the staff. They talk to you boys too?"

"Who, the police?"

He hummed a "*mmhmm*" while puffing on his cigar.

"Yeah, man, crazy shit. You heard from any of the crew?"

Spitting a bit of tobacco from his lips, he said, "I'on't even got any of they numbers… They sure as shit don't got mine." He offered the boys a puff and they declined. "But, nah… Haven't heard shit. Just assumed they give as hairy a rat's ass about being here as me an' stopped coming in. Wuz thinkin' 'bout playin' hooky *myself* tomorrow. Who the fuck gon' bring their kids to sit on fake-Santa's lap on Christmas eve?"

"Yeah, yeah," Marvin jumped in and Shawn nearly cringed. "You should just bounce out now, man. Fuck this place. Shit's gettin' weird, right?" His eyes screamed "get the fuck out!" and Grandad wasn't stoned enough to not notice.

"You a'ight, young blood? Look spooked…"

Marvin's jaw froze partly open with the words, *he's on to me,* echoing in his mind, so Shawn jumped in.

"This fool just sick. Came in anyway to kiss that white woman booty." He puckered his lips to add to his show. "Gave him some pills to keep in the game an' this fool took too damn many."

Grandad stared into Marvin's eyes, searching for the truth behind them before Marvin shrugged nervously and the old man laughed.

"Bahahaha! You tweaked the fuck out, ain'tcha?!" He shook his head and Marvin nodded strenuously. "Boy, you two young niggas is a mess!" He exhaled an amused sigh. "Takes me back… Shoulda seen me in Nam – woulda shit yo' fatigues lookin' in my eyes with an' M16 wrapped around my neck."

Shawn chuckled. "Fuck that shit… You scary as fuck dressed as Santa!"

They all laughed, some more genuinely than others. Then Shawn went on, trying to smooth out the rough spots.

"F'real, though… He ain't wrong – shit's gettin' strange 'round here, man. You gotta gun?"

Through a cloud of smoke, he said, "Hell yeah, I got guns… My RV is fortified, lil nigga."

"*Sleep* with that shit tonight, Grandad—"

"F'real," Marvin added.

"Them colors you wearin' is bad luck right now," Shawn continued.

Grandad nodded and put out his cigar. "Don't you worry about me, young blood. Ain't nobody dumb enough to fuck with *this* nigga."

"I'm sayin', though…" Shawn held out a paw for departing gestures.

"Yeah, I hear ya." He extended his mitt to them both as they started on their way. "An' you ain't wrong… Shit's startin' to smell funny 'round here, an' I ain't talkin' 'bout that leftover Booboo Express in these dumpsters…"

"So, you'll watch yo' back, then, yeah?" Marvin needed to throw in his extra two cents before it was too late to make change.

"Yeah." His answer was dim with consideration. It seemed the boys may've gotten through. "Yeah, I will." He reached in his pants to pull out and straighten his beard. "You two stay sharp now, too, ya hear? I know you ain't wearin' read and green, but you boy's is practically one'a *us*."

They waved their affirmation as they started off, sullen to his words. It never occurred to them that *they* might be in the line of fire – whoever was doing this could just be saving them for last...

Their walk around the outside of the mall was a dour and gelid battle against icy wind and gut-wrenching guilt. So far, they'd had it easy considering the corpses they'd disposed of were hardly more than acquaintances... But the thought that Grandad was likely on the list was one that neither could attempt to bare.

"Yo," Marvin finally broke their silence when they made it inside the truck. "How 'bout I crash at yo' pad tonight?"

Shawn revved up the old Datsun, not sure how to respond. "I'on't know, man... If that shit follows you to my crib, we fucked."

"It won't, man... Yo' house doesn't have an open backyard like mine. You surrounded by other homes an' shit. And, if nothin' else, maybe with all them folks around, someone'll catch 'em in the act if they try..."

"And if we wake up to my mom and pops dead under my tree?"

Marvin shook his head. "You know that shit don't fit the M.O. Not unless yo' pops is plannin' on rockin' red velvet 'round the house..."

"It's risky, man..."

"C'mon, man, I can't sleep in that house tonight. I can't risk wakin' up to that shit again. I gotta better chance of gettin' some sleep if I crash witchoo."

"And you okay with leavin' yo' moms and baby bro by theyselves?" His eyes made his point as clearly as his words did.

"I don't *want* to... But they prolly safer without me. Not like I can do shit against whoever the fuck is stringin' up bodies like Christmas lights, anyways."

A long pause with Shawn's fingers nervously fidgeting against the wheel finally came to an end. "A'ight, man..." He threw the truck in reverse and started home. "I jus' hope this don't make shit worse for me..."

Marvin nodded. "Me too, bruh..."

DECEMBER 20ᵀᴴ

12 AM

2 hours after meeting Grandad:

Red, green and white lights like a galaxy of yuletide stars submersed them in holiday cheer while silver and gold tassels dangled from the tips of heavenly bodies to bring joy to all. Snow speckled rumps thumped to an EDM baseline, muffling the cry of the faithful as they chanted *"Daaayyyummm!"* in unison, awed by the spectacle.

"Yo, you know who that is?!" Shawn had to shout over the loud music, seated between Marvin and Grandad Santa around the stage at Tango's Foxtrot: Fine Drink and Dance.

"You don't know her, nigga, quit playin'!" Marvin brushed his friend off with a banana daiquiri in one paw and a fistful of ones in the other.

"That's Bry's ex-girl, fool!"

"Shut yo' mouth!" Marvin wasn't buying it.

"F'real! 'Member we seen her a few years back? She used to be at his crib all the time, just…with more clothes and less…" He threw out the universal gesture for big boobs.

Marvin's interest was piqued, eyeing his friend for signs he was screwing with him, then, when he found none, examined the facial features of their entertainment more carefully. After several trying seconds of not staring at her mostly-naked curves, he was beginning to see the resemblance. When the light caught the glitter on her cheeks just right— "Oh, shit…" but he wasn't entirely convinced. "Nahhh, nigga! It's *dark* in here! You trippin'!"

Shawn shrugged and nursed his piña colada. "A'ight, bruh. But it is." Marvin not believing him only made the reality of it his alone. He knew it was her because he'd heard she worked here before coming in. He just thought it was a rumor until he laid eyes on her. "I'm pretty sure Bry paid for those, too!"

Marvin laughed. He didn't believe it, but the thought that it might be true made the show that much more intriguing.

It was an ongoing Christmas party in the Foxtrot with sultry flavored merriment abound. As it turned out, Grandad Santa used to be a bouncer here for thirteen years and had no problem getting his "nephews" in for their early Christmas present after Marv's long first day in the mall. The joint was filled with the afterhours crowd, most with festive trimmings to fuel the theme – the Arctic Click had been a big hit the past few nights, especially the little elves (who were apparently big tippers). And when the alleged Bry's ex-gf came in for the kill on all fours like a cat stalking a mouse, Marvin helped to lure her in by playfully waving his bills and pulling them slowly toward him.

Corn silk hair down straight to one side, she leaned over the stage into his personal space and licked his daiquiri from stem to rim. Frozen in salacious shock, he couldn't lift a finger to stop her when she bit into his four-dollar spread, yanked it from his grip, then crawled off, ass high in a concupiscent sashay.

After a few seconds of trying to maintain dry underpants he muttered, "Holy shit, that *is* her…"

Shawn laughed, threw a few bucks on the stage for the show and howled like a horny coyote ready to hump a full moon.

Marvin eventually regained his composure and turned to the elder in their midst. "Yo, Grandad! This is the coolest shit I ever seen!"

Santa hat still adorning his skull while his coat draped the chair, beard firmly in his back pocket, he raised his 20oz mug of ale to toast to his new young friends. "Ho-ho-ho, little niggas! Looks like you just made my naughty list!"

"Fuck yeah!" Marvin hollered, and Shawn followed suit, all three drinks held high to clank on queue.

A chug, sip, and a slurp down the hatch and Shawn got up from his post. He smacked Marvin on the chest and headed for the men's room, high-fiving several of the Christmas crowd on his way. Marvin took the opportunity to slide on over next to Grandad to be sure he had someone close by to share in his experiences.

"F'real, man, this is fuckin' lit!"

"Huh?!" The old bruiser had to lean in to hear.

"I said this shit's off the chain!"

"Ain't no thang, young blood! This place is like a second home to me!"

Marvin laughed. "You ever take any of these girls home?!"

He nodded under his sip of beer. "Hell yeah! Used to be a *few* who I'd escort outta here."

"Nah, I mean—"

"Yeah, son, I know what you sayin'! And I'm sayin', shit yeah! Most the times I'd just walk 'em out or give 'em a lift home, but there'd been plenty over the years who wanted to keep the party goin'!"

"Any of 'em still here?!"

Grandad almost choked on his beer with a laugh. "Hell nah, son! They'd be thirty-somethin' by now! Ain't a dime in here over twenty-four!" He raised his chin toward the back corner. " 'Cept maybe Alley, back there! She gotta be pushin' thirty!"

Marvin followed Grandad's chin to find a marginally larger woman shrouded by the shadow of someone's husband flirting in the back. "I'd hit that!" He admitted, and Grandad went on.

"I don't even think she dances no more; jus' works on the marks for free drinks an' tips! Think she works at the grocery store on Market in the day!"

Now it was Marvin's turn to spit up his drink. "Oh, shit! I seen her last week!" He laughed. "God damn! These ladies livin' whole other lives up in here! Can hardly recognize 'em with the wigs and makeup an' shit!"

Grandad chuckled. "You be surprised whose mommas you know used to work up in here when they was young…"

The thought started as a laugh then morphed into downright paranoia. "Hold up… You ain't sayin you know my moms!"

He shrugged, "Maybe I do, lil nigga!" then covered his smirk with his glass.

Marvin paused in some estranged purgatory of his own making before catching the grin under Grandad's mug. "Motherfucker!" He punched his antagonist in the arm and laughed.

"I jus' might be yo' daddy, boy!"

Marvin shook his head and smiled. "The fuck outta here, Grandad!"

They both laughed.

"Yo, Migi!" Shawn shoved the men's room door aside like he owned the commode, alluding to Miguel, Santa's little miscreant still rocking the elf-wear. "How's it hangin'?!" He laughed at his own cheesy humor with Miguel standing on his tippy-toes at the urinal, all three-foot-seven of him with a Heineken warming up in his palm.

"It ain't!" the little guy replied. "I'm just trying not to piss up my nose!"

"AhHaaa! Whooo! This shit was a good idea!" He went for the stall to handle his business. "You dudes is some cool peeps, man!" He heard the toilet flush before Miguel responded.

"I'm glad you boys got to hang! I'll introduce you to my lady when we go back out. Just make sure you wash your hands!"

Shawn hissed an intoxicated laugh. "Aww, man! This night's been fuckin' bonkers, bruh! I can't believe I'm here right now!" Zipped up and adjusted to stroll, he headed for the sink to clean up while catching Miguel inhaling a white rail from the counter. "Damn, fool! That shit bigger than yo' arm!"

The frosted elf snorted, conquered the drip, then shook it off with a primal, "Ahhhh! Shit, that's nothin'!" He wiped the snow from his nose. "But I gotta keep my head on straight around these broads, man." Offering Shawn the rolled-up bill, the young party animal declined.

"I'm cool, man. I keep it all na-tur-al!"

"What're you, a fucking hippie?" He smacked Shawn on the thigh with a swat from the back of his hand. "How about rolls, man? You wanna *really* have a good night?"

"What, you mean molly?"

He pulled out two capsules filled with white powder. "If that's what you kids're calling ecstasy these days." He juggled them a little in his palm. "Pure MDMA, my man. It doesn't get any cleaner than this shit."

Shawn hesitated...but couldn't bring himself to turn down the opportunity. "I ain't never rolled before..." Fingers reaching, he asked, "This shit gon' fuck me up?"

"One pill will do you right, get you in a good mood. Two will have you rolling around on the floor making carpet angels and kissing peoples feet who walk by."

He laughed and shook his head. "Two it is, then!" He grabbed the other one, but Miguel slowed him down.

"Stick with the one, my man. You're still soaring from your trip earlier. One'll set you straight."

Almost disappointed but slightly relieved, he said, "A'ight, Mig." He pronounced Miguel's abbreviated handle like it was short for "midget" – an irony the little guy reveled in. "Good lookin'." A handful of tap water drowned the pill into oblivion. "You gon' roll too?"

Miguel pulled the pill apart and dumped the powder on the back of his hand. "I prefer to take mine to the head." With a voracious snort, the little powder-mountain disappeared in a whiff.

"How long's it take to hit?"

"For you? About thirty to forty-five. Let's get out of here, though, before people think you're in here blowing me for drugs or something."

"Pshhh! Like they'on't know I'm all about the ladies!" He followed his new friend out into the happiest place on Earth. "Yo, I need another drink!"

Miguel shook his head and waved for him to follow. Shawn saw Marvin hanging with Grandad back at the stage and hollered at his boy with a fist-pump before finding his way to a table with Xavier, the other little guy, and another elf who he couldn't remember the name of. She was in her twenties and obviously into women, stuffing someone's panty-line with a few ones when they sat down.

"You havin' a good time, young playa?!" She asked with a bright smile, her elf hat on the table to let her dirty-blond hair down.

"Oh, hell yeah! This shit is insane!"

Miguel slid him over a bottled water. "Here!"

Shawn looked at it like he'd never seen H2O before. "What about my piña colada?"

He shook his head. "It'll dull your roll! Trust me! Stay hydrated and you'll thank me later!"

Shawn shrugged. He figured the little guy knew what he was talking about so cracked open the Glacial Springs at his behest. A few minutes later and a Latina goddess glided over to their table with a waitress in tow and a serving tray hosting an ice-bucket full of Coronas. "Damn... Y'all know how to get down!"

The goddess circled the table, sliding her fingers across Shawn's back until she came to Miguel who put his arm around her waist while she de-capped his beer.

"This is my special lady! Candeleria!"

"What?!"

"Candeleria!"

Shawn wasn't getting it. "Nigga, I'on't know what the fuck you sayin', but goddamn, you got it good!" He eyed the slender, sensual deity, her body covered in gold glitter with a gold choker matching her under garments. "Whatchoo supposed to be?" he leaned in and asked.

Her smirk led her lips toward his ears, close enough that he could feel the warmth of her breath when she said, "Your dreams come true."

He raised a knuckle to his teeth and bit hard. Miguel smacked her on the ass then slid up to the table. "I'll be sure you get a dance with her later when your rolls kick in!"

Mouth wide in utter amazement, he held out his hand. "My nigga!"

Miguel responded with his own mitt in Shawn's and Xavier leaned into the conversation.

"My man! You got more…?" He put two fingers to his lips to symbolize a spliff.

Shawn nodded. "Hell yeah! You wanna smoke?"

"Does a midget love to eat pussy?!" was his rhetorical reply that always brought the house down.

"I wanna come!" the dirty-blond elf called out and Shawn was happy to contribute.

"Cool! Let's roll!"

Outside, the wind was sharp but refreshing. Shawn took a deep breath as he noticed the lady-elf kissing a bouncer on the cheek behind them. Xavier was well on his way to the parking lot beside the building so Shawn followed once the straggler caught up.

"What's up with dude?" Shawn wondered, tilting his head back toward the bouncer.

"That's my man," she answered, closing a coat over her elf costume and shivering at the wind.

"Oh, like yo' *man* man?"

"Yeah. Why?"

"Jus' thought you were…"

"What, gay?"

He shrugged. "Looked like you were really diggin' the ladies."

"I was."

"So you Bi?"

"Pan."

He had to take a second to let the concept of pansexuality sink in. "What, you mean, like, you into everything? Chicks with dicks an' all that?"

"It's more like I don't discriminate when it comes to sexuality. But, yeah… 'Chicks with dicks' if that makes it easier for you." She smiled.

"You know there's no such thing, right?" Xavier joined in on the conversation from about ten feet ahead of them, zeroing in on his ride.

"What, 'chicks with dicks'?" Shawn asked.

"They're all just dudes with tits, man."

"So, you think hermaphrodites are a myth, or what?" She figured she'd bait him a little and see how he responded.

"With an actual functioning cock and vag? Yeah, for sure. Why? You know different?"

"Nope," she shrugged. "I spend too much time having actual sex to spend any searching the internet for that kind of thing."

Shawn chuckled then dropped his jaw at the sight of Xavier's 1959 orange Cadillac. "Whaaaat?!" Fist clenched over his gaping maw he asked, "This yo' ride, bruh?!"

"My pride and joy." He unlocked the driver's side and flipped the seat forward for his troop to pile in. (No one noticed Big Red Bryan chatting up the bouncer at the front entrance while Shawn followed lady-elf into the back.)

"*Who-oo-ooo!* This is *tight*, man!"

Xavier jumped into the front and shut the door, turning on the engine to rev her up and get some heat in the cab.

"Shit! Marvin's got the pen…" He checked his pockets, only to discover he had a big bag of weed and nothing to smoke it out of.

"It's cool. I have papers. You want me to roll?" X reached into his glovebox for the appropriate paraphernalia.

"Go for it, bruh." He threw the sack onto the front seat. "Seriously, though… How the hell you afford this ride on an elf's salary?"

"Maybe he built it in Santa's workshop," lady-elf grinned and leaned forward to finagle her iPod into the renovated dash. She was petite, hardly more than one-hundred-ten pounds, and pretty, even without makeup.

"*Pffft!*" Shawn tried to hold it in.

"You know I out rank you in the Elf Order, right, El?"

Ellen! Tha's her name!

"You and your 'elf seniority' jokes…" She leaned back, iPod plugged in, thumbing through her playlists. "That's all I hear, all day long…"

Shawn chuckled.

"No, but I bought this beauty from my great uncle years ago. Fixed her up with my dad before he passed."

"Y'all did a hell of a job."

"Thanks, man."

Then the beat kicked in and Shawn was once again in blissful wonderment – Jarren Benton's *Money Bag* tantalized in base and rhythm.

"What, girl?! You like rap?!"

"Fuck yeah!" Her head nodded to the beat.

"Shit, this girl blew my mind the other night," breaking up buds for his roll, Xavier looked back. "What was that, yesterday?"

"Wednesday, I think."

"Yeah, Wednesday."

"Why, what happed?"

"Man, you gotta hear it to believe it… You wanna show 'im your skills, Grandmaster El?"

Shawn couldn't believe what he thought X was suggesting. "Noooo…" he started, in shock to the thought.

"I don't know if he's ready for this," she teased.

"Oh, I *know* he isn't," X chuckled.

"Alright, alright, let me find the right beat…"

"I'll do you one better." He licked the spliff to seal the deal, lit the end, took a puff, passed it back, then turned the music down. "You ready for this shit, man?"

Shawn let El hit the joint first, then accepted it with a cheery grin. "I ain't even sure what 'it' *is*… But hell yeah!"

X cleared his throat and raised his fists, beatboxing stance initiated to hit them both with a beat that neither expected.

"*Ohhhhh!*" came a unified exclamation from the bedazzled crowd.

"Okay, okay…" After composing herself, El rolled her neck and found the rhythm. "Check it…" When the beat came back around, she let 'er rip. "I wreck rhymes and catch dimes while all these kittens sweat mines. Hot ass lines droppin' fireballs on landmines!"

Shawn was beside himself, bobbing his head along with their performance.

"A dragon on the mic, eradicating mice. You're a rat full of lice that even cats wouldn't bite! So say goodnight before it's over, I could clobber you drunk or sober. Don't argue with your Queen, I teach lessons with a flamethrower! Scorching all humanity! I'm a sorceress with the profanity! You're desperate for a taste, but you can't *catch* young Calamityyyyy!" She threw two thumbs up to point back at herself to end her verse.

"Ohhhhh! She killt it!" They laughed, and X brought the beat to a close. "Is that yo' rap name? Calamity?"

"You know this, dawg!" She grabbed the joint then passed it up front.

"Hahaha! Nice! That shit was lit!" He was having more fun than he could ever remember. "Y'all are fuckin' cool, man... Really turned my night around."

"Dude," X tried to get a word out through a lungful of smoke. "You were so fucked earlier!" He laughed and choked at the same time.

"He *was*, right? What was Damon calling him?"

Both X and El remembered together— "Black the Tripper! Hahahaa!"

Shawn shook his head and pulled at his shirt, airing himself out. "Crazy fuckin' night, man. I was out my *mind* earlier." A warmth rolled over his body, a sense of relaxation that tingled when X turned the music back up. "Damn... Think that pill is kickin' in..."

"Dude, you're still going?!" El was aghast with amusement. "What'd you take?"

He rolled his head around, taking in the tingles and the warmth, suddenly feeling like he could just melt into the upholstery. "M-molly..." The music was banging its rhythm on his bones... "Oh, *shit*, this feels good..."

They chuckled.

"You ever rolled before?" El wondered.

"Nah..." he managed to say while slipping into his high.

"C'mere." El adjusted herself to sit facing him and turned him around. "You're gonna love this..." She blew on his neck and started working her fingers on his upper back and shoulders.

"Holyyyy *fuck*, that's the shit..."

"Take off your jacket."

She didn't have to tell him twice. He disrobed and took a swig from his water; it tasted like life itself... He drooled a little in his enthusiasm. "Oh, god..." Entirely disarmed with a sudden urge to go out and roll in the sleet, he murmured, "I think I love you, El."

She cracked a laugh. "Well, who doesn't?"

It wasn't long before an intrusive knock on the window brought the doorman – aka, El's burlier half – over to break up the good time. She looked back over her shoulder to see him towering outside the Cadi and figured she'd better pay him some mind.

"Gotta go, guys..."

Marvin groaned.

"...Duty calls."

"Aww, mannnn... What's that big ass ogre got that I don't?"

She smiled, leaned forward to kiss Shawn on the cheek, then crawled into the front seat and exited stage right. "See you fellas inside."

"Damn..." Shawn sunk back into the upholstery. "Dudes is always hatin' on a nigga's good time..."

X passed him back the joint. "You'd do the same if she was your girl."

"Hell yeah!" he admitted. "Still, though... That shit she was doing with her hands was magic!" He took a huge drag, hardly able to feel the fire, and blew the biggest cloud of smoke he'd ever seen. "God damn, this molly is the shit!" Lazily, his limb extended to hand the joint back to his host.

"Shawn. *Dude*... I got arms like a T-Rex... You're gonna have to try a little harder than that."

Shawn giggled like someone poked him in the dough-belly, then leaned forward. "Yo... Let's go outside, man..." Gazing through the windshield at the snowy wilderness obscured by shadow, he abruptly felt a call to the wild.

"It's colder than a witch's tit out there!"

"Yeah, but," he aired himself out, "it's hot as fuck in here... Need some fresh air."

After much consideration: "Alright, alright... Just don't go running off. I'm too damn short to run after you, and your ass'll freeze to death if you get lost in those woods."

He waved his hand out, dismissing the notion. "Nah, man, I ain't going nowhere. Just hard to breathe in here right now…"

"Don't make me regret this." He got the feeling he'd need a leash to keep Shawn out of trouble but could tell he was in the "roll" stage of his trip and would be mostly floored for at least another ten minutes.

So they entered the dark World of Winter with intentions on getting air, which, to a smoker, meant it was time for X to light up. He offered one to Shawn, but tobacco wasn't his thing. He shook his head and stretched his arms, taking in the chilly wilderness with a deep breath and a satisfied sigh of release. The sterling flavor of nature was like imbibing pure refreshment. His hot breath on the breeze rolled away from his lips and stayed visible for twenty feet, dancing in the current, spilling whisks of his imagination into the night air.

"*Wwwahhhwahhhwahhhwahhhh*…." The noise amplified the experience of the puffs of mist released from his throat as he created whole scenes in white clouds that disbanded into the wind like a dream. It took him a minute to realize that most of the clouds were coming from X's Winston's. "Oh, shit," he giggled. "I forgot you was smokin'…"

"E is a hell of a drug…" He blew another thick white billow to the delight of his young associate.

"I'ma have to get some more'a this shit…" He shuffled back up against the warm hood of the car. "Oh, god…" Cheek to the hood, he whispered sweet nothings into the Cadi's ears. "You feel so good, babygirl… I could just sleep right here tonight…"

"Hell no, you can't," X assured him. "But Mig got those pills from me. You want more, I'll hook you up. I'll give you four for fifty."

"*Dayuumm*… Ain't that a little steep?"

"Dude… They go for twenty a roll. I'm giving you the wholesale price."

"A'ight, a'ight…" Hands clumsily finding his pockets, he pulled out about eight dollars and took five minutes to count it. "Shit… I wasn't prepared for this kinda night, man…"

"You got money at home?"

"I can get it."

X shook his head. "I don't want you stealin' from your momma, now…"

"Nah, fool! She broke as *shit*… I work with my uncle doin' graphic design."

"Seriously?"

"Yeah, man. Since I was fourteen. Gonna be a game designer. Already takin' college courses an' shit."

"Damn, kid… You gotta leg up on me at your age. I didn't have a job 'til I was twenty-two…"

"*Pfff!* Hahaha! Aww, man… Fuck you was doin'?"

"Drugs." He laughed, and Shawn did too.

"Oh, shit… That's priceless, nigga…"

X slid over to the passenger side of his ride. "I'll front you fifty's worth and just pay me by Christmas, cool?"

"Fuck yeah, man. You the shit, f'real." He was starting to get a grip again, refueling his cells with fresh oxygen. He'd been so relaxed his eyes were barely open for half their conversation, so when he opened them he was taken by the vibrancy of the night. "Whoa…"

The forest was vast; trees like an army of Ents standing watch to safeguard the winter realm. These frosted giants spoke in the language of the wind through their leaves, a soft blue aura radiating from the cold they'd collected. The Eldar were there too. Their long white strands of timeless elven hair providing the perfect camouflage amidst the snow. They hung back in the shadows that shielded them from the eyes of men, reassuring the safety of the forest and its benevolent inhabitants. But in every fantasy world, no matter how elegant and virtuous, there would always be an enemy seemingly too great to defeat. One more powerful than all the armies of middle Earth combined. A beast whose puissance rivaled the gods with an unquenchable thirst for life's succulent nectar…

Its breath blew snow from the leaves of trees in swirling gusts of heat, its lionlike back gracing just below the forest's top. The softness of its padded feet was nearly undetectable, but the sway of the Ents song of rustling branches told no lies.

It moved like it was stalking prey, melting the frost on the brush that trickled in streams to the forest floor.

Until it stopped.

Shawn's eyes were as wide as hubcaps. He wanted to call out but knew better than to make a sound. This thing was enormous… Blueish fur that shimmered with the slightest touch of the moon light, he could see its musculature ripple under its coat as its lowered, feline face turned to spy who'd spotted it.

Jaw dipping at the utter helplessness of being caught in its stare, he was so taken by the beast he couldn't tell if he was afraid or mystified... It had to have been fifteen feet tall, with tiger-like stripes of blue on blue – rippling...*glistening*... He could almost hear its purr...

When the door slammed shut behind him he jumped at the sound, looking back to see what manner of lumbering oaf would dare cause such a ruckus.

"Here." X walked back around with a tiny Ziploc bag that held four little white capsules. "Remember... Fifty by Christmas eve." He held it out for Shawn to accept his generosity and noticed the look of utter betrayal in his gape. "What? The mall's *closed* on Christmas..."

Astonished at the audacity, he quickly whipped his head back around to gaze once more at the marvel his eyes had been blessed with...but only found the after-shimmy of the trees waiting to be seen.

"That..."

"What?" X was lost...

"Did you...?" He started to ask but knew better. If he'd seen it too, he wouldn't be chirping about future payments.

"Bro, those shrooms kick back in or what?" He noticed the bewildered gleam in Shawn's giant eyes.

"Dooood... You got no *idea* what I just been through right now..."

X laughed and smacked him on the elbow. "Let's go back in, man. The ladies are waiting."

Almost with reluctance, he shuffled behind the little elf on course for boobs and butts, still caught in the dream of the beautiful blue beast set off to conquer the world...

The remaining witching hours of sweaty, glittery turpitude were a vibrant haze smeared by intoxicants and heightened by colorful lighting and resounding music. Marvin and the old man bonded for most the night – he was the unruly father-figure he had always yearned for. When they weren't laughing, chatting, or outside blowing smoke, they were neck deep in hot, feminine flesh; lap-rides aplenty. The ladies seemed to get a kick out of the kick the underagers got out of them. The boys' youthful jubilance was intoxicating, not to mention they were both *monumentally* playful drunks.

At some point, Shawn managed to get a lap-dance from three of the clubs finest all at once (taking the smashed-goggles into consideration…), buried in the scented bliss of their most pertinent of parts. It was the most scintillating two-and-a-half minutes of his existence followed by a shower from a bucket of ice courtesy of Marv to cool him down – Shawn almost enjoyed the ice bath as much as the triplets.

Marvin blew his proverbial load (of cash) on three dances from Bryan's ex and she may've thrown in a fourth for fun, he wasn't sure. But when he was engrossed in her eyes, lips and curves, time seemed to have slowed for him; it was like a first, second, and third date all in one night, every succeeding encounter going a little further than the last. Needless to say, his boxers weren't the only casualty of the evening; his heart felt the loss of her departure nearly as deeply as his pockets had.

They managed to make it home before four in one piece, per se – a rather *mushy* piece, without much resilience to offer the harsh reality of consciousness, but capable, in that they figured out how to operate a door knob and bedding (to some degree). The night they'd endured was one they'd never be able to duplicate but would likely spend years trying. Nights like these were without equal. Conversely, some may say something similar about the mornings that followed.

Eventually, noon reared its cantankerous horns and stuck Marvin square in the gouch to say good morning. He stared that irascible beast right back in its fuzzy chasm of lost time for a face and swore to it he'd never drink again in exchange for another hour of sleep. But the beast relished in his agony and would agree to no such arrangement, twisting at the wound instead, forcing his victim to surface from his black slumber and take his place at the porcelain alter.

Marvin heeded the call and went through the motions, but come time for worship, he threw a wrench in the works and refused to kneel, squatting over the cold shrine instead and offering it his pasty penance for all it was worth. In the end, the victory belonged to him, his 4am Quick Stop meal still on the path he'd set it on, his last four dollars and some-odd cents money well sacrificed for sustenance to soak up the spoils.

He could nary recall the details concerning the ride home. He was pretty sure he didn't drive, *damn* sure Shawn couldn't…yet, when he made it back to his room he realized its occupancy was plus one more than usual, and not one he'd have bragged about to friends…

Shawn laid splayed atop four or five pillows on the floor, still fully clothed and faced down – a sorry sight to be seen. Confused, memories stirring like old beef stew in a lukewarm pot, Marvin left the scene of the mystery to cast some light on it from outside, pushing a curtain back in his living room and uncovering Shawn's truck at the curb, entirely in one piece and lightly sprinkled with snow. A few seconds of struggling to fill in the blanks brought a clue into view: a note clamped in the top of the passenger side window. After finding appropriate footwear to brave the ice-slicked front walkway, he shuffled into the chilly afternoon and down to where the answers he sought may be. Tugging at the rolled sheet of paper protruding from the vehicle, he ultimately had to rip it free for fear of otherwise taking the damn window with it. When he finally had the answers to his quest in his hands, he chuckled at the scripture it contained:

> Ho ho ho, lil niggas! Keys are in Shorty's jacket.
> GS

"Good shit, Grandad."

The old, jolly bruiser must've done them the honor of driving them home, then whisked away on a sled full of booze and blunts being hauled by strippers with antlers atop their melons back to wherever he crafted his Christmas miracles. Suddenly, the frigid aftermath of a night of utter debauchery didn't seem so cold.

After a breakfast run in the truck while Shawn still snoozed, he woke his friend with the alluring aroma of ninety-nine cent tacos and seasoned curly fries. A few woozy hours of half-assed gaming and chortling like Beavis & Butthead at the events of the prior night led Shawn to depart for a bed between more familiar walls and Marvin to a steamy shower that melted away the glitter and perfume he was still happily saturated with. He was back in uniform and on the clock at the parlor ten minutes early and eager as a zombie beaver to sink his teeth into his second shift with the boss.

"Good time last night?" Vibrant eyes and full lips flashed his way, and a goofy grin gave her her answer, but he proceeded to respond nonetheless.

"It was okay," he shrugged, playing it cool, tying his Tasty Cream apron loosely around his waist.

"Uh-huh." She knew that look. She'd seen it plenty of times in the expressions of young men she'd been courted by before marriage. "Well, hopefully I'm not keepin' you from *too* much fun... Just enough to remind you I'm still the boss." She winked at him and suddenly there wasn't another woman in the world.

"Yeah, well, there's about a zillion other cool things I could be doin' right now, but I'd hate to take torturin' me fo' *kicks* away from you."

"Good. 'Cause it's the highlight of my night. Pushin' 'round the little people's what I got in the ice cream business for, ya know."

"I figured it wasn't fo' the money."

She smiled, impressed by his witty repartee, setting a fresh container of Peppermint Christmas Blizzard into its slot. "So, do I get to hear about yer night?"

That goofy grin came back in full swing. "Ahhhh..." His hesitation radiated embarrassment. She had him squirming like a worm on a kitten's claw and she loved it. He washed his hands to divert from making eye contact. "There's nothin' to tell. Jus' hung with some friends."

"Girlfriends?" she baited.

He giggled, getting a flash of Bryan's ex on his lap staring so deeply into his eyes he couldn't think of anything else...until now. "There mighta been a female or two hangin' 'round. S'not like I need a lady present to have a good time, though."

She feigned seriousness. " 'Course not."

A few seconds ticked by and the silence between them winded their lips into big, luminous grins. Her penetrating eyes eventually made him laugh and he had to turn away.

"Stop!" he whined while she kept poking at him with her stare.

"Aww, but embarrassin' you is the only form of entertainment I got!"

He covered his smile with his hand, tugging at the corners of his mouth to try to rearrange his cheesy grin into a manly scowl.

It didn't work.

"Stop, f'real!"

"Never!" She pulled at the hand that hid his embarrassment. "Not until you give me her name!"

"*Pshhh!* I didn't get her damn name, shit…"

Her mouth sprung into the shape of an amused O. "You are somethin' else, ya know that?"

"What? That's how us playas roll." He pinched at his shirt to facetiously cool himself off.

"Right… 'Cause you love 'em and leave 'em, don't ya, playa…" A playful scowl attempted to tear through his defenses as she crossed her arms, her ass against the freezer, ice cream scooper like a weapon in her hand.

"Tha's how the game is *played*, boss-lady! I'on't make the rules." Arms folded to match her stance, he wasn't about to budge.

"Oh, so you just benefit off 'em… Is that how it is?"

He put two hands up to his sides. "When in Rome!"

She shook her head with eyes like slits that could pierce the heart of any man in striking distance. "You know Rome fell in the end, right darlin'?"

He sucked at his teeth with a soft shrug. "All the more reason to cash in now while the gettin' is good."

She tried not to smile… She tried *really* hard… But eventually her stern demeanor cracked, and she had to laugh. He smiled too and flinched at the swat of her hand he'd earned.

The rest of the night went better than he'd ever bothered hoping for. They laughed and worked and worked and laughed. He hardly noticed his hangover, putting aside all pain and anguish for a smile and the chance to further flirt with the unattainable. Eventually, taking a Thirty to get some grub in him, he wondered why he was torturing himself by having such a grand evening with a woman he'd never have a chance at getting closer to than incidentally brushing up against. But a good time was a good time, regardless, and he enjoyed every minute he got to spend with her.

He convinced himself the only thing that really mattered was that he'd get to pass the time with a gorgeous, funny, sweet, and impossibly cool older woman and, if nothing else, it was doing all sorts of good for his self-esteem. If he could keep up with a goddess like this then he could flirt with anyone. The warmth of her empowering presence seemed to just melt away his inhibitions and leave behind a stronger, more chiseled foundation in which to build a man. He felt like he was growing with every tease or joke they exchanged and he'd only end up a more confident person because of it.

Everything was coming up Marvin. It didn't even bother him when Mr. G showed up to escort his dashing better-half out of the mall after they closed up shop. Marvin had joy enough for everyone and gladly extended it to the man who put him in the position to delight in her company.

At home, he didn't once waste time longingly flipping through Snapchat stories to covet the events he wasn't a part of or the teenage girls he hardly knew, but instead, ripped a b-load and opened a book for the first time in over a year. A sense of fulfillment imbodied his mind-state that led to classic literature from H.P. Lovecraft and a marginally early bedtime. Sleep was a cherished reunion with an old friend.

Yep. Everything was coming up Marvin.

Five more days until Christmas…

Next on the list: A Happy New Yeaaarrrrrrr!

DECEMBER 22ND
10 AM

An alabaster December morning – as if God partook in the previous night's escapades and cracked open a leftover, city-sized pill to gently sprinkle its contents over the town of Winterset, Iowa – treated the two young go-getters to a wintery fresh start sometime just prior to noon. They likely could've slept until nightfall and awoke to the hooting of great gray owls – the so-called Phantoms of the North – with a stretch, scratch and a yawn, stumbling into form with brunch burgers in their eyes. But the chime from Marvin's cell denoting a text from last night's willing participant, Shandra, that read: Had fun last night. C u at the mall later, with a winking, kissy-face, disturbed his slumber and, in turn, stirred that of the sleeping Ewok's nuzzled on the couch.

Marvin's room was well-equipped to handle guests, being the domesticated basement his distant older brother had once ensconced. The upstairs only had two rooms: one for mom, the other for baby bro, but the basement was equal to them both. It was a smorgasbord of gamer paraphernalia, beanbags, and a bong for every occasion, from small, artfully blow glass to his narrow, six-foot, gray acrylic he'd named Slender Man. It was the type of room you'd likely find him still in in his early thirties, playing Call of Duty: Black Ops 17 with a hover-bong floating over his domed helmet filled with statically charged THC vapors.

He grinned at the text, then turned his attention to Shawn buried under a brown, fuzzy blanket.

"Bruh..." He kicked off his sheets and started layering clothing to brave the mid-morn. "*Bruh…*" Another call to the rustling grump under covers did little else but lead Marvin to take more palpable action. He looked around for a means to his end and called upon a lonesome Converse to be the agent of his intent. Hoisting it by the shell toe, he lobbed the shoe like a stun grenade, landing it on its mark and coaxing a primal groan from the little, forest dwelling critter.

"*Mmmmnnaaahhhh…*" came its response to the egregious attack, flipping over as if it'd disappear from the sights of its enemy if its back was turned.

"Bruh! The fuck *up*, man… Got shit to do…" Struggling to find a foot to fit in his Timberland, he eventually rose from his nest and pounded what was left of the two-liter bottle of Mountain Dew on his nightstand.

"Fuck you mean? I ain't doin' *shit* today…"

Holy hell… It speaks!

" 'Member? We promised my moms we'd salt the walkways. Gotta do that shit 'fore I go into work. Need yo' truck to go get the salt."

"Take it, man. The fuck you need me fo'?"

"I ain't haulin' twenty bags of that shit all by myself, fool! You helpin' was part'a the *deal*."

"Yeah, yeah…" It rolled over to face its responsibilities head on, still nestled under warm furs. "Damn… I *hate* the fuckin' snow…"

"It's about to hate you too, nigga. Get yo' ass up so we can go an' kill it."

Dozily, the thick-coated mammalian rose with naught but its face visible under its fur to eventually rejoin the Resistance.

It took the boys about two hours total to make the supply run and get the job handled, all walkways and steps de-iced and protected against further, frosty buildup. Finding a spot for their rears on the back steps, they figured they'd earned what they had coming: a gutted and finely rerolled Peppermint Maccabi courtesy of old Grandad Santa – bless his stoner heart. They both chuckled with enthusiasm for their ensuing high, eager to get toasty to counter the cold. It wasn't until the moment Marvin was about to light up that his eyes caught the snowed-over shed in the distance, the walkway toward it still buried beneath last night's flurry.

Marvin's shoulders deflated under the weight of utter depression;

Shawn didn't see what the hold up was.

"Dude...*now* what?"

Marvin shook his head and sighed. "The shed, man..." He lazily gestured fifty feet out. "We forgot to salt the path to the damn *shed*..."

Shawn gazed, not entirely concerned. "Who gives a shit? S'not like you ever go in there..."

"Yeah, man, moms said she needed to – that's what started the whole damn conversation."

Deflation was going around like the flu. Shawn hung his head and Marvin heaved himself onto two feet.

"C'mon, man. It'll just be another twenty, then we'll light up."

A sigh like a gut-wound poured from Shawn's mouth before he joined his friend to finish what they'd started. "We only got two bags left, man."

Marvin shrugged. "It's gon' have to do..."

And after about fifteen minutes of shoveling, the salting commenced. They sprinkled it sparingly, which they likely should have done from the start, and just about covered the walkway and the small cement slab in front of the door.

"The fuck's in here, anyways?" Shawn went for the knob, quickly discovering it was locked.

"Christmas shit. Decorations an' all that."

"Bruh... It's three days before Christmas..."

"What, nigga...? Moms is lazy, shut up." He reached in his pocket for the key she'd given him to retrieve the box of decor and proceeded inside. "What—?"

"Aww, dude..." Shawn gaped alongside his friend at the broken window and disheveled storage. "You got *jacked*, fool!"

"Aww, hell nah..." Marvin walked in and tugged on the light-string, illuminating the disorder – the results were disheartening. "The fuck, man? What kinda Christmas tweaker jacks a buncha ol' ornaments an' shit?" He approached the split open boxes to see a handful of broken Little Drummer Boys left to rot in their grave of demise.

"That's fucked up, yo..."

"*Damn*... I *thought* I heard some shit out here last night..." Eyes lifting to inspect the shattered glass, he caught the remains of stolen tinsel glimmering on the sill. "Hold up..."

Shawn followed Marvin's inspired hustle out to the side of the shed where, if they looked closely, a trail laid in silver and gold, leading into the trees behind his house.

"C'mon, man. Bring yo' shovel."

Shawn did as he was told, unsure of what Marvin was meaning for him to do with it if they happened across the caperer: dig himself a hole and hide?

The trail was nearly invisible without eyes specifically looking for the mostly snowed-over glimmer. Every ten to twenty feet the sun would catch the lingering evidence and highlight their path, taking them through the trees directly behind his house and further into the snowy woods.

"Yo, whatchoo expect to find out here, man?" Shawn wondered, trailing a little further behind than he probably should. "S'not like they gon' be camped out in a tent decorated with yo' momma's shit."

Marvin hardly cared for Shawn's naysaying. Something just seemed odd – like the trail was *meant* to be followed. He found himself taken by its mystery. "I'on't know, bruh... Shit's weird. Why the hell they go inna woods? There ain't another house back here fo' miles..."

Shawn couldn't bring himself to respond; Marvin had a point he couldn't think of a rebuttal for.

Five minutes later brought their hunt to a halt when the tinsel trail landed them at the base of a giant pine. Marvin circled the bulky trunk, searching for reason rounding the mysterious tree while Shawn hung back, not too eager to dig deeper.

"Mystery revealed!" He teased, playing off his discomfort while Marvin continued to pry. "Godfather pine done stole yo' momma's shit!"

Marvin proceeded to pay him little mind, crouching down to the base of the tree.

"What...? You gon' taste the powder and say some shit like, 'There was *three* of 'em: A righty and two lefties. One with a bum knee, the other, bad breath and an orange mullet'?" he snickered.

Marvin fondled the tinsel and brushed away some frost at the roots...

Nothing.

"C'mone, man! Shit's cold out here. You ain't gon' find *shit* in this snow..." He waved his arms out to encompass the vastness of it all. "Ain't no evidence left to be...found..." Eyes spying a pinch of green that was too bright to be foliage, he shuffled over to inspect it. "The fuck's this?"

Gloved fingers reaching for what looked like a bit of cloth, he picked at it with a few flicks of his index, uncovering more green below. Eventually he clutched enough fabric to pull it from its icy slumber, lifting the snow-covered object to eye level. The frost cocooning it made it difficult to make out, so he brushed at it until green turned to red. "Dude…" Unsure of what he was looking at, he kept up the dusting while he caught Marvin's attention, slowly revealing the pulpy, burgundy base of it. Marvin wandered over in the process and gaped curiously.

"Lemme see…" He reached for it and Shawn pulled away like he'd claimed salvage rights.

"*Chill*, man." Staring into the maroon center, he turned it over and started working on the other end, picking away while Marvin lent him a hand…that he obviously had plenty of already— "FUCK!"

He dropped the bloody stump when discovering cramped fingers at its opposite end and they both fell flat on their asses like someone tossed a bomb between them.

"WHAT THE FUCK, MAN?!" Marvin yelped – tone like he'd just graduated fifth grade – and Shawn responded astutely.

"It's a fucking hand!"

"No *shit* it's a fucking hand! Why the fuck you touchin' it?!"

"You touched that shit too, fool!"

"Nah! I di'n't touch shit!"

"You *touched* that shit, nigga!"

"Nah, *you* touched that shit!"

"Fuck!"

"Fuck!!"

Bloody stump erect in the snow, they stared at the human bit until it occurred to Marvin that, somewhere, there had to be the rest of a person who was *missing* it. When he found his voice, he muttered,

"Whe…where's the *rest* of 'em?"

Shawn's brows twisted in the middle. "The rest'a *who*, nigga?!"

"Him, fool! …The fuck? Mommas don't give birth to baby *hands!* There's uh, uh, whole 'nother *person* 'posed to be attached!"

"Fuck, you think I don't *know* that?!"

"Then why you askin', fool?!"

"Nah, man, I'm sayin', who! Who's the *person*?!"

"Fuck I look like, forensics?!"

"Shit!"

Panting, but catching their breaths, Marvin eventually grew the testicular fortitude to (ironically enough) crawl on all fours toward it, hoping to shed some light on their scenario.

"Don't touch it, nigga!"

"I ain't! Stop yellin'!"

"Man, it's a fuckin' hand, yo! The fuck you think I'ma do? Be cool?"

"F'real, man, keep yo' scury-ass voice down!" He got close enough to start searching for details. "Whoever did this shit could be close..."

"Wh...wh..." Shawn was having trouble making sense out of it all. "...Why they steal yo' Christmas shit and leave they hand, man?!" he whined.

"Shhhh!"

Head on a swivel, Shawn barked, "Thought you said you ain't forensics!?"

Ignoring him, Marvin straddled his focus and followed a strange line of logic that insisted the hand had to have come from somewhere, so he looked up—

"OH SHIT!!"

Shawn's gaze followed. "AHHHHH SHIT!!"

"Fuck no! RUN!!"

"Fuck!!"

On pace to make it to the Canadian border in T-minus thirty seconds, the two speedsters took off like rats on a sinking ship, headed for the illusion of safety of four familiar walls. But before they made it screeching back inside, a moment of reality-based paranoia flashed in Marvin's mind and he leaped onto Shawn's back to drag him to the snow.

Arms flailing like an octopus in hot water, Shawn had no idea who or *what* had tackled him and didn't care to find out. He commenced with the screaming that led Marvin's hand to muffle his cries.

"Stop, fool, stop!"

When Shawn realized what was happening, he yanked Marvin's hand from his mouth.

"Get off me, man, what the fuck?!"

"Just *chill*, a'ight?! We can't go bustin' into my pad all screamin' 'bout bodies an' shit!"

"The *fuck*, man, why not?!"

"Because, fool! They in my backyard! Those're my decorations all over that tree and the trail leads right the fuck back here!"

"*So*, nigga...? We di'n't do that shit!"

"Bruh... You see who was up there?"

He tried to make sense of the image in his mind. "Chr-Christmas peeps..."

"Yeah, fool. And we was the last ones to see 'em alive! 'Member, Grandad said they never showed up to work!"

The words were sinking in, but... "That...that don't mean we killt 'em!"

"But we suspects. And they in my fuckin' *yard*, nigga." Shawn pushed him off and Marvin went on. "We gotta think this shit through... We can't just go runnin' up in my momma's crib with this shit." He could see he was starting to get through. "Look, man... We innocent, so in the end it won't matter... But only if they can pin it on someone else. If not, we the one's gon' get *fucked*."

"N-nah, man..."

"Yes, fool! Couple young black kids with no friends and a shit load of drugs in they system? Buncha bodies turn up in they backyard and they the last ones to be seen with 'em?"

"F...fuck, man...tha's..."

"You gettin' me, man? We need to think about this shit... Gotta chill, a'ight?"

Swallowing hard, he said, "A-a'ight, man..."

Marvin slumped into the snow in relief. Now all he had to do was get his head on straight enough to decide on a course of action.

"What we gon' do?"

"I..." He didn't have a clue... "I'on't know... But we can't have this fuckin' trail leadin' to my house."

"We..." Shawn looked back at the path they'd wrought. "We can't...*un-fuck* the snow, man... No way we can c-cover that path... Not all of it..."

Marvin hated the thought, but... "Then we gotta go back..."

"Aww, man... Nah..."

"We gotta go back, man, an'...an' take that shit down. *All* of it..."

"Tha's...tha's tamperin' with evidence, yo!"

"I'll take 'dumb kids tamperin' with evidence' over 'juveniles convicted of first degree'."

"How the fuck they gon' convict us? There ain't no murder weapon—"

"Bruh, whoever did this shit, did it to us *specifically*. They tryin'a set us up, so who *knows* what evidence they left out there…"

"Fuck…" He hated that that made even the slightest bit of sense. But, in the end, he figured Marvin was right: They were innocent. Being scared kids trying not to get convicted of a crime they didn't commit wasn't going to get them life sentences in a concrete Hell, but if they were falsely accused and imprisoned when they could have avoided it all from the start… "A'ight…" He couldn't believe the words that were about to come from his mouth… "Let's…c-clean it up, then." He was trembling, but he wasn't cold. Heart racing, he asked, "You…you gotta ladder?"

With eyes not so focused on the trail, when the giant pine came back into view from several hundred feet away its icy grotesquery demanded their awe—

Body parts dangled from tree limbs, wrapped in soppy Christmas garland while blood-splattered, sliver ball-ornaments scintillated in what little sun still shone through the clouds. Frosted intestines draped the circumference of the tree with one of the Santas' hatted heads set fifty feet in the air to top the display like a morbid Christmas star. And blood seethed into the snow dripping from the needles leaving streaks of murder in perfect contrast with the season's white and greens.

"Oh, hell nah…" Shawn stopped dead in his tracks, unable to stomach the death in their path, but was pulled forward by the front half of the ladder Marvin carried. "We can't do this shit, man. *I* can't do this shit…"

Marvin was entranced, not even hearing his friend's mutterings. The sight before him looked like a spectacle of hatred… Whoever did this was doing it to make a point. …But one that escaped him entirely, as did his brunch burger when he got close enough to make out the expressions on several of the hanging faces. Maws all gasping in fear, the sight of terror in their eyes was worse than the terror their butchered corpses presented like an anti-Christian shrine of aversion.

Shawn's stomach turned after Marvin's, as much from the gore as from the sounds of his friend's guts wrenching at the sight of it. Several minutes post vacating their breakfast into murky, steaming swamps of vomit at their feet, Marvin proceeded on their path.

"Ho-hold on, man!" Wiping his mouth on his sleeve, Shawn hadn't picked up his end of the ladder yet. "We...we seriously gon' do this shit?"

"We have to..." He didn't even turn back to respond.

Shawn shook his head with putridity carving lines into his brow. "Shit, man..." He stomped on through the twelve inches of last night's snowfall and lifted his end of their shared felony. "This shit gon' take all *night*..."

"S'why I called in sick."

"I'm sayin, though... Maybe I shoulda brought my truck around—*hurrghh*..." He heaved when he caught a whiff of spilt insides spoiling the breeze. "Oh, fuck... The wind's turnin'..."

"C'mon, man. We gotta hurry."

"But what about my truck?"

"We'll bring it 'round when it's dark. Can't have anybody seein' us haulin' out big-ass tarps full of bodies. First we gotta get this shit down—*hrrng*..." He swallowed, barely managing to keep his guts inside him. "S...spread these tarps out like we said."

They dropped the ladder and unzipped their overloaded backpacks, reluctantly getting to work.

Four large tarps were spread flat around the base of the tree so they could cut down the messy bits and they'd splat right into position to be rolled up and dragged out. Pruning shears, hack saws, twine, rainslickers, and rubber gloves were the bulk of their carcass-scaping tools. They planned to not touch any fleshy remnants of what looked to be four of their new friends by cutting off the branches they were strung to and collecting the fallen trimmings. They needed to gather everything, including his mom's ornaments, and move them as far away from them as they could get without being gone for long enough to be suspiciously absent. Shawn spoke of a ravine he'd been to two summers back, deep in the woods up the 169 freeway, sixty miles north at Pilot Mound. He said the trail was nearly invisible and he found it by accident when he pulled over to relieve himself coming back from his cousin's in Rochester. If all went well, they'd bag up the bodies, drive an hour out to drop them in a ditch big enough to conceal a corn silo, then be back in time to take ten showers and smoke themselves stupid enough to fall asleep.

All did not go well...

Shawn feigned a fear of heights to start, putting Marvin on the spot to get up close and surgical with Operation Hack & Grab. The ladder got him to the lowermost branches, but when he braved their limbs to de-carcass the giant, Christmas murder-beacon, he realized quickly he was not equipped to do the job – at least not safely. Trying to prune the branches with sheers you needed two hands to operate when, coincidingly, he'd needed both those hands to keep from falling to a chilly doom, wasn't a functional diagram for being proficient. The sight of him attempting to hook his arm over one branch while reaching to cut another – legs spread between two more – would have been laughable if Shawn wasn't so engrossed in the suspense of the resulting *splat* from whatever may fall to the forest floor next.

"Man, *f'real...*" After the recovery of two arms and a leg, Marvin got to thinking. "What the hell you 'posed to be doin' down there? Piecing these dudes back together?"

Shawn suddenly realized he hadn't bothered pretending to help enough to get away with not doing anything. "I'm coordinatin', fool! How you gon' get alla'em if you can't see where they at?!"

"They everywhere, nigga! The fuck... You think I need help findin' this shit?! I'm swimmin' in *dead* folk up here!"

Quick, think fast, Shawn! He's not buying it!

"And what happens when somebody walks up and we both up there cuttin' down bodies with tarps full of people's legs an' shit?!" He let Marvin sit on that thought for a minute, hoping it wouldn't occur to him that anyone walking up would likely see what was in the tree anyway. "I need to be down here to cover this shit up real quick 'fore somebody sees it!"

After half the contemplation someone who wasn't perma-baked would pore over, Marvin sucked at his incisors and got back to work. "Fine... Stay down there, then. I hope this shit falls on yo' *head*, nigga..." Someone should have taught him to be careful what misfortunes he'd wish on others...

Shawn sighed internally, relieved he didn't have to climb through the crooked limbs of Hades' deranged forest to snip at intestines and saw through wet wood to get to frozen bones.

Eventually it became apparent Marvin couldn't get the job done without getting his gloves a little bloody. When it came to clipping the garland-guts, without a precise hand to release them slipping between branches, they'd just get stuck on more twigs below the higher he'd climb. Getting covertly vengeful, and a little delirious, he made it a surreptitious game of his to try dropping pieces through the maze and land them as near to Shawn as possible. He caught him off guard a few times, chuckling when he'd jump at the *thwap*, but it wasn't until near nightfall when he was sure he had him lined up for the ultimate Christmas goring.

Shawn had made it his duty to shovel the parts into piles so to be quickly tied off, breaking the branches mixed within for easier consolidation. He was getting good at organizing it all, putting thought into fitting the mess together like some horrific knot of the macabre. He was also charged with keeping count of the bits to be sure, in the end, they had collected all four complete sets. This, unsurprisingly, was not a task that particularly agreed with his attention span, but he'd started leaving tallies in the snow to assist in the endeavor – improvising in a crunch seemed to be his enduring strength.

From a Marvin's-eye-view, the fuzzy red, pompom top to Shawn's Storm Trooper, Christmas beanie was a gleaming bullseye eager to be plundered. He'd realized the problem before with hitting his mark had been the slimy intestines weren't bottom-heavy enough to not whip around and screw with his trajectory...so he extemporized—

Insensate to the dreadful, and on the bitter end of their engagement, he discovered the creative fortitude to keep a few of the hooks from ornaments he'd recovered and entangled them to secure a booted foot as an anchor. The contrivance was appalling...but structurally sound. And when his target was absorbed in his headwork, Marvin stealthily lowered the heavy end into position, calculating the drop, then waited for the precise moment to release...

The boot fell on its intended path, thirty feet or so before impact, pulling the wormy guts from the upper portion of the tree, gradually slithering closer to Marvin's shoulder. When it brushed against his neck, it suddenly occurred to the prankster that, in his enthusiasm, he'd forgotten to clip the other end.

At first, he jerked from the gut-serpent's closeness as it slipped between the crook of his neck and shoulder, still trying to maintain radio silence so not to alert the enemy. But as it became more apparent he'd royally screwed the pooch, with branches crackling above and the remaining bits higher still beginning to fall, he yelped at the happening with a swear and a spasm of his hands.

"Shit! Get off!"

Shawn looked up at the rustling outburst, spying the falling boot on course to leave its tracks on his befuddled face—

"Fuck!"

He dove from his post into the snow, a crater left under his weight... but without cause. The boot faltered in its path before reaching the ground, dangling from what it got caught on.

"What the hell, man?!" he hollered skyward, adrenalin spiking his voice.

Fighting the dimming sunlight to see through the foliage, Shawn traced the intestine-rope back to the object of its hang-up, somehow tangled in the gore, frozen like a spider being attacked by its own web...

Twenty-some-odd feet overhead, Marvin was face-to-crotch with the one-legged pelvis of George St. Nick and, incidentally, the thorax-source of his would-be entertainment.

"H...help..." he uttered softly, afraid to move for fear of setting further comeuppance into motion.

Shawn *heard* him...but was more engrossed in the dangling foot at the end of the insides Marvin was entangled in. He stood from his snow bed with his head tilted in perplexity, moving slowly toward the floating boot to investigate.

"The fuck is this...?" Gloved hand reaching to explore, he gave it a push, watching it swing – mystification consumed him.

"H...help..." came a cry for assistance again like the cooing of a pigeon caught hopelessly in the plastic of an improperly discarded six-pack.

Shawn eventually gave up on the enigma of the swinging boot to gaze high. The debacle he witnessed from his roost safely below put the mystery of the shoe to shame.

"The fuck happened to you?"

His explanation was brief and unconcise: "H...help..."

...In fact, it was no explanation at all.

"Icy Hot, nigga," Marvin wheezed through the white cloud in his lungs with a grin, referring to the refreshing combination of sensations their peppermint blunt provided.

Shawn giggled, as stoned as a heretic in the Medieval Inquisition, and inherited the ass-half of their source of Zen. "Hot an' Spicy," he countered, sampling the burn.

Marvin cheesed.

They'd managed to bag up four bodies in twenty-some-odd pieces into four separate tarp-loads in the rear of Shawn's Datsun and felt compelled to release some tension before setting off for Pilot Mound and the dense region of forest they were headed an hour north for; a discreet trail of snowed-over shrubbery they'd soon become all too familiar with. Bloody gloves and rainslickers packed into a trash bag, it was just passed sundown and a clearer night than most.

"Maaan…" Eyes lost in the stars while seated on the open gate next to his smoking companion, Marvin's gaze accompanied his thought. "…if we was on Mars right now, we'd be like, *twice* as high… An' that shit would prolly last twice as long."

Puff, puff… "Whatchoo mean?"

"Thinner atmosphere, bruh. I mean…if it had one we could *breathe* in." Shawn wasn't following. "Less gravity, yo. Prolly means the air wouldn't be so thick, so we'd be gettin' higher off less weed cuz there'd be less oxygen, like what they say about smokin' up in the mountains an' shit."

"F'real?" He passed the thinking torch back to the budding philosopher in their midst.

"Uh-huh…" Puff, puff… "At least, I think so…" Exhale… "Shit makes sense to *me*."

"If you say so, nigga…"

"An' them plants would be like the size of *houses* – less g's to weigh 'em down."

"Damn… Tha's a trip, though…" Astronomy was more of Marvin's thing, but Shawn was just as much a dreamer in his own right. "What about on Venus, bruh?"

"*Pshhh…* That place a wasteland, nigga. Ain't no weed plants growin' over there. It's too hot – shit snows metal."

"Fuck outta here, man…"

"F'real, dawg… Read somethin' about it blowin' outta volcanoes inta the atmosphere, then cools down and lands on mountaintops like snowcaps."

"That's nuts, yo…" He took another pull then caught a whiff of their cargo. "Almost as nuts as us *talkin'* 'bout this shit with four dead Christmas peeps in the back'a my truck."

"Damn…" Marvin shook his head. "You right, though. We need to handle this shit. …Prolly shoulda waited till after we was on the road to light up… M'high as *fuck*…"

Shawn chuckled. "Me too, bruh… It's the only reason we chill right now. Prolly a *good* thing."

"Yeah…" Marvin nodded, flicking the roach into the frozen wilderness. "You right. …Gotta stay sharp, though. We should grab some coffee when we gas up – stay alert, an' shit."

"Yeah… Oh, fuck!"

"What?"

"Maaan… We *stupid*, fool! We shoulda filled the tank *before* we loaded a bunch bodies in here… Now we gotta pull up to the station all stankin' like ass an' old meat!"

"Fuck!" Marvin threw his head back, astounded by their lack of higher reasoning, not even realizing he was leaned up against Larry the Elf's bag of mutilated pieces. "How much gas you got?"

They made their way to the cab to answer that query. When Shawn turned the engine over, they both watched the gauge slowly rise; every notch higher it climbed from E became more suspenseful. It cleared a quarter-tank in the first three seconds, then insipidly floated higher, conquering a third until it leveled out just under a half. Shawn tapped the plastic covering a few times to try to jar another eighth out of it…

It dropped one instead.

"Awww, maaan!"

"Can we make it on that?" Marvin inquired hopefully, stoned eyes as naïve as a child on Grandad Santa's lap asking for toys.

"I'on't even know, man… You gotta gas can in that shed?"

"Gogogogo!" Marvin squeezed the full gas can into the truck bed sandwiched between a tarp and a hard place while cracking open the door and— "Stopstopstopstop!"

"Fuck, fool, hurry yo' ass up!" Shawn jumped the gun and gassed it before Marvin made it back inside.

He hopped in and shut the door with vehemence. "Nigga, I almost ate yo' dust! The fuck is you doin'?!"

"You said *go*, fool!"

Marvin looked over his shoulder at the gas station fading off their list of to-dos behind them.

"Shit, man... I swear I could smell these niggas from the pump..."

Furtively, the sly duo had stashed the truck off the road behind some shrubbery across from their stop while Marvin walked the five-gallon container over. He'd topped it off and slithered back into the shadows afterward without a hitch...for the most part.

"Anybody see you?"

"Bruh... I paid *cash*. You know I ain't got a bank account..."

"Man, there's a cash thing between the pumps! You ain't hafta go in!"

"Whatchoo mean 'a cash thing'?"

He shook his head. "Forget it..."

"I ain't gotta car, man... How the fuck'm *I* 'pose to know 'bout that shit?"

A sigh as long as a sentence filled the cab. "Yeah yeah..." At least he didn't have to pony up for the petrol... "What happened? He say anything?"

"Nah... Lookin' at me like I was gon' steal his *cat* or some shit, but nah."

"Man... You wasn't supposed to be *seen*..."

"An' how the fuck I'ma do that? You gotta fuckin' invisibility cloak in yo' glove compartment, Scary Potter?"

"Shut up, man..." Shaking his head, he looked down at his hardly-a-third-of-a-tank. "Damn... We suck at this, fool..."

"We made it this far. As long as you don't get us lost in them woods we should be home free."

"Yeah..." Marvin's optimism was a breath of fresh air – Shawn gladly inhaled.

Their long drive was an arduously quiet one. Shawn never pushed the truck over sixty-five miles an hour and Marvin's heart jumped at every vehicle that passed them by, but they made it to the state forest in just over an hour. The tricky part, they realized while navigating the winding road, would be finding this nearly impossible, hidden trail of Shawn's...

"I think this it right here..." He slowed to a stop off to one side on the two-lane route.

"You said that the *last* three times..."

"You want this shit to be easy to find?"

Marvin gazed out the window as they pulled over. "Jus' sayin'... you marked yo' territory... Can't you sniff that shit out?"

"Fuck up, man... Shit was like two years ago..." When his headlights caught the yellow deer-crossing sign, the dim memory clicked into place. "Yeah... Yeah, this it. Watch..." He drove the truck deeper off-road, headlights beaming into the overgrowth, then stopped. "See that shit?"

Marvin peered intently. "I'on't see shit..."

"Exactly." He grinned, then started forward.

"Hold up, hold up."

"What?"

"Tha's a road?"

"Yeah, man. This it right here."

Rusty wheels grinding in his mind, he said, "I got an idea... C'mon."

They hopped out of the truck, boots crunching the white medium below, and Marvin reached behind the seat into the duffle bag that kept their pruning shears.

"If we cut these big ass pieces off and set 'em aside, we can put 'em back after we leave so the road stays covered insteada jus' bulldozin' over that shit."

"Yeah... Yeah, good shit. A'ight, let's do it."

It wasn't difficult to carry out Marvin's plan, and fifteen minutes later they were headed into darkness toward snowy ambiguity. The overgrowth hounded the Datsun's paintjob all the way through until the road abruptly ended with a makeshift, log barrier.

"The fuck this road even for?"

"I'on't know, man. Maybe they was gon' put a rest stop here or somethin' – picnic tables an' shit."

"A'ight, well where's this big-ass cliff you pissed offa?"

"Watch… This shit crazy."

They started on their way, walking perpendicular to the path, not making it very far before realizing they should've brought flashlights.

"Damn… Can't see shit…"

Marvin used his phone's flash to illuminate their course.

The forest was immense. They could hardly see the clouds through the trees above.

"Why you walk all the way over here to take a piss, man?"

Shawn shrugged, leading the way. "Just high on nature, bruh. Shit was cool as hell – like a secret spot where it was just me an' the trees."

"You scared to piss out in the open, huh?"

"Nah, man… Just trippin' on all these greens – unexplored territory."

"Shit's dense as fuck…"

"But, yo…" He figured it was time they were serious for a minute. "We ain't even really talk about this shit yet… Too busy tryin'a figure out how to clean it up…"

"Whatchoo mean?"

"Like, who the fuck *done* it."

"How the hell would I know?"

"Cuz it was at yo' crib, fool! Somebody obviously did this shit to *you*, right? Left that trail, an' shit. Killt them Christmas peeps we was chillin' with…"

"Yeah…" His guts clenched at the thought. "Fuck, man, I don't even wanna think about it. Makes me sick picturin' that mess in yo' truck as people."

"Yeah, but—"

"Nah, man… *Seriously*. Let's just get this shit over with."

Shawn knew how he felt – he felt the same way. "A'ight, man… We'll talk after we handle this shit."

"Tomorrow, man."

Shawn conceded. "Yeah… Tomorrow."

They walked for ten more muted minutes, the only sound between them their boots depressing snow. Marvin realized he would have likely fallen off the cliff and into a soaring, one-hundred-foot plummet if he'd been out there walking around in the dark without his guide.

He met Shawn at its edge to peer, his line-of-sight swallowed by the mouth of the abyss. Without the moon in the sky, it was too dark to clearly see the bottom – a perfect chasm in the middle of nowhere for abandoning your most fettering of carcass complications.

"Goddamn…" He got a little dizzy staring into its solemnness. "Nobody gon' find shit down there…"

"Like you said:" Shawn threw a little optimism of his own Marvin's way. "We home free."

Almost enthusiastic, they marched back the way they came, clearing a path the best they could in route. They agreed they could get the truck nearly through to the cliff if they chained the tires and avoided a few trees. They'd probably end up just short of the ravine by about a hundred feet. Dragging hefty piles of body parts that far wouldn't be easy, but it was *loads* more doable than attempting the same thing over grounds eight times as distant.

Slowly, Shawn maneuvered the terrain like a kid who'd never taken his truck over an obstacle bigger than a curb, climbing bumps in their path at a stoned snail's pace and cringing at the drop. But even moving slower than a three-legged tortoise was preferable to lugging corpses over the same impediments that deterred them. It took them longer to get there by truck than it did by foot.

"It's all downhill from here."

Comfortably near, they parked close enough to see the dark consume their headlights at the edge of the gorge before setting foot back on the path. Shawn gazed outward, double checking their route – it more visible now with the truck lighting the way – while Marvin went straight for the corpse-sacks in the rear, desperate to get his uneventful life back on track.

The irony was torturous… He'd had more fun these past few days than he could recall having in his entire life: Getting to work side-by-side with a stunning older woman; meeting Grandad and partying out of his mind at a strip club months before turning eighteen; hooking up with Shandra after a wild party and getting his V card punched… Weighing it all – it was horrible to think, but – at this point he probably wouldn't take any of it back. He'd gladly trade it for the lives of the four folks in pieces wrapped in tarps in the bed of the truck, but if they were going to be killed anyway, and everything turned out alright for him and Shawn in the end, cleaning up the most heinous mess on the planet for the few days of utter glee he'd gotten to enjoy was a price worth paying. But, if that price got any steeper…

Approaching the truck gate, his drifting mind refocused on its dilemma and his heart started pounding in his chest at a glimpse of what he hoped was just a trick of light. It wasn't until he made it all the way around when a whole new predicament cackled in his gaping grill like Satan's crack whore with a shiny new rock.

"Shawn!" His shrill holler made his friend wince.

"*Shhh!* Damn, dude, don't be yellin' right now… We probly alone, but no reason to draw attention." Shaking his head, he didn't bother to get worried until he saw Marvin's glazed, wide eyes. "What…?" He stopped short of a sentence as he rounded the truck. "Where's…" There were only three tarp-sacks in the back. What Shawn didn't know, and Marvin could hardly believe, was that when Marvin came to unload the first of their haul, the truck's gate was already open… "What…?" He still couldn't bring himself to string together a question; he had no idea where to start.

Marvin tried shedding some light. "The gate was open."

"Whatchoo mean?"

"The *gate*, man, the fuckin' gate! *I* didn't open that shit! It was open! We left it open!"

"Naw… No fuckin' way…"

"Fuck!"

"Naw…wait… When…when you open it last?"

"Man, I'on't know! I…I never did!" He'd removed the gas can at the station just by reaching over the wheel well… As far as he could think, they must've—

"Wait… You sayin' it was open this whole time?!"

"I don't fucking know! Did you close that shit 'fore we left?!"

He racked his brain. "Nah, you did, fool!"

"Nah, man, I…don't think I did!"

"Why'n't you close the gate, man?!"

"The fuck you mean?! It's yo' truck, nigga!"

"But you was the last one in back—!"

"We jumped off together, fool!"

Yelling wasn't getting them anywhere. Shawn looked back behind them, starting to work his way through the situation.

"Maybe... Maybe it fell when we was driving over here – all them bumps in the trail—"

"And if it di'n't?!"

"Fuck!" Shawn started heading back on foot the way they came, illuminating their path before Marvin pitched in.

"Wait, man, wait! ...Let's...let's dump these three first—"

"But—"

"If it ain't right behind us, nigga, we can't be drivin' 'round all suspicious with three piles of dead folk in the back!" His point was slowly sinking in. "And if it *is*, it can wait."

Shawn stomped back in succession. "*Damn*, man... This some fucked up shit!" He may've spoken too soon...

"C'mon, man..."

Four hands to a tarp, they pulled the first one down and started dragging it by its top. "A'ight, let's think back: Only place we stopped was outside the gas station, right?" Shawn was way off. It's a wonder they even made it to the forest...

"Nah, man... We stopped three times on the main road when we was lookin' for this shit—*Oof!*" His heal kicked a sizeable rock and his ass hit the frost.

"Get up, nigga! Damn... You clumsy as hell..."

"Yeah, I'm clumsy... You left the goddamn gate of yo' truck open with fo' dead bodies inna back..." He regained his hold and they carried on.

"You the one wanted to smoke that blunt, fool! Got me all high, an' shit..."

"Oh, you di'n't wanna smoke that blunt?"

"Nah... I'm sayin'—"

"You di'n't wanna smoke that blunt..."

"I mean, yeah, but we shoulda waited, man..."

"And that shit's on me?"

"Nah—*Oof!*" Ass, say hello to snow.

"Who clumsy now, fool?"

"*Shit...*"

Twenty minutes of more of the same brought the two do-dumbers back to their previous path. They realized it was the right move to bring the truck so they could haul the load if and when they found it – if the police hadn't already... And after carefully retracing their clandestine route back to the main road, they discovered their search was not yet over. Their missing Mr. Clause – good old George St. Nick – was yet to be retrieved.

Twenty bickering minutes more and they found themselves at their first off-road stop of the night – a shoulder off the road that still bore their truck's tracks in the snow. It didn't take more than one pass to see the blue tarp-lump festering a few feet from where they'd lost it.

"That's it!"

"Oh, good fucking *lord*, that shit was intense..." Marvin put his hand to his heart, hoping to help steady its beat.

They jumped out of the truck and reloaded its back with the wrapped up pulpy pieces like they'd found a laundry sack full of cash. Shawn and Marvin *both* had a hand on the gate as it shut, and Marvin gave it an extra rattle to be sure it was latched good and tight. Afterward, they took a moment to catch their breath before languorously shuffling back inside. The whole ordeal had taken so much out of them they could hardly climb their asses into the cab. But their work was far from finished...

"C'mone." Shawn grabbed a handful next to Marvin when they'd made it to the end of the line.

"Whatchoo *think* I'm doin'?" Marvin's hands were just as full of tarp, both working together to pull it off the bed.

"I'm coordinatin', nigga! Damn..."

"Oh, cuz that's yo' thing: 'coordinatin'...'"

"Dude..." Shawn stopped pulling, stood up and looked down at the bent over pissy-pants he had for a partner.

Marvin recognized the glare right off and took a breath. He knew Shawn was doing his part – they were in this together and each handling it the best they could.

"Sorry, man... I'm jus'...too *sober* for this shit right now..."

Shawn accepted his apology with a shake of his head. They were both sobering up more than they'd prefer to while doing a job as sucky as this one.

"A'ight, man... Let's jus'...*handle* this thing an' get back on the road."

"Yeah..."

They reestablished grips and proceeded to de-carcass their corpse-filled evening. Considering ol' George was the heftiest sack of the three, around half way to the cliff they seemed to catch a break, sliding along more easily than the previous times…until the load seemed a little *too* light for Marvin to accept as "smooth sailing".

"Hold up… What…?" He looked up, then walked around the backside of their haul. "Aww, *hell* nah!"

Shawn wasn't ready for another hitch in their plans. He plopped onto his ass even before Marvin could explain his cry. Leaning back into the snow, he asked reluctantly, "What the fuck now, man?"

"Maaan… There's a goddamn *hole* in the tarp's ass! We been shitin' out dead Santa all over the fuckin' place!"

"Awww, maannn…" He didn't even have it in him to raise his voice. "How much we lose?"

"I'on't know, man, shit…" He looked back, then forward…then back… "Fuck… We gotta open it up and see…"

"You f'real, nigga?" Still lying in frosted wrong-doings, Shawn was almost unsurprised at the new kink in their hose.

Marvin went for the tarp's top and tried working the twine to get it untied. "Fuckin' gloves, man…" He couldn't get his fingers in deep enough to pull at the knots. "Lemme see yo' knife."

Shawn dug in his pockets then hoisted it high. Marvin aggressively snatched it from his hands, mumbling like an old grump with an infestation of grade-schoolers on his lawn, then got to cutting. Tearing the twine from his path, he whipped open the tarp to a nose full of rancidness and an eyeful of repugnance. The proceeding up-chuck was instantaneous.

"Aww, man, don't—*bluuuaahhgg!*" Shawn discovered he was not immune to the universal Lardass-effect.

After exercising their gut-demons, Marvin managed to look back at that horrendous mess piled at his feet, hand over mouth to stunt the stink. There was a one-legged pelvis, a two-shouldered arm, a booted foot, another arm and leg…

"Man, we missin' two hands, a foot and a head."

Wiping his mouth, Shawn declared, "I ain't touchin' the head."

"You can't call 'not it' on collectin' body parts, fool! That shit disrespectful."

"Maannnn…this some *fucked* up shit, right here."

"C'mon…"

The search wasn't too difficult a thing considering all they had to do was retrace the path that was clearly gouged behind them. They found the missing extremities with little effort, but one piece of the person-puzzle remained elusive: George St. Nick's hatted and mangled melon.

"The fuck, man, that shit roll away?" If they could catch a break just once this night, Marvin would put his PS4 aside for a month and take up a real sport…like *golf*… "Some land crab need a new home and take off with it?"

"Oh shit… What if a deer got that shit or somethin'?"

"Goddamn… You f'real?!" Marvin was astounded. "Deer's is *vegans*, fool!"

"Nah, man, I said 'or somethin'', shit… A fuckin' bear or beaver or some *other* asshole animal…"

"Damn… Then we gotta spread out—"

"Hold up…" A thought occurred. "You got that shit from off the top'a the tree, right?"

Brain as soggy as his socks, Marvin pondered the question, going over the effort to de-murderize the Christmas pine in his mind until deciding—

"FUCK!!"

Figuring there was no use in wasting an hour's drive being sober, feeling out of sorts, edgy and irritable, they hotboxed the cab so intently the *Datsun* was likely high. After a brief discourse angling the blame – the so-called "coordinator" catching shrapnel from discharge of his own rendering – the remaining cruise was somewhat blithely. Since it was dark when they left Marvin's, they knew no one would see George-a Clause's de-bodied dome dripping Salisbury Santa from the treetop. Their only current concern was getting back in and out without looking as guilty as they felt.

Sleuth-like in their maneuvers, they cut the lights and parked several houses down, dastardly on approach like a couple of raccoons looking to thieve their meal out from under the nose of momma Rottweiler. A graceless foursome of feet tiptoed over egg shells to slither alongside the home, retrieve the ladder, and then clop through the snow passed the shed and into the woods. They easily followed their own sloppy trail back to the Tree of Degradation and set up shop with only marginal clumsiness slowing them down.

A murder of crows flew the coop when the ladder hit the trunk but circled above in the dark like a bad feeling. Marvin tried playing the "I went last time, you go this time" card, but Shawn used his height disadvantage as a point of debate claiming he wouldn't be able to reach the top from the last bit of branches that were sturdy enough to hold him. Marvin gave up without much fight, figuring he could do it faster anyway since, at this point, he and the pine were practically going steady. True, their relationship was full of distrust and prone to violence, but they knew each other's numerous quirks intimately – there was likely to be less friction if *he* did the dirty work.

Scaling the branches like a pro got him to the top without much plight. But upon arrival, he had to assert his dominance on the food chain in the face of a lingering, winged scavenger the size of a Cocker Spaniel. With pruning shears poised like a bird's beak, he swung viciously for the feet of the morbid fowl and proved to be the King of Carrion: the most savage hoarder of the freshly dead.

Strategic in his advance, he'd purposely approached the noggin from the back so to not have to stare into the eyes of his recent acquaintance. He didn't want to have to imagine what George would think of what he was doing – or George's loved ones – so he threw a trash-bag over the last horrid box on his list that needed checking and unstuck the deceased from his disgrace. One day they'd sort all this out, he thought. And when whoever was responsible for this atrocity was caught and convicted, they'd disclose the location of the bodies to have them retrieved for a proper burial: justice and dignity restored to all.

One day…

The bagged-up head landed in the snow with a *thunk* and Marvin made his way down.

"You carryin' that shit." He wasn't going to let Shawn get away with anymore malingering. Unless he no longer had use of his hands or feet, his ass was handling the head from here on out.

Hoisting the back end of the ladder, he followed his friend away from the worst night of his life. But before the tree was out of sight he looked back, perturbed by a sudden inquisitiveness. Even in the dark, the fading red could be seen haunting the white that covered the frosted needles, but less pronounced than before a fresh layer had danced over it in a new evening's squall. Who the hell could *do* something like that, he wondered, and why the hell would they do it to him? Maybe he was merely the audience they chose. Maybe his involvement was entirely inconsequential – just the guy who happened to be hanging around the right group of people at the wrong time. Maybe it had nothing to do with him at all…

They stuffed the head in the bag that carried their tools and drove north once again, quiet and morose. By the time they made it back home it was nearly midnight. Shawn dropped Marvin off and went on his way – just another Monday night. They both found their own way to their rooms and beds to look for sanity in a normal routine. But sleep evaded them like an electric rabbit racing around a track. They chased the elusive bastard for hours until night turned to morn.

Maybe the new day would bring peace, balance and tranquility. Maybe a fresh flurry would cover their sins and they could forget any of it ever happened.

Maybe tomorrow would be different…

DECEMBER 21ˢᵀ
9:23 AM

Yep. Everything was coming up Marvin.
    Well rested, refreshed and resurfacing into the morrow like a daffodil blooming in spring, the day's chilly morn had never looked so promising. High on life and weed, his first bong load balanced his ambitions and set him on a cool path for coffee and eggs. Mom and baby Chris were particularly agreeable, reflecting his own good mood with a smile and a cordial, "Good morning". Shawn texted to say he'd be by the mall later and Holly left a message asking if he could come in an hour early, her voice the sound of birds singing on a lake shore.

He texted back with a playful, "I'll do it for a raspberry-vanilla Holy-Cone special" and she responded with, "U sure ur ready for another life-changing experience?". He figured the reasonable answer was, "Only one way to find out".

Chuckling at the exchange, he found himself exhilarated, so dusted off his older brother's long-since abandoned dumbbells and maxed out on two sets per bicep. He even hit the deck and threw down a solid twelve pushups with his form as taut as a spaghetti dinner, then spent more time shirtless and inveigling the mirror than he did working up a sweat.

A hot shower called to him like the moon calls to a wolf: tauntingly and beyond reach… The pipes were so cold it took fifteen minutes to coax any heat from the damn things, but once he established steam he turned the bathroom into a sauna. A half-hour later momma wasn't so cordial any longer, banging on the door and vocalizing some colorful rant about a tropical rainforest.

After twisting his curls on top to accentuate his fade, he decided it was time to shave the dust off his upper lip and stop pretending he had presentable facial hair. Armpits like black moss, it was apparent some man-scaping was also overdue, so he spent forty minutes lining up his nether regions, indulging in the art, and getting lost for a stretch in the details.

When the time came he was back in the race, he realized he was going to be late at being early if he didn't get his ass in gear.

"Ma!" he hollered while tossing his dresser for fresh garments. "Ma, we gotta go!" Where was a damn fresh pair of boxer briefs when you needed one? "MA!"

"Boy! Quit yo' hollerin' 'fore it's the *last* thang you do!"

Reluctantly, long underwear was his only clean option, so he pulled them on in a rush, tangling his feet and tripping over his haste. *"Oof!"* Kicking his way in, he jumped up afterward and continued to plow through drawers for a wrinkled pair of khakis. "Ma! I'm gon' be late!"

She moved to the stairs to address her ecstatic offspring and cooed, "Child, what are you yellin' about?"

"I'm 'posed to go in early! Gotta be there by four!"

"Well, why ain'tchoo tell me sooner?"

"I forgot—*Oof!"*

She sighed. "You also forget you got two legs?" Shaking her head, she wandered off, figuring he'd be struggling to get decent for the next five years of his young adult life; no sense in waiting on him now…

Once he'd conquered his most recent footwear debacle, he grabbed what he needed to handle the cold and jackhammered up the stairs—

"MA!"

Basically on time, given an unspoken ten-minute grace period by default of being a teen, he made it to his third day of shoveling sugary goodies with an invigorated sense of willingness, eager to tackle his responsibilities and handle the shop on his own for an hour until Holly could make it in. It only took forty minutes of non-stop scooping for him to be drained of his zestful enthusiasm and reintroduced to a more familiar sense of indolence… But it was worth every nettling moment of facing down the line of a Thousand Salivating Mouths to see her smile proudly when she arrived, hair pulled back and ready to hop to his aid.

"Mah hero!" She leaned in and gave him a peck on the cheek then turned to address the crowd. "Thanks fer yer patience, everyone – yer second scoop is on the house!"

The delightful buzz among the patrons was the same sound Marvin's heart made as her hand drifted from his shoulder across his back.

Within seconds her apron was wrapped around her and tied tight; plastic gloves buffering skin from cone, scooper locked, loaded, and ready to serve.

Reinvigorated, Marv found his second wind and the two of them tackled the attendants with inspired charisma. Thirty minutes later they'd obliterated the invading forces of lapping pallets and found themselves with a moment to breathe. Holly took the opportunity to whip up something special for her wingman.

"Don't forget the cherry," he teased, watching her add the finishing touches – or, to be more accurate: watching her *figure* add the finishing touches while she plotted to spoil *his*.

"Oh, you are just *lovin'* the special attention, aren't ya, Keeper." Cherry placed artistically atop the swirl of whipped cream, she handed him a waffle cone that would shame all others. "I give you, Holly's Life Changer."

"Should I clap? I feel like I should clap..." He took the cone with wide eyes. "F'real, though: this thing's beautiful."

It truly was a sight to behold.

She grabbed a pink plastic spoon and stuck it in the top. "Why, thank you, young man. You deserve no less." He went for the spoon and she smacked his hand. "But you can't eat it behind the counter. So either get yer butt in back or on the payin' side of these freezers."

"Yes, ma'am." Deciding to keep her where he could see her, he exited through the counter and grabbed a table. Hand finding the spoon, the spoon nearly found his mouth before his eyes found hers staring his way, drawing him to a pause. "You ain't gon' watch me eat it, are you?"

She almost laughed. "Fiiiiine..." With a smile, she buried her eyes in her work, wiping up spilt ice creams and rinsing used scoopers.

Then the feasting began. Knowing she was eager to sample his reaction, he made it a point to exaggerate every experience.

"*Mmmm*...oh god...just...*mmm!* Wow..." He kept the corners of his eyes on her to be sure she didn't look up. "*Unnnff*...yeah, tha's

it right there…*ahh!*…cold!…*mmm*…*mmhmm*…so good, though…"
She tried to retain her laugh, restocking cups and cleaning the top of
the glass. "Ohhhhohoho…ahhhaha…*Mmm!*" His exclamation was
of perverse delight, emphatically slurping between more definable
groans. But he stopped abruptly when he caught her eyes angling his
way. "F'real?" One eyebrow raised, he sucked his teeth in offense.
"You jus' can't help yo'self, *can* you." Head shaking, he scolded her
with his tongue-in-cheek disbelief.

She chuckled reservedly under a humbled head. "I know, I know!
…So inappropriate… M'sorry, okay?"

"Am I gon' have to take this outside?"

"Course not…" She waved a hand at the thought. "I just…had a
little moment of weakness, is all."

"Uh-huh…" Eyes like rubber daggers, he stayed fixed until she
was back to work, then further indulged. "Oh…oh god…*nnnnnff*…
this is changin' me…*mmm*… Lord, fo' once in my life I am truly alive!
Unh!"

Eventually, after embarrassing the boss-lady for a solid ten
minutes with immature dude-humor and possibly scarring a family
of three who tucked tail before setting foot inside, Marvin got back
to work, reloaded and ready to do battle. It was only another hour
and a half of sugar-crazed customers he and his CO had to take on
to stop the Zombie-Glutton Apocalypse dead in its tracks before it
spread throughout the city. Brave in the face of certain doom, they
stuffed the gaping grills of the mindless hordes with a frosty sedative
and proceeded to herd these deadly cattle in ugly Christmas sweaters
into manageable clumps to be picked off one-by-one like soda cans
on a wooden fence. A job finely orchestrated – the town of Winterset,
Iowa had been spared.

Shawn showed up fifteen minutes before Marvin had a dinner break
and wasn't entirely out of his skull, but decidedly baked and properly
caffeinated. He bought a triple-scoop (that he coaxed into a quadruple)
on a chocolate-dipped waffle cone laced with Oreo crumbs like salt on
the rim of a margarita glass. He was all over the menu with his mashup
of toppings – who else but a weed-head would think to mix gummy
bears with cashews? The finished product was an abomination of the
most glorious sort… It appeared their fight for survival against the

zombie-glutton hordes was merely a warmup for this final showdown with the ultimate boss baddie: Shawn Gargantuos-Apatitous!

All may soon be lost…

The valiant duo threw the book at him; everything they'd learned in their time on this twisted world. And an arsenal of mixed sensations encroached on the beast with its first bite, but it was hardly fazed. It took to the deadliest dessert ever made like it was swatting a fly… It wasn't until Marvin nearly went mad with desperation and made a move no one was prepared for that the beast even noticed the sting of impossibly-sweet—

Holly eyed her trusty righthand man as he dove toward the candy toppings. When his hand reached out, she shrieked at the danger it could pose. It was *insane*… Downright delirious! Chewy Red Hots on top of caramel sauce and cookie dough balls?! Appalling! It couldn't be done!

Arm flailing outward to impede his efforts, jaw practically scraping the floor with her cry, she leapt for her First Lieutenant in a hopeless push to prevent the greatest disaster ice cream had ever known…

But it was too late.

"Oh, hell yeah, man, good lookin'. Pile them sexy lil red devils on top… Yeah, tha's it…"

Sweat beaded at Marvin's brow, hand shaking at the weight of the responsibility he wielded. This abhorrence he'd constructed was reckless and impulsive…but what did he have to lose?

Swallowing hard, he dug deep and found the courage to taunt the beast upon its completion. "G'ahead, bruh. See how that shit sits in you." Lines forming at the corners of his eyes, all he could do was watch…and wait…

Holly was nearly in tears. Even if Marvin's daredevilry worked to subdue the tyrannical brute, neither of them would ever be the same… They'd crossed the line. Civility would be forever outside their grasp.

Spoon-hand tight, elbow preloaded for torque, Shawn Gargantuos-Apatitous! stabbed at the colossal dessert to tear away a mouthful that could destroy an entire society if improperly handled. And the two desperate, terrified grunts observed with glossed-over lenses, wet with their final hopes, as the glutton voluntarily shoveled his maw full of his own undoing.

Its reaction was almost imperceptible at first – it had finally met a dessert it didn't understand. Slowly *–miraculously* – it took another bite, while the Commander and her champion entangled in an embrace that was meant to see them into oblivion… But when the monstrosity ceased its forward approach and gingerly started its retreat, they knew they'd accomplished the impossible.

Shawn Gargantuos-Apatitous! had been subdued…

The city had been saved.

"I can't believe he's eatin' it," Holly whispered as Shawn numbingly drifted into a seat in the corner.

"I could slap some pepperoncinis on top'a that shit right now an' he'd still smash on it." He observed his friend through mostly sober eyes and shook his head. "Dude's *unconscious*…" then he wondered, "That how I looked on my first shift?"

"No," she assured him. "He's just high as a kite… You were sick as a dog *and* high as a kite."

He laughed, then thought out loud, "S'miracle you ain't fired me right off…"

Her finely polished, glittery blue nails tossed the concept aside. "You and yer friend make this gig more bearable than it's been all month."

He squinted, remembering she hadn't been at this for long. "Tha's right… You and Mr. G jus' bought this spot."

"Sure did. I told him I couldn't move here unless I had somethin' to keep me busy. But I wasn't about to work fer no gropy, so-called entrepreneur who'd wanna keep me overtime four outta five nights a week in hopes of wearin' down my defenses to 'make his move'. I had to be my *own* boss."

"So he just up and bought the joint for you?" He was surprised by the concept of having that kind of cash lying around.

"I have my own money, you know," she pointed out. "It was a joint endeavor. But he'd lived here all year so got to know the place and found this dreamy little parlor. I'm a people person and have a *voracious* sweet tooth, so it was perfect."

He wasn't sure he agreed with her idea of perfect. "But for how long? If it was unbearable before me, how you gon' feel when I'm gone?"

"Heartbroken, I'm sure," she pouted. "But we usually don't stay in one place very long. Clint wants to be a college professor and he's more than qualified. This is just to pass the time between towns."

He was trying not to show how depressed the idea of her leaving made him feel. "Well…I hope you don't skip town befo' Christmas, cuz a brotha gots'ta get paid!"

"Oh, you'll get what's comin' to ya, darlin'." She playfully punched his shoulder. "Just you wait'n see."

A wink and a smile fluttered his stomach and he figured he'd better take his break before he confessed his undying love.

"Cool if I take thirty?"

"Now's as good a time as any." She smiled.

"Thanks, boss-lady."

Apron set aside and wallet retrieved, he sauntered toward Shawn to nudge him on the shoulder: a friendly heads-up for him to follow along. Mastering the plastic spoon while placing one foot in front of the other would be a hell of a hard row to hoe for the toasted teen, but he took it in stride and managed to keep pace while they meandered toward the food court.

Marvin almost admired his friend's determination to not spill a single rainbow sprinkle. He chuckled a little at the sight and shook his head. "Man…you gon' hurl if you try'n smash that whole damn thing."

In between spoonfuls, Shawn countered, "I ain't eat since breakfast, bruh. Been thinkin' 'bout this shit all day…"

Marvin let the air out through his teeth in an amused *tshhh*, then asked, "You got the pen on you?"

"Mmhmm."

"Cool. Let's roll out back, right quick. If I'on't smoke I'ma start gettin' angsty."

"You worried 'bout what Mrs. G gon' think?" he teased, smiling goofily under syrup and whipped cream with eyes as slim as coin slots.

"Nah, man…"

"Quit lyin', fool. You sprung as hell."

"She my boss, nigga, shit…" he shook his head. "Don't wanna fuck this job up…"

"So you gon' get baked?" He laughed and spilled a little glob of ice cream with his jubilance. "Awww…*damn*…" He felt the loss like he'd known the drip since they were kids.

"Better to be a lil lit than all moody an' shit. You know one bowl ain't gon' fuck me up; just set me straight."

Their trek took them passed the mall Christmas tree; a line as long and as thick as a bus festered restlessly. Only one elf held the fort when there were usually three, and Santa's velvet throne sat vacant without a lap to grant Christmas wishes to squirrely little kiddies.

"Damn... Them dudes must be partying even harder than *we* is. They been droppin' like it's hot since the titty bar..."

Marvin hadn't been up to speed. "Whatchoo mean?"

"Was chillin' with Grandad an' that cat Kevin earlier." His head gestured toward the lone elf on-call. "Said dudes's been no-shows; Mig, X, El...George, and like three others."

"Damn... So Grandad's workin' again tonight?"

"Mmhmm... Prolly out back smokin' right now."

It didn't take long to find Shawn had accurately surmised the old man's whereabouts.

"Speak'a the devil...and here this nigga is, all dressed in red an' blowin' doj!"

They'd made it out back to where the mall workers would go to smoke, rustling their jackets around themselves to contest the cold.

"Sup, young fam?" Grandad was as cool as a cucumber, not even wearing his Santa jacket, letting the hot smoke from his roll keep him warm.

They exchanged hand-slaps while Shawn handed Marvin the G-pen, and Marvin asked, "They got you here on yo' day off, Grandad?"

"Fuggin' goldbrickers..." He shook his head while taking a puff. "They ruinin' Christmas! Been nothin' but one no-show after the other..." He spit a bit of loose leaf and went on. "Only three'a us Nicks lef' now, an' four elves. It's gon' be a long-ass three days till we c'n hang it up."

Marvin clicked his pen on and took a drag while Shawn fought the chill, working on the crunchy bits of his cone.

Grandad continued.

"S'all good, though. Long as I got my weed an' my whiskey I'ma be cool. Ain't no thang to hang wit these young chidlins. Jus' like when my gran'kids would come an' see they poppa. 'Cept my lil girl moved away wit her ol' man an' I ain't seen 'em *since*." He sighed.

"That why you doin' this gig?" Marvin wondered while working the chamber for every hit he could siphon in the fleeting time he had. "...You miss yo' gran'kids?"

"Uh-huh." He blew a thick cloud into the nippy air. "Ain't nothin make this ol' vet happier'n'a youngin's smile..." He trailed off, seeming a little sad at the thought. " 'Cept maybe babies laughin' – happiest sound on Earth. Spent four years away from 'em before I realized there ain't nothin' in this world I miss more."

"How old they now? Yo' gran'kids..."

"Nineteen, seventeen an' twelve." He didn't miss a beat when answering. "I call 'em on they birthdays an' on Christmas, but I ain't seen 'em in seven years now. The youngest one...she don't hardly 'member me."

With a mouthful of who-knows-what, Shawn offered, "Tha's fucked up."

And Marvin added, "Rough shit, Grandad. Why ain'tchoo go an' see 'em, then?"

"Never have the funds. Can't stay at they crib – even they *couch* occupied with this nigga's lil brother outta work. An' I sure as hell can't afford no roundtrip ticket an' a motel."

"Ain'tchoo gettin' paid from Uncle Sam for bein' in the war?"

"Ain't gotta dime *yet*... Been tryin'a get what's comin' to me for three years, but it ain't come through. It's always some other bullshit wit these assholes, findin' ways not to put out, hopin' you keel over dead 'fore they gotta pay up."

"Shit's twisted, man," Shawn decided, shivering while still going strong, nearly finished with his treat.

"You gon' *show* these assholes, Grandad. You gon' live till a hundred-and-twenty-six'! Cashin' in on that government cheddar fo' sixty years of retirement. Get you a RV, move out 'round yo' family and spoil that youngest one rotten! She gon' know yo' name..."

"Heh... You a'ight, young blood." He gave Marvin some extended love through his palm. "Both you lil niggas is good peeps. Make *damn* sho' you stay that way, cuz I *will* kick yo' skinny asses, I find out different."

"We straight, Grandad," Marvin assured him while returning the love. "We silly as shit all weeded up, but we ain't hoods."

"Nah," Shawn agreed. "We gamers, dawg. S'all 'bout that high score!" He chuckled and slapped hands with Marvin.

"Nigga, you know I kick yo' ass erry time we play," Marvin clowned with a smirk.

"*Pshhhh…* Yeah, you keep tellin' folks that. Only bit'a win you gon' get is "when" you bullshitin'."" They both laughed. Shawn generally had the upper hand in the gaming world, but Marvin wasn't about to go around admitting it.

"Y'all stay on that path." Grandad's voice turned more serious than it normally would. "Better to fuck around on them games than fuck around on them streets." He leaned in a little closer and softened his voice. "But don't sleep on gettin' you some nookie 'tween them rounds'a GTA. Ain't nuttin' better'n this world than a good woman you call yo' own."

If only, Marvin thought, picturing Holly's smile, then quickly discarded the image to stay in touch with the real world.

They funneled back inside and while Grandad went to pose for pics with the town's tots, the boys followed their noses toward the mall's conglomerate of fast food franchises. Marvin ordered something that could pass for a burger and Shawn found a mini-mart that sold Flamin' Hot Cheetos and energy drinks. Mealtime was mostly quiet other than their shared chuckling at mall customers who resembled cartoon characters. They spotted the Tasmanian Devil eating a soft pretzel, Shrek holding hands with Olive Oyl, and Jessica Rabbit pushing a double stroller in yoga pants…

Nice.

"Yo, whatchoo doin' for Christmas, man?" When no other recognizable animated folk were spotted, Shawn's mind started to wander.

"You mean besides kickin' it with moms and baby Chris?"

"Yeah, bruh – afterwards."

"Prolly just post up and kick yo' ass in Black Ops. You wanna roll through?"

"Hell yeah! My sister's comin' in from Michigan – girl got seven kids… I can only take so much'a that bullshit 'fore I need to chief some."

"Oh shit… You can't blaze while they there?"

"Nah, man… My brother in-law a cop. Mom's said I gotta keep the weed out the house for a few days."

"S'not like dude's gon' arrest you in yo' own crib on Christmas… is he?" He thought better of being presumptuous were "Five-Oh" was concerned.

"Nah… But you know how moms is: always tryin'a put up that front like we the perfect family…"

"Yeah…" His mind wandered, thinking about the blinding contrast between his household and Shawn's. "*Pshhh*… You know *my* moms ain't frontin'." He laughed. "She that black woman in curlers inna grocery store changin' a damn diaper 'fore she even *pays* for 'em."

"AhHA! Nah, quit playin'…"

"Serious, dawg. Embarrassin' as fuck. I stopped goin' to the store with her when I was ten, like, 'hell *nah* I ain't bein' seen witchoo in public'!"

"She did that shit? F'real?"

"No shame, bruh… She cool as hell when you need somebody to get yo' back, but you can't take that woman no place without her makin' sure errybody knows she don't give a fuck."

"Haaaaaa! That's some shit, though. Sometimes I wish *my* moms was more hood, just so she ain't so uptight alla time."

"Yeah, I'on't know if I'd like that shit either. Guess it's a fair trade: embarrassin' as hell, but chill, too."

"Yeah, yo' mom *hella* cool. We been chillin' over there gettin' high since eighth grade an' she ain't said shit but 'pass the spliff.' "

They laughed. Then Shawn thought,

"Yoooo! We should get Grandad to chill on Christmas, bruh!"

"What, at my crib?"

"Nah, fool! See if he can get us back up in that club" —he did a little dance with his fists near his chest— "get our twerk on one last time 'fore the New Years!"

"*Chhhhh*… *Bitches* be twerkin' fool, not dudes." He shook his head. "I'on't know, though. I ain't tryin'a be 'that kid', askin' for favors an' shit."

"You trippin', man. Grandad is all *about* us! He ain't gonna think we buggin'!"

And as the thought marinated in his blunted lobes, "That shit *would* be tight, though…"

"Aaahhh? *See*, fool?! We should holler at dude later. I'll try'n hit him up while you back kissin' up to yo' boss."

Marvin didn't mind the sound of that. "A'ight. Don't be skeevy, though. Old dude's gotta lot on his plate right now with all these fools not showin' up to work, an' shit…"

"Yeah, yeah... Quit bein' all scury. You worry 'bout shit too much, bruh – you obviously ain't high enough right now."

Marvin tilted his head, finishing his last bite of burger. "You ain't wrong." Dusting off the crumbs and washing down the lump, he got up to head back. "A'ight, I gotta roll. Shoot through whenevs, man. Boss-lady's cool with you kickin' it."

"Cool, bruh... Oh shit—!"

Marvin froze at his outburst. "What?"

"Look who's 'bout to warm up Grandad's lap, yo!"

Following his not-so sly pointing finger, Marvin caught the slightly awkward sight of Shandra and Yvonne in their sultry Little Helpers outfits, shuffling toward Grandad for a playful photo op. His mouth gaped before he slapped Shawn's hand from its stiffly erected pointing-posture.

"Don't be all obvious, fool!"

Shawn lowered his hand, taking his friend's advice. "Damn, they look good..." Candy-cane striped thigh-highs below a ziz-zag hemline on very short green skirts had the moms in line sneering and the dads envious of Ol' St. Nick. "I'ma hit 'em up—"

"Nah, yo! They probly still pissed—!"

"At *you*, nigga!" He laughed. "I ain't do shit."

"But—"

"*Chill*, man. I got this. I'ma fix whatever it was you fucked."

The old Marvin would've argued further, hiding his embarrassment and lack of confidence behind reasoning filled with holes... But then he remembered he had a goddess who was eager to have him back in her company waiting and decided not to sweat it. "A'ight..." he nodded. "Handle it, then. I'd watch yo' ass trip over yo' own words if I ain't had to go back..." He snickered, and they slapped hands. "Jus' don't forget you my ride home."

"Nah, I got you. Don't trip."

He had his doubts, taking Shawn at his loosely-reliable word, but wasn't going to sweat that either. If worse came to worse he knew Mr. and Mrs. G would take him home after they shut down shop.

But Shawn would be there. He didn't have anywhere *else* to be.

Marvin made it back to the parlor two minutes before his break was over as Holly was finishing up with a family of four. He loved to watch her work – he'd never known a person could be so socially enchanting. He hoped he could be as graceful with people as her someday... It was all in the *smile*, it seemed, and the brightness of her eyes when her lips peeled back to present it. Without kidding himself, knowing his cheesy grin wasn't nearly as appealing as hers, he could still see a time in his future when he was fulfilled enough in life to smile just as brightly, and wondered if that time would be of his own making...or someone else's... He figured Holly was as content as she was because she loved her husband, and he loved *her* – very outwardly – as much as she deserved. So, could a person ever be so happy without finding their perfect match? Or were we all born as broken halves to a lost whole that needed to be reunited to finally be complete?

If that were the case, he figured he'd better get his head out of the clouds and back in the game. Mrs. G wasn't on the board... But there were plenty of *other* pieces left to play with that were only a roll of the dice away.

Orange Cheeto-fingers waving like a stoner-flag in the air, proclaiming his purposed declaration of truce, Shawn called out to his two classmates after they made Grandad Santa's night and were moving on.

"Yvonne! ...Yvonne!" He figured the smart money was on addressing the one who wasn't directly pissed at his taller friend. " 'Eyyyy! What's up, girl?!"

He didn't bother getting up, sitting sideways in his seat with one elbow on the table and one on the chair's back. Yvonne smiled and started to wave, but Shandra sighed and pulled her in the opposite direction.

"Shit..." They're getting away! Do something, dude! " 'Ey, hold up!"

Now wasn't the time for playing it overly cool, he decided, and got his ass up to show his determination by catching them in their path—
"Hold up, yo, damn!" —but he wasn't about to grovel...*yet*...

Shandra cocked her hips and rolled her eyes, and Yvonne put her serious face on in support of her friend. "Your boy's an asshole, Shawn," she led with.

Her move had been made, and he quickly decided he shouldn't back off just yet.

"Yo, I know he *dumb* sometimes, but he ain't no asshole. Shandra... you *know* he cool. He always been nice to you."

She still wouldn't allow him the satisfaction of eye contact.

"Yeah, well, he straight called us hoes," Yvonne countered. It was a powerful stroke... Shawn would have to dig deep to combat against *that* fuck-up on Marvin's part.

"Damn... He said that?" ...*cuz he was just repeatin' what I said*, he didn't bother mentioning.

"Uh-huh," Shandra finally confirmed.

Think, man! And make it quick! You're losing them!

"Yo, you know he was shroomin' right?" Noticing a flicker of hesitation in her eyes, he started to lay it on thick. "He was just gettin' loose an actin' a fool... He'd neeeeever say some shit like that an' mean it. Y'all been cool since seventh grade!" The red heels at the base of those cocked hips that'd been tapping to the tune of Aggravated started to slow in its rhythm as her eyes moved to Shawn's, looking for sincerity. "F'real... You really think Marv would disrespect you like that? I mean, really? Marvin? Silly-ass, hardly-can-talk-around-you-cuz-he-shy-as-*hell* Marvin?"

Her pursed lips started to ease into what could be mistaken for a hint of a smile, and Yvonne watched her reaction closely, hoping for the same outcome Shawn's was.

"Yeah, I guess he just dumb sometimes..." She looked down, hiding a subtle change in disposition.

"Yassss! Tha'swhat'msayin'! You know my boy... *Been* knowin' my boy. He sweet as hell and feels like a dick, f'real."

"Then why he ain't say he sorry?"

He set up a sympathetic pair of brows to put the cherry on top. "Between this new job and bein' all scury with girls, he was worried he'd lose you as a friend an' ain't got the balls to say it, yet."

"What new job?"

"He's workin' here at Mr. G's ice cream spot."

"With his wife?" A salty look replaced her hopeful one.

"Yeah. He workin right now." She rolled her pretty eyes... He was losing her again so had to act fast. "C'mon. We'll go see him and you can see for *yo'self* he's sorry for sayin' that stupid shit." He shifted his attention to Yvonne to see a hidden smirk waiting for him, hopeful and appreciative of his efforts to get them all together.

"He was shroomin'?" Still going over Shawn's story in her mind, Shandra hadn't yet decided if it was reasonable to give him another shot.

"Shroomin' *balls*... First day'a work too. Dude was out his mind!"

She smiled and Yvonne's eyes got brighter.

"A'ight... But he *better* be sorry."

"He will! I mean he *is*... C'mon, let's roll." Slyly slinking next to Yvonne, they started back on their way with Shandra *mostly* on board. "So, whatchoo girls ask Grandad for Christmas?"

"Who?" Shandra snapped.

"Oh... Tha's what we call ol' dude inna Santa suit. We been chillin' with him since Marv been workin' here."

"Why you call him that?" Yvonne chimed in, needing to be a part of the conversation.

"Just cuz he old and black an' cool enough to be fam. Dude's been smokin' us out after work like every night."

"F'real?"

"Yeah. He cool as hell."

"You been smokin with Santa Clause..." She was playfully doubtful.

"Hell yeah! My man's been rollin' up peppermint blunts daily! Shit's smooth as ice!"

"Damn... I ain't gonna lie... I'ma little jelly right now..." Her mixed-ethnicity graced her with reddish curls under her elf hat and a lightly freckled nose. "Shandra... You *know* you wanna smoke with Santa Clause," she teased.

Still not ready to lighten up yet, she shrugged. "He seemed cool – not too handsy when we was on his lap..."

Shawn shook his head. "You two seriously had alla us dudes eyeballin' that whole situation like, dayum!"

She smiled at that, and Yvonne remarked, "Well maybe when you're old enough to grow a beard I'll wanna sit on your lap too."

"Ohhh! So you into them old dudes, then, huh?"

She blared out an exaggerated laugh, then countered with a, "Well, if they grantin' *wishes*, shit..." She moved a hand toward Shandra and wiggled her fingers for some love. "Ain't that *right*, gurl?"

Shandra reached out and mixed wiggling-fingers with her friend. "You *know* this, gurl!"

Shawn felt the covert triumph of Yvonne's to get her friend to come out of her skulk and play along. "Whatchoo ask for, Shandra?" He figured now was the time to get her talking.

"Lil Xan." She smirked.

"Whaaa?!" Shawn nearly choked. "Quit playin'! You like that fool?!"

Embarrassed, but feeling the need to defend her celebrity boy-crush, she offered, "What? He cuuuute!"

"Aww, c'mon... Dude looks like he twelve!"

"That's what I said..." Yvonne puckered her lips like it tasted bitter to think it.

"The boy got style, though!" They laughed at her attempt to rationalize it. "Whatever... He fine."

"And what Grandad say?"

"He said he'on't know who that is but he gon' find 'im and wrap 'im up in a bow for Christmas for me." She pouted as they continued chortling at her expense.

After recovering his composure, he turned to Yvonne. "Aight, so what*choo* ask for, then?"

"A chocolate Labrador puppy," she answered, sounding a little hopeful she might get one.

"An' what he say?"

"He said he think he only had two left in his shop but if I was good he'd save me one."

"Haha! Smooth, Grandad! I *like* that ol' dude!"

"Yeah, he cool," she smiled. "And he a black Santa so we *had* to get that pic."

"Yeah, no doubt. Me and Marv got mad selfies with him at the club."

"*What* club?" Shandra unfurled a mouthful of doubt in her tone.

"His ol' ass got us into Foxtrot's on Friday."

Yvonne wasn't buying it. "No he di'n't."

"*Pshhh*...please..." he pulled out his cell like it was his VIP pass and started flipping through pictures.

Yvonne grabbed his phone in disbelief and Shandra spilled over her shoulder to gape. "Ewwww! Y'all'er scandalous!" she cried, scoping the photos they took with the girls, and Yvonne added,

"These girls're ratchet!"

He sucked at his teeth. "Jus' cuz they strippers don't mean they ratchet!"

Yvonne cultivated a matter-of-fact look in her eyes. "Uh, yeah, it *does*."

"It really does," Shandra of course agreed, and Shawn thought better of pushing it.

"A'ight, they were *kinda* ratchet… And dumb as slugs…" That one scored a few points back in his favor. "But fine, though."

"Tha's just the makeup and wigs, fool."

"And the lighting," Yvonne pointed out. "It's dark as hell in there…"

"That's what Marvin said…" he reminisced.

"See?" Shandra jumped on that, feeling better about Marvin with that little piece to add to his chances of redemption. "Even yo' *friend* know they ain't that fine."

"A'ight, a'ight… They ain't all that." He took his phone back and put it in his pocket. "But they got *moves*, though."

He had to get the last word in and Yvonne wasn't having it. She went straight for a handful of his jewels to get his mind on the right girl, squeezing as a playful threat.

"Boy, you wanna see moves? I got your moves right here!"

"Ahh, ahh! Ok, ok, shit!" He played along, throwing his hands up high.

"Say they ain't shit."

"Damn, gurl!" Shandra was shocked her friend made such a bold move.

"Say it!"

"A'ight! Damn! They ain't shit, ok?!"

"Say, 'they ain't shit compared to you, Yev'."

"Girl," he countered, "I'on't even remember who we *talkin'* about right now…"

"Say it!" She squinted and squeezed.

"Ahh! Shit! A'ight! They ain't shit compared to *you*, Yev!"

"Damn straight, they ain't…" She let his twig and berries shrink back into the bush and Shandra looked away, embarrassed.

"Goddamn…" He adjusted the goods while trying to think of something smart or clever to say. "I ain't even gon' play witchoo…

That was sexy as *fuck*." It was neither smart nor clever…but it was all he had. If they had been keeping score, Yvonne just slam-dunked on his ass to take a commanding lead.

"Well, you act *right* and you just might find out what other moves I got."

He bit his knuckle with exploding eyes and Shandra laughed.

When the crew made it into the parlor, Marvin looked halfway impressed Shawn had wrangled the angered livestock into a calmly herd – they even had *smiles* on their faces… At least until they saw grins to surpass their own on the two ice cream gurus behind the counter.

Holly was as bright and friendly as ever and Shandra instantly felt the sting of Marvin's apparent delight being beside her. Instinctively, she perked up every curve under her command – especially her lips – to the threat of another beautiful woman, so Shawn quickly broke the ice—

"Cream Team!" he beamed. "Look what I found under the tree!"

"Hey, girls!" Holly smiled, wiping down the counter. "You two look gorgeous!" She turned to her favorite Jedi in training. "Don't they, Marvin?"

Marvin caught the glimmer of the light against Shandra's lip gloss and smirked, recognizing the extra effort she put into being noticeably alluring. "Yeah…she does…" He stared right into her eyes with a confidence he'd never known, then, when he saw hers waver at his intensity, he strategically eased off. "I mean, yeah, they *both* do." He gave Yvonne her just dues and Shandra smiled. Marvin smiled back.

"My man," Shawn started, facilitating the healing process, "I told our girl Shandra how shitty you felt fo' runnin' yo' gums on Friday and she said she needs to hear it from the source."

"Uh," he glanced toward Holly, "Yeah…yeah…um…" A little head tilt from him and a nod from her and he stepped outside the counter to make his apology more personal while Shawn escorted Yvonne two booths down.

Shandra's eyes were on the wall, arms crossed in front of her; breasts plump, hips angled to stop traffic. Holly had a wry smile on when she turned to mind her own business, and Marv stepped closer than he'd usually have the cojones to.

"Hey…" Her eyes didn't budge from the wall, lips as kissable as ever. "I was bein' stupid, okay? I known you fo' years an' never thought you was anythin' but beautiful." He could see her defenses weakening. So could everyone else. "You strong, an' cool, and sexy as *hell* an' I was actin' a fool. …I jus' got all excited you wanted to kick it an' thought I was the shit for a minute." She almost laughed. "But then I remembered I'm jus' silly ol' Marvin, an' all I wanna do is make sure we still friends." Her eyes slowly shifted to meet his and he smiled softly. "Is that cool? Can we still be friends?" He held out his hand for her to take him up on his offer.

She looked to her girl who was *more* than satisfied with Marvin's apology and said so with her "nudging" eyes, pushing her to answer him with a, "Yeah… We can be friends." She smiled reservedly and took Marvin's hand.

He held it like it was made of papier-mache, then said, "C'mere," getting the vibe that a hug was on the negotiating table.

She allowed him his hug and did her best not to cheese too gleefully at their reunion. She'd never had *anyone* apologize to her so genuinely before…

"*Awwwww*…" Shawn spilled, "That's so sweeeet…" He laughed, and the girls giggled. "Told you my boy would set things straight!"

Holly chimed in. "Darlin'…*that* was beautiful," she looked back and forth between the girls, "but if I were *you* ladies I'd put him to work makin' you some ice cream." Then she playfully divulged, "I'll take y'all's orders outta his paycheck."

They laughed and Shandra thought bossing Marvin around a bit would be her cherry on top. "You heard the lady, Marvin. You gon' have to buy me some ice cream to make that apology official."

"*And* me…" Yvonne jumped up eagerly and they started eyeing the freezers with enthusiasm as thick as syrup.

Making his way back to the serving side of the counter, Marvin mouthed the words "thank you" to his favorite older gal and she winked while handing him a set of plastic gloves. They geared up to get down and handled the purposely, overly-indecisive teens like seasoned vets: with endless patience and a "thank you, come again" smile. The tag team of Holly and Marv operated like a well creamed machine; all minds were set right, cheery and in good spirits.

Holly handed Yvonne her cup of Christmas Cookie-Butter Delight after Marvin dispensed his subject with the physical manifestation of an apology and Yvonne accepted it with hungry orbs glowing white… until a tickle caught her nose and a squint turned into a sneeze.

"Oop! Bless yer little heart," Holly offered, along with the treat, but Yvonne wasn't done.

An adorable onslaught of squeaky nasal eruptions burst from the tip of her snout, drawing the eyes of the entire gang.

"Gurl…you allergic to sweets or somethin'?" Shandra wondered, not waiting for her friend to find her bearings before indulging in her freebie.

Eight to ten sneezes later and Marvin alluded to the napkins at the counter while Shawn decided to take the next stab.

"…Or white women?"

Marvin held in a laugh and Holly grinned.

"No…" napkin muffling her response, she said, "*cats*…" She looked to Holly from under her suddenly watering eyes. "Do you have one or somethin'?"

She chuckled a little. "Not as far as I know, darlin'. And you'd hafta have a purty darn sensitive sniffer to be goin' off like that if I did… Does this happen all the time?"

"No…" She made it back to her booth and sat down next to Shawn. "Not unless I'm in somebody's house who has one." A little embarrassed, she kept the napkin over her face to hide.

"It's true," Shandra pitched in between licks. "I got two and she never goes off like that 'round me."

"Can we go?" Eyes still glossy from the peppering, she looked to Shawn for an escape from her predicament.

"Yeah, cool." He got up to escort her out with Shandra not far behind. "Yo, I'll be back 'round 9:30, bruh." He called out and Marvin threw up the deuces.

"Peace, fam."

Shandra turned back while sexily strolling from the parlor to make sure she left her mark. "See you later, Marvin."

The words were almost a warning. The young man had no idea what he'd gone and gotten himself into. *Holly* did… She had a knowing smile waiting for him while he tried to avoid eye contact but proved unable considering she wouldn't stop eyeing *him*. When he finally looked her in the peepers, she raised her brows twice with a half-moon smile and, once again, he felt blessed to not have to suffer the awkward congenital condition of involuntary blushing.

Shop mopped, prepped, and locked up for the day, Marvin was surprised at how fast his night flew by. Mr. Greggerson showed up as punctually as a monthly bill; cowboy hat and boots rearing to ride regardless of the weather, arm raised high and ready to swing atop his dashing bride the instant her key left the parlor door behind.

"Howdy, there, kitten." He tilted his head to receive his welcome.

"Hiya, cowboy." She pecked him on the cheek before stashing her keys in her bag.

"Sup, Teach?" And Marvin slid into his coat, draping his gamer scarf around his neck.

"How goes the Battle of the Horrid Holidays, Mr. Jones?"

"Ain't no thang," he shrugged. "Yo' wife's a master of the people arts – ain't nothin' she can't handle."

Holly wasn't about to let him get away with not taking any credit. "Not while Ah have my righthand guy." She smiled.

"Seems you two make a helluva team." His eyes narrowed. "Careful she don't get attached – when this one gets her claws in ya, only way out is to buy'er a ring."

Black skin, be praised! Only thing giving away his reaction to flattery was an unmistakably tickled grin.

"You be *good* now," Mr. G went on. "Old St. Nick checks that list *twice*."

"*Chhhhh…*" amused, Marvin had to add, "Me an' Santa is boys, yo! I gotta lotta pull with the jolly ol' dude. Ain't nothin' but love comin' for *me* this Christmas."

"You know what they say…" he cocked his head and winked. "Careful what ya wish for."

"Ahhhh, they do *say* that, don't they, Teach! Ahaa!" He gave him more credit for that one than was called for, feeling especially humoring. "Peace out, then, G fam!"

"Bye, Marvin," her voice sang, and he did his best to hardly notice.

After braving the whipping winds and cursing the cold, he joined his thinning flock at Shawn's truck for a snowy winter smoke-off. Grandad Santa, Kevin the Elf – a thin, nineteen-year-old flexible-sexual with sleek cheekbones – and the blunt bearer, Shawn, were already tits deep into a conversation when Marvin strolled into it, looking to get warmed up with a pull from their peppermint roll.

"...thought I'd harass El before I came in since she didn't show up yesterday," Kevin was saying, "but she wasn't there."

"What about her man – the bouncer dude?" Shawn had a hint of worry in his tone as he gave Marvin a heads-up greeting along with the blunt.

"He's got his own place. I don't know where it is. Hopefully she's there, because her roommate hadn't heard from her either." He shivered when he talked, a little from nerves building at the thought of nearly all the pre-holiday hires missing, and a lot from the cold. "Hopefully she's just too over work to answer her phone... Weird, though... She really seemed like she liked helping out."

Marvin took an extra pull, catching up to the rest, then turned to Grandad with the torch and a query. "You been back to the club? Seen any of 'em there?"

He shook his head. "Ain't been back since you skinny niggas had me out 'til fo' inna mo'nin'." He took a hit, not at all worried. "They's just kids, man. 'Cept for George an' Larry. But Larry's hitched – a good Christian. He don't go to the club. Ain't nothin' strange for a buncha college kids to not show up fo' work." Passing the doobie, Kevin picked up where Grandad left off.

"Well, if they're just screwing us off, that's fucked." Puff, puff, puff... "Today was fucked... That line was more than one elf can handle..." Puff, puff, pass. "I don't think I ever wanna see another mother and her little brats *again*..."

Shawn exhaled an airy laugh before inhaling smoke. "Yo, on another note: guess who *we* chillin' wit tonight." He raised his brows insinuatingly at his bestie.

Marvin almost forgot... "Shut up... Them girls wanna kick it tonight?"

Grandad chuckled at Marvin's change in tone, going from bleak to chipper in less than a pull.

"Yeah, bruh! Well," his head gestured toward Kevin. "Kev's got a Christmas thang goin' down and invited alla us; the girls too."

"They looked too cute in their little elf coses," Kevin admitted. "I had to invite them – they'll fit right in with the rest of the crowd."

"What crowd?" Marvin wondered.

"It's a work party." They all looked at him like he was dense, wondering if he realized no one was likely to show, and he rolled his eyes. "My *other* work, guys… I work at Tarnished—"

"Oh shit! The porn studio?!"

"Adult video and *entertainment*… God…" he feigned offense. "But, yeah. I'm a photographer."

Marvin hardly saw the point of him working at a place with so many… "But you ain't…"

"Into girls?" He shrugged. "I'm gay, not blind. Girls are hot – just not my thing *personally*. But they're a much better medium to shoot – more versatile."

Shawn chuckled mischievously. "You comin', right Grandad?"

"It's a naughty Christmas party, ain't it? What's a naughty Christmas party without a grimy ol' St. Nick?"

"Hell, yeah!" He slapped hands with his hero while Kevin went on.

"Hopefully some of our missing peeps will show. They all know it's going down. I know a few of them wouldn't miss it for the *world*."

"So when's it poppin' off?"

They all turned to Marvin and grinned.

"Three days!"

"What?!" Marvin *thought* he heard him, but couldn't believe he heard him *right*…

"Three days!" Kevin repeated louder from under his elf hat, melodious voice competing with the music. He'd had on the same outfit from the mall minus his white collared shirt, still sporting the green vest with suspenders over his bare chest and his pointy elf shoes.

"Gotdayum!" Confirming what he thought he'd heard was a jaw dropper: it seemed the party hadn't stopped for three days…

"Peeps are coming and going but we got every fly DJ within two hundred miles to rotate in and out of here! My boss went all out! Invited talent from all *over* the Midwest!"

Eyes full of holiday cheer reflecting off sparkling skin, the two gamers were enamored. There were five times as many girls prancing around the house-party as there was at the strip club. Apparently the yuletide groove-bug had been spreading throughout the town's in-crowd, cultivating masses of its elite. The hired muscle at the door almost didn't let Grandad in, *despite* his jolly ensemble, but Kevin had the final say – he was on "the list".

The house was huge; one of those million-dollar homes that would be ten million in a costal state. Two stories and sixteen rooms, it had everything from an indoor pool to an eight-car garage. It was a bit of a drive to get there, a half an hour from the outskirts of town, but had been professionally decorated with icicle-blue lights lacing its every horizontal edge and enough silver garland inside to stretch from one end zone to the next and back. Mistletoe hung from one-out-of three door frames but most didn't bother to limit their necking to beneath traditional shrubbery. Sexy, sweaty bodies grinded through every corridor while three different baselines (from three separate DJ's) vibrated all walls glowing with a red or green hue.

Shawn turned to Marvin, both nearly drowning in giddiness but trying to keep their cool "This is fucking insane!" he yelped in a pitch like a little girl's, and Marvin giggled in kind.

"Yo, Grandad!" Marv turned to spray his enthusiasm on the elder in their midst like a cat sprays piss in heat, but O.G. Clause was already on the move. He'd grabbed two bottled brewskis and jiggled his way into the cluster of college girls getting their freak on on the dance floor. "Check this nigga out!" He pointed to the life of the party being surrounded by five nearly nude ladies in heels.

"Hell yeah!" Shawn resurrected the fist-pump. "Yo, we gotta get in there, man!"

Marvin chuckled. "Fool, you know you can't dance!"

"That shit don't matter!" He pointed to his Christmas headdress. "It's all about the hat, yo!"

Marvin chuckled goofily while Shawn made his move for the center of the crowd. Being tall and awkward, Marv still hadn't quite grown into himself and had never been comfortable being the center of attention, so he hung back and just watched with a jubilant grin, marveling at the red-and-greened themed debauchery. He knew the score. When you're a weed head at a party like this, all you had to do was light up and you'd get *plenty* of stray love, even while on the sidelines.

But he didn't feel the need for love just yet – he was too enthralled by the turnout. Also, the thought *did* occur that he was still walking a thin line with Shandra. If she was already there or showed up while he was bumping and grinding, it was likely his shot at getting a little more familiar with her lady places would be out with bedazzled tees and the early 2000's. It was hard for him to look at her now like he had before Holly and the titillating events of Christmas break, but he knew she was still his best bet for playing the long-game. He might be able to hook up with a random girl tonight who could rock his world, but it would be back to small town options the next day, and there wasn't much more going for him than the one he'd had his eye on since the start of high school.

There was no shortage of friendly faces, however. He found himself on a couch hanging around Bry and his bro with three delightfully shameless "ladies of the industry", passing around dabs in a vaporizer. Bry was trying to talk the talent into accompanying him up north for Christmas to hit the slopes; rather indiscreetly insinuating a hotel ski resort and an eight-ball of fresh blow. They seemed more interested in getting what they wanted without having to pack a bag and hit the road with a fiery-bearded stranger and his skater-haired hangabout. When one of the girls started to scoot closer to Marvin, leaning over him while holding the vape pen for him to hit from her hand, he had to go and be "that guy" and let her know he was meeting someone. He explained he was already on her shit list and had to play his role cautiously; at least until she showed up and he screwed his chances by opening his mouth...

"Why, what's wrong with your mouth?" the petite, twenty-two-year-old Filipino girl wondered, still testing Marvin's resolve by rubbing her tiny frame against him on the couch.

"I'ma massive geek..." he admitted. "I get ripped and start spacing out, talkin' 'bout aliens and gamer shit. Instant chick repellent."

"Awww..." She gave his arm a hug, one leg over his thigh. He could feel the warmth from between her legs through his jeans... "That's adorable!"

Oh, good Lord, give me strength!

"Thanks...uh..." He took one more look at her thigh over his, angling up her body and into her festively dressed hair. "I should dip, though, before I end up hangin' 'round *you* all night..."

"Would that be so bad?" She pouted.

He threw his head back, cursing the prick above who put him in this twisted crucible, and she giggled. "Nah, it'd be fuckin' great, but... Like I said... This is my shot at somethin' special..." He wasn't sure he believed Shandra was really something special but had to play that card to avoid the God's honest: that she was his best bet for getting laid on a reoccurring basis.

"Ok, cutie." She caressed his thigh with hers then removed it. "But if I see you all alone later, I might not be able to control myself." His stupor was so blatant she laughed at the look in his face before she stood, showing off her ass in those tiny, red velvet shorts. "Bye, gamer boy."

Breath still stuck in his throat, it took him a minute to get his head out of his urethra. When he felt it was safe to stand, he found Shawn watering his hole with something that wasn't likely to be water and pecked at his arm, gesturing for him to come out back and get some air.

As the music diminished with their retreat, he turned back and exclaimed, "Bruh… This shit crazy!"

"Fuck, dude, I ain't *neeeever* seen no shit like this befo'!" They made it out back to gape at a wooden-roofed yard with three kegs being cooled by a pile of snow and another hundred people.

"Yo, you heard from Yvonne?"

"Shit!" He'd forgotten to check his phone. Pulling it from his pocket, he unveiled a ten-minute-old text. "They *here*, man." His fingers tapped at the screen. "I'll tell 'em to meet us out back."

"Nah, it's *cold* out here. They in skirts, bruh—"

"Man, see? Tha's yo' *problem* – always actin all nice an' shit." He shook his head. "You too considerate, man… Makes you seem desperate."

"F'real?"

"You know chicks ain't into nice guys, bruh! S'why you ain't never got laid…" Marvin looked around, hoping no one overheard that. "Gotta stop givin' a fuck about 'em for a minute an' then they'll be comin' to *you*."

"That shit don't even make sense, man…"

"Just trust me, a'ight? Who got 'em to hang tonight?"

"Yeah, yeah…"

"A'ight, then. Follow my lead an' you'll be cool. Just let 'em show *us* they down by comin' out in this cold. If they don't show then we got options." He looked around at the hordes of eye candy before he got a text back.

"What she say?"

He looked at it for a minute, then, "She said it's cold out there and she wants us to meet them upstairs."

"Hahahaa! Awww, dawg... You had me goin' too..."

"Shut the hell up, man, I ain't wrong. You too *nice*... Just put yo'self *first* fo' once, a'ight? Don't be a little bitch tonight."

He'd argue, but... "A'ight, man. Don't even trip, though. I'm in a good ass mood – ain't even nervous."

"Yeah." He nodded, seeing the indifference in his man's stance. "Yeah, you been cool as hell since you been buddying up with Mrs. G..." He lifted a brow. "You fool around wit her inna back or somethin'?"

"*Pshhhh*..." He grabbed him by the shoulder and spun him toward the house. "You stupid, fool... Let's go holler at these ladies 'fore they get tired'a *waitin'* fo' yo' suave ass."

Shawn led the gotta-get-some march back inside and up the stairs with Marvin close behind. The two being as slender as noodles allowed them to slip easily through the crowd, but they had a hard time keeping their forward momentum with all the enticing action they passed. It wasn't until halfway up the stairs that Marvin came to a dead stop, eyes caught in the light of Her radiance...

"Oh shhh..."

There she was: the lovely and talented, Texas, Holly-Cone Specialist getting loose in the center of several dozen gyrating bodies, brown hair down and whipping around as lively as the most spry of her college equivalents. He didn't even notice the cowboy hat at first until it noticed him. Mr. G lifted his head while boogying down and spotted the stunted teen staring back. He raised a finger like a pistol with a smile and shot Marvin right between the eyes. Holly noticed the gesture and turned back to wave. Marvin waved in response, trying to avoid looking like he was stalking her from afar. He reached up and grabbed Shawn in his climb so to have evidence he was just passing through and pointed the two of them out. Shawn threw an amazed fist over his mouth and a pointing-finger of his own, shocked at seeing his favorite teacher getting his groove on in a house-party like this one. He exclaimed his appreciation with a fist-pump and Marvin pushed him along, playing the part of "having places to go" seamlessly. The two groovsters waved back, neither especially Christmas-y in their attire, but spiritually above reproach. Marvin's sly coverup went so well he felt Holly's stare stick to him as he moved on, noticing the absence of his divided attention... Afterward, Mr. G grabbed his wife's hand and spun her back into the music while the boys leveled-up to the second floor.

Braving the long voyage through perilous anarchy to seek out their festively garnished, sexier halves immediately scored the boys points with the damsels. When they found them in a room filled with more smoke than Chong's van, Yvonne threw her arms around Shawn and guided him down to a designated make-out sofa while Shandra grabbed Marvin and pulled him right back out the way he came.

"Let's go dance!" she insisted.

Marvin felt the pinch of that impending, downstairs conjuncture almost instantly. Hesitant, he asked, "Right now?" hoping to stall for long enough to give Holly and company a chance to take a breather.

"Yeah, why not?" She halted at his stagnant progress.

"I'on't know..." *Shit...* "I just seen Mr. G down there with my boss... Might be awkward..." The truth sprinkled with a touch of misdirection always seemed to spell Convincing.

"Kev said they've been here every night this thing been goin'. ... They cool. Don't worry." She noticed he still wasn't convinced, so she turned around to face him fully and stepped close, looking up at the lengthy teen who stood at least a foot taller. *"Pleeeease, Marvin?"*

Her body brushed against his and he was putty in her hands.

Her big eyes were even more seductive than her begging... He did his best to not cave in in under two seconds. He literally counted to five in his mind after he knew he was ready to go wherever she wanted and even looked around with "reluctance" to further stall. When his eyes finally found hers again with a sigh, she bounced in excitement and yanked his arm like it were a leash and she a sprightly pup.

She led him through the raucous masses like a young woman possessed by the rhythm and right to a spot beside Holly and Hubby. He saw it coming halfway through the dance crowd and mentally prepared himself to lift a hand for a friendly high five with the G-man so when it came to that, it was a natural a thing as if it never crossed his mind to *not*... Holly smiled as brightly as a star without a cloud in the sky, but Marvin wasn't ashamed to admit *his* catch looked mighty fine in her scant, holiday elf getup.

The ensuing get-down brought the four of them near enough that the thought of a Shandra/Holly threesome naturally slipped around in his sticky little mind. At least until the 'Stache of Infertility peaked over Holly's bare shoulder and the image of an unwanted, pierced phallus with ball-chaps and a cowboy hat destroyed his partial chub… Mr. G winked before he did some sort of showboating twirl that had no place in dancing to Trap music, but Marvin rooted him on nonetheless. He'd already murdered his fantasy-boner… No sense in letting his antiquated dance moves ruin his high.

Three tracks later and Marvin wondered where the hell the buoyant, older couple out-partying them cultivated all their exuberance and if he could get it in pill form along with a liter of water.

"Let's chill for a minute, yeah?!"

Shandra nodded and led him from the center of the crowd. It wasn't easy not to turn back and say bye to Holly but he knew better. Instead he kept his eyes on the rump clearing a path for him until an unrefined, right hand met his chest and stopped him in his gait. He followed the scratchy mitt up its cotton trimmed, red velvet sleeve to find Grandad just over its shoulder, buttery teeth cheesing under his voluminous strap-on beard.

"Careful with this one, now, young blood." He alluded to Shandra who had stopped and looked back to see why they weren't moving. "Girl knows *exactly* what she want." He chuckled and Marvin played along.

"Ahhhh!" He slapped hands with the old man and Shandra squeezed in afterward for a hug. "This Grandad!" he introduced, while the seasoned man-of-the-hour got his second sniff of her.

"I heard!" she smiled. "Shawn said you been kickin' it together!"

Grandad leaned in to covertly exchange hellos. "You still gon' want me to wrap up that Lil Xan fo' you fo' Christmas, babygirl?"

Her eyes moved up to Marvin's who waited patiently for them to have their secret rap and then— "Put 'im on ice, Santa-man. I gotta good feelin' about this one."

"Oh, okay," he nodded dramatically, "okay…" Turning to Marvin now, he warned, "Boy, you in *way* over yo' head with this little thang! Haha!"

Marvin chuckled in embarrassment as Shandra's libidinous eyes narrowed, and her holiday gold and red nails squeezed at his hand, dragging his virginity toward its doom.

After collecting the smooching sofa-rollers, four teens crammed into one rickety Datsun and headed for Yvonne's unsupervised hacienda. She lived with her older sister who was away for the weekend, as she often would be, leaving a marginally well-kept abode ripe for hormonal befouling. The preceding hotbox made for a smoky arrival that B-Real would be jealous of, and when the four, arrantly blazed crusaders stepped onto the sidewalk outside her home, a frigid gust of wind erased the cloudy evidence and sent them all shuffling for the front door, "oh, shits" and "goddamns" flying as free as birds.

The ladies didn't waste time with host-like courtesies that the fellas may have bothered with. They led their horses to their preordained watering holes post haste, figuring they were thirsty enough to drink whatever was there, romantic trimmings or no. They were likely right, although Shawn did feel obliged to point out the lack of effort—

"What, no candles?"

Yvonne pushed her boy-toy onto the bed after locking her bedroom door. "Shut up and fuck me."

Forgoing the instinct to haggle, he thought it best to save the gritty details of their negotiations for the aftermath, whispering atop battered pillows.

Marvin, on the other hand, had to wrestle the urge to yammer on about the icy oceans of Enceladus as soon as Shandra's elf hat hit the floor. It was like the flowing of her wavy hair prompted some geek defense-mechanism that warned him of ensuing sexual turbulence – direct human female contact was, at this point, unavoidably inevitable—

Red Alert! Red Alert! All hands, proceed to escape pods! Impact is imminent! Repeat: Impact is imminent! Abandon ship! For the love of James T., abandon ship!

Perched on the edge of the bed in the master bedroom, he watched while she approached her Chosen One a single stride at a time, losing an article of clothing with every step.

After the pointy hat was flung away, so to was the bra; she maneuvered it from under her costume to get comfortable which teased the hell out of her nervous spectator. One red heel flew off next, then the other, bringing her shortened frame to within groping distance.

Instincts kicked in and the fate of the starship *Enterprise* no longer held sway, so he reached for her hips to guide her in – safety regulations be damned – but her hand slapped his before he could make contact. He forced a smile, letting her take the conn, and watched while she reached under her jagged hemline to roll down a very festive pair of red and gold-laced panties that likely cost more than the whole Christmas ensemble. Eyes following the garment's decent to the floor, when they made it that far, she reached for his hand and guided it under her dress…

Eureka! First contact!

O, what enthralling alien wonders would await! Strange new furls and slippery libations!

Her moist warmth to his touch sharpened his breaths so acutely they had edges. His heart swelled with the pumping of his excitement when he explored inside of her, mouths gaping together at the sensation. It didn't take long before she wanted more, so forced him on his back to crawl into a position of dominance above.

He knew he shouldn't say it, but—

"I never…"

Her lips gave him his response when they shut him up. Nothing other than their two bodies mattered now; two bodies that would soon be one…

Her hands worked at his belt, and his never left their new home between her thighs. She moaned at his touch while voraciously working to uncover more of him. When she was finally able to fill her grip with what her body craved, she returned the pleasurable favor of priming his pump before putting it to work.

His only recourse was mental distraction—

Call of Cthulhu gameplay… Baby Chris's shitty diapers… Mr. G's prickly mustache… Holly's ass moving around in that tight—

"Waitwaitwaitwait…"

"*Shhhhhhhhhh…*" she shushed him with a finger to his lips. "Just let me, baby…" Ignoring the warning, she did as she would with him, sliding a lit dynamite stick between her walls like she had a fetish for exploding mortar.

Marvin's peaking moans of helplessness were four seconds of elation that erupted into ten more of pulsating release nearly a decade in the making. His swollen gamer joystick filled her lovely alien corridor with a passion so thick her breaths shortened and heart sped to a sprint. Blindsided by the opportunity, she pounced into a rapid rhythm atop the defeated explorer while the soldier in him still held out hope. Confused, he watched from his place of surrender as she gave no quarter. Hands reaching to disarm her defenses, he pulled her front armor from her chest to unveil her forward weapons, and had a *hell* of a time deciding if he wanted to subdue them or just let them run their course...

In the end, his training took over and he found the courage to launch a counterstrike, cupping the two WMD's in his palms and guiding them to a safe harbor. His touch gave her the support she needed to let go – her explosive foray nearly rivaled his own.

Afterward, she slowly fell over him like a feather from the sky until they embraced; she slid beside him with one thigh still adorning her conquest.

Eyes unsettled, examining the ceiling for conversation, he couldn't help but say what was on his mind:

"Ok, this is gon' sound retarded, but—" Then don't say it, dipshit! "—are you on the pill?"

She squeezed out a laugh with her head on his chest, contemplating messing with him for fun but decided not to screw with the ambiance. She lifted her head to look into his eyes, giving him an honest answer. "Yes, Marvin... That *did* sound retarded..." she chuckled at his confusion. When his eyes still begged the question; "And *yes*," she promised. "I'm on the pill." Her head tucked back into his chest. "Can we go back to cuddling now?"

His sigh was a gust of wind that cleared the air, allowing him the freedom to breathe. "Yeah..." He smiled and let his body untighten, arm snugly around his new— "Wait, so..." Just stop talking, dude... "...does this mean we—"

"No."

Told you.

"Right... Nah, it's cool. Heh..." He loosened back up. "I jus' wanted to be sure, y'know? So I didn't crowd you or nothin'..."

"Boy... Yo' pillow talk needs work..." She looked up and smiled a little then pecked his lips. "Lucky you got it where it counts..."

There's nothing like complimenting a man's johnson to set him at ease.

The rest of the evening was mostly uneventful. Marvin woke up Shawn a few hours later so they could make their way home before things became awkward. The driving conditions weren't ideal, but neither was the thought of overstaying their welcome. He figured it best they didn't have to do the "morning after" thing – no toothbrush on-hand meant no conversations with ladies at daybreak. And who *doesn't* have to take a frightful dump when they get up in the morning? All logic and reason pointed to a timely departure, and all parties seemed to quietly agree.

Besides, Marvin had promised his mom he and Shawn would salt the paths around the house in the morning, and Shawn agreed. He'd volunteered to crash at Marvin's so they could get the job handled first thing. Whether or not he'd recall this when the time came to get his ass hauling twenty-pound bags would remain to be seen...

When the clock struck four, Shawn was out cold. But Marvin couldn't help but be wired from the past few nights' events. Recounting his life's turn to fortune – from hanging with Grandad at the club, getting to work side-by-side with Holly, and navigating the halls of the wildest house-party he'd probably ever see – he wondered what a new day would bring; also, when the hell his cheeks would finally give in and stop pulling his lips into a cheeseburger grin...

He laid for at least an hour with his eyes wide, fantasizing about future possibilities while listening to the flurry picking up outside. As snug as bug under a rug, when what sounded like glass breaking out back spiked the cry of the wind, he perked his head up in the dark to listen...but didn't think much of it. It was probably just the shriek of the storm through the trees, he figured. No sense in getting out of bed. The only things rustling around outside in *this* weather had four legs and fur hides. So unless a posse of possums were planning a heist, he thought better of worrying about it.

Yep. Everything was coming up Marvin...

And sleep nestled his conscience into a restful daze.

DECEMBER 24TH
2:34 PM

Sullen and morose, unnerved by what wretched reality had made them its own, the two hapless screw-overs gawked in a daze at what would push most into a spiraling, cataclysmic meltdown wrought with projectile juices from any number of effusing orifices.

A three-faced snowman of frosty repugnance – six human arms atop six legs, like two spiders humping – sat waiting for the two teens to turn up in Marvin's backyard. And Marvin, numb from the icy morbidity that'd become his life, couldn't help but think the snowy death shrine awaiting them was somehow fashioned playfully; scampish in its revulsiveness…

Staring into something that should've made him run screaming in the opposite direction, he took a close account of it all, allowing its design to manifest fully in his mind—

The bottom bulge of its base boasted its devilish overtures with Ol' St. Larry's red-velveted thighs protruding to form a lap in which to sit (if one were so inclined), while the four, candy-cane-striped gams with all too familiar red pumps were crossed on each side, personifying flirtation and femininity. Cruor soaked this segment so thoroughly it resembled a malignant tumor, with a small pond and rivulet of grume bespeckled by the morning's recent fallings trickling toward the woods.

The middle bulge of this seasonal horror was predominantly Larry's – his unanimously admired as the jolliest of the Santas' paunches. Belly as pristine as a present under a tree, it seemed great care was taken when constructing this horrid warning… But what that warning conveyed was still as much a mystery as who or *how* anyone could have done it. Packed in snow for spherical symmetry, his arms were left attached to his torso: one hand on his lap, the other reaching out for the "so inclined".

Four more naked arms of a feminine persuasion rounded this same segment, each in a position of terror, clawing or shielding or flailing or reaching for mercy... These bare limbs were gouged to the bone where signs of struggle were apparent; purplish and vascular in others from the cold... But the twenty festive fingernails that garnished them were perfect; not even a *chip* to their merriment, as if the assailant had no form to be assailed. The sun was setting...and the twinkle of its retreat bouncing off the tips of fingers that had been so recently intimate with the boys' bodies was hypnotic... Neither Marvin nor Shawn could say for sure how long they stood and stared.

Triple-tongued, the three faces of the snow-grotesquery's top segment had all been made to gape and lap provocatively, as the girls so often would in the selfies they'd post to aimlessly stimulate their following. Tongues frozen blue and split down their centers, despite their skanky gape, their eyes told of the chilling truth; capillaries burst, lids hiding beneath brows, pupils dilated to consume the iris...

That they'd died in horror was gut-wrenchingly evident.

Their eye makeup was smeared to resemble demonic tears, lipstick pungent and embossed with layers atop layers, cheeks rouge and plastered with glitter... Either the killer added his own finishing touches to their visages for artistic flare or the two girls planned on being noticed when they left their home (which wouldn't be a stretch considering Marvin's last words to them; namely two that began with the letters F and O, delivered exuberantly, without consideration of how they'd be received.)

And then there was the head of Ol' St. Larry, the eldest of the "hired Nicks". A good Christian, as was told through the words of Grandad Santa, with naught but kindness in his heart and ham in his belly. Mouth pried so wide his cheeks were ripped into a Joker smile, his store-bought, one-season-a-year white beard was now suffused with coagulated red... Frosted snot dripped from his nose and clumped the fibers of his mustache, and his teeth unfurled with lips frozen in a forced snarl. Tongue disturbingly elongated, it protruded from his throat to extend nine inches passed his jaw. His eyes were rolled so high into his head only a glimpse of his blackened irises could be seen; neck so ragged it must have been torn from his shoulders with brute force. And set carefully at the apex of it all was the hat he'd worn to transform himself at this time of year into the joyous embodiment of the Christmas spirit, its white cotton tip perversely spattered with the evidence of his slaying.

After a dismal night's rest at Shawn's – but likely a better one than he'd have gotten at home – when they got up to *not* find any flagrantly festive corpse-sculptures festering close by, they were naïve enough to allow themselves to think they were in the clear. If Marvin would have been wearing his head on straight he'd have called his mom the minute he woke to save himself the trouble of freaking out when he got home and she wasn't there. Because if she *had* been, he likely wouldn't have risked going out back to find what he had… He may've never set foot out back again, just for the sake of not wanting to try his luck.

But, no… Head swirling with carcasses and motives and dots without lines to connect them, it never occurred to call ahead, so when he stepped foot inside and no one answered his hollers – his mom's car still parked in the driveway – he fought the urge to not go out back, and did so for the sake of needing to know…

The bodies of his family were not amongst the carnage; he'd learned they'd gone a few houses down to babysit a neighbor for a few hours. That was the extent of the bright side of this curdling scenario.

"I'll…go get some tarps…" Sedated with the lack of bothering to hope for this to be over, Shawn shuffled away while Marvin just stared.

Something inside him was beginning to turn.

Broken corpses anonymously retired to a crowded ravine ripe with red and green dead, Shawn and Marvin now found themselves manning a life-or-death quest on Christmas eve; newly discovered Resolve in full swing.

Shawn was entirely on board – rejuvenated by the determination in Marvin's tone when he made it clear they were going to Grandad's to stop this thing – but wanted to be sure they had all their corpses in a row before showing up to haphazardly save the day.

"So, what we gon' tell him?"

"*Everythin'*," Marvin droned. "It's the only way he'd even bother listenin': if we come *clean...*"

Shawn's grip on the steering wheel tightened. "You think he'll believe us?"

"Don't matter... Whoever's doin' this shit'll be comin' for 'im. He'll believe it *then*. We'll jus' stay with him till he do."

It sounded simple enough, but—

"So...you think we gon' fight this shit, then? Us against them?" It was apparent he didn't think that scenario would end well.

Marvin didn't answer. He honestly didn't know.

"I'm sayin', man... I'm *with* you; this can't happen again... But... How we gon' stop it?"

Still no response.

It seemed Marvin had discovered the resolve to make his bold move toward redemption but hadn't yet manufactured the focus to plan ahead... "We're winging it" appeared to be the unspoken rejoinder.

He hadn't bothered calling out of work. He was so intent on saving a life that disappointing Holly was as trivial a thing as what shoes he'd wear to do it. And if he could somehow manage to save Grandad from whatever dark force was stalking him, then it was likely this whole ordeal would come into light, so him skipping out on a shift would ultimately be shrugged off as the price paid for doing a hero's duty.

The mall had closed early anyway, being Christmas eve, so by the time the two had deposited their troubles and then made it back to town, Grandad was already getting settled into a snowy night alone with his blunts, meatloaf and whiskey. His delight upon having visitors was evident but dissipated quickly at the sight of a world's worth of worries weighing the two of them down.

"I ain't never seen two niggas needed to get high as badly as the pair'a *you*..." Relaxed in civilian gear, Grandad opened the screen door to his mobile home for his wayward guests to come in. He could tell from the looks of them that asking if something was wrong was a waste of whiskey-sipping seconds. He knew they'd get to it when they were good and ready.

They both meandered into the home of someone they'd come to think of as extended family and found a couch that fit their asses. Shawn watched as Grandad scanned the front of his abode for trouble then locked the door for safe measure. Figuring this stage of the game was The Marvin Show, he just stared into the depth of the off-white wallpaper while Grandad refilled his glass at the kitchen counter. The old bruiser pulled two more glasses from his cupboards then brought them and the bottle to the coffee table that hosted his teen guests. Two-fingers per glass, he figured the young'uns could use some lubricating to shake loose what it was they came to say.

Shawn made the whiskey disappear in a single tilt and Marvin took a few seconds to decide he should do the same. When Shawn's throat closed up faster than a virgin sphincter getting poked at by a finger, he jumped up and bolted to the sink to chase the burn with tap water. Marvin hardly budged at the sensation.

"Now…" Grandad settled into his lazyboy beside the couch while Shawn wandered back over. "One'a you two's gon' have to tell ol' Grandad what this is all about 'fo' that bottle goes hollow." He gestured with his eyes to the already half-spent quart. "But until then, I got time, so go ahead an' take y'alls."

Shawn waited for Marvin to make a move, and when he didn't, reached to wet his glass with another two-fingers to occupy the silence. But Marvin's purposeful hand stopped him in the act, lenses still staring into nothingness when he finally said,

"We know what happened to the Christmas peeps."

Eyes jumping around the living room, Shawn suddenly felt the pressure of their confession on the rise and clammed up, leaning back with his arms tucked inside him as if to not touch anything he could be blamed for murdering.

Grandad took a sip of his Johnnie on the rocks while relaxing into the chair with eyes that said, "nothing you can say to me will shock me, so go on and spill it".

After a few grim seconds, Marvin just came out with it.

"…They… They dead…"

The twitch in the corners of Grandad's eyes was near imperceptible. He wasn't sure if he should believe it at first, but after weighing the demeanor of his guests – Marvin apathic and numb, Shawn breaking into a sweat – he decided to take the words at face value.

"…Alla 'em?"

Marvin nodded.

Grandad took another sip.

"You boys seen the bodies?"

They both nodded.

"You know who killt 'em?"

They shook their heads.

Reaching for the bottle (and time to let the news sink in), Grandad treated his tumbler to a healthy refill, set the bottle back down, then settled in for story time.

"Go on, then. Lay it on me."

Marvin did as asked and spilled the human beans. Shawn pitched in on occasion to help him keep the details and body count straight while Grandad threw back two more glasses, "rocks" absconded.

When it was over, the old man sat calmly, contemplating the existence of his coffee table, pulled into the wood-grain patterns that told the illustrious tale of its lifelong journey...

The boys were attuned to the silence to start, finding solace in its uneventful nihility. But eventually the time came when it was counterproductive and nerve racking... Something had to be—

"I'on't blame you boys fo' not goin' to the police," he finally said. "Findin' a buncha bodies in yo' backyard when you black an' on drugs is enough to make *any* nigga wanna run fo' his freedom. ...And seein' as how they was decorated in yo' momma's shit, and you the last to see 'em alive?" He softly shook his head, eyes still lost in the table's woodwork. "I can't say *what* the law mighta made of it..."

Marvin felt he had more to add to that point. "And if the killin's stopped when we was in *custody* – like, this all some sick attempt to frame us – then there woulda been nothin' we coulda done but hope they found somethin' else that proved us innocent."

Grandad nodded. "Does *look* like whoever done this was lookin' to set you boys up..." He shifted his stare, finding Marvin's tired, but determined, bloodshot eyes. "But I'll tell you this: I seen some shit in my time in the Bush..." His eyes tightened. "Shit I woulda never believed another human would do to one'a they own..." letting his stare go, he finished with, "but what you boys is describin' sounds like somethin' else entirely..."

"I ain't never seen some shit like this in the *movies* even..." Shawn groaned, and Marvin added,

"This some twisted, evil shit, f'sho..."

But Grandad hadn't quite made his point. "Twisted ain't the word for it..." He trailed off with telling eyes.

When Marvin caught on, he asked, "Whatchoo mean?"

"I mean, I'on't know how this shit even humanly *possible*. I ain't seen it with my own two, but in this weather, in the time frame it happened, the murder scenes constructed like you said...? It'd take a whole *team*'a niggas *days* to set some shit like that up."

Shawn felt the tingle of paranoia, thinking what Grandad was saying was that they must've been making it up. "But it *happened*... Jus' like we said." He looked to his grown stoner-mentor, hoping to find trust in his eyes. "...You believe us, right?"

Grandad lifted his gaze and there was no doubt behind it. "Oh, I believe you. Like I said: I seen some *shit*," he reminded them. "But this may be some *other* kinda shit... Shit tha's not 'posed to exist, if you hear what'm sayin'..."

"You mean, what? Voodoo or somethin'?" Marvin guessed. "Some witchcraft type shit?"

The hairs on the back of Shawn's neck stabbed at his coat to try and flee the conversation.

"Like I keep tellin' y'all lil niggas: I seen some shit..." He finished off his glass and sighed after a traditional whiskey pucker. "...but what's happenin' *here* is somethin' else." Head tilted, savoring the taste, he *hmphed*. "Guess this explains why you two been all sketched-the-fuck-out these days... Thought you mighta been smokin' them bath salts'r some shit." He put his glass down and lifted the empty bottle to mourn its passing. "Yeah... I think I'm 'bout liquored-up enough to pop a cap in some goth-hippie ass, he come gunnin' fo' me." With that, he stood tall, his next move very clear.

"Where you goin'?" ...Or not so much, as made apparent by Shawn's confusion.

"Get me my shottie an' a box'a *shells*..." Face like he was talking to imbeciles, he added, "Where you think I'm goin', Popeye's Chicken?"

Armed and geared for riding a sleigh through moonlight, Grandad eventually turned up in his red-velvet suit, minus the beard; double barrel in hand, peppermint blunt between lips—

"Whoa... Grandad... You think that's a good idea?" Marvin became unsettled at the sight of the warmongering St. Nick.

"Hell yeah, I do! How you think I'ma shoot me somebody and not be high?" Eyes soaked in bafflement, he awaited a reasonable response.

"Nah, I mean the *suit*... Whoever doin' this is killin' folks in they costumes."

That concern seemed to make more sense to the blunted old vet. " 'Xactly! We wanna find out who doin' this we needa chum them waters." He raised his arms and smiled behind the blunt in his teeth. "You ever seen a hunk'a chum so plump fo' killin'?"

"Jesus..." Shawn hung his head, distraught his group of do-gooders consisted of a teen who just had his cherry popped (then seen the girl dead two days later), and a stoned-off-his-rocker, ex-military Santanator smiling in the face of certain doom. "Jus'...tell me you straight enough to hit what you shootin' at."

"Don't gotta be. This here ol' fella spits buckshot – spray anythin' I'm aimin' fo' to damn-near *dead*."

"Well, you got one fo' us?" He figured why not throw the thought out there.

"I ain't *that* drunk, young blood." Shaking his head, Grandad sat back down to warm his blue-collar throne. "Whatchoo boys come up wit while I was gearin' up to save Christmas?"

"We ruled out Bry. Unless he smarter than he look..." Marvin was only partly enthused about their progress.

"That big-ass, Arian lookin', ginger-beard-havin' security nigga? Why you think it mighta been him?"

Shawn took the reins on this one. "Cuz Marv got cozy with his ex at the club... But he been in Minnesota since Monday."

"How you know?"

Marvin lifted his phone. "Social media. Dude 'checked in' from St. Cloud three hours ago – been there fo' three days..."

"I'ma act like that makes sense to me so we can move on... Who else on yo' list?"

Marvin figured he'd give Shawn a little taste of what he gave. "Shawn got close to El out in the parkin' lot an' her man ran interference... Don't know why he'd have beef with *me*, but he was around all them peeps when we was."

"You mean Derrick?"

"Never got his name," Shawn admitted, not much help.

"Derrick is El's man, so you must mean Derrick" he confirmed. "He work nights, mostly. That shift end at 4am. I c'n call the 'Trot and see if he been workin' them hours. If he has, he ain't our man."

They both nervously agreed, Shawn reaching for the strain of Blue Dream in his pocket and the G Pen.

It didn't take Grandad more than a few minutes of sweet talking to find out Derrick had been as punctual as ever; not in any position to be carving up death shrines during the witching hour. He made up some line about a bet on a ballgame to quell any suspicions before giving the boys the news.

"Damn..." Marvin shook his head, running out of options.

"Now, if y'all're acceptin' an outsider's eye... I seen some shit that should *definitely* put yo' boss's *hubby* on yo' list."

"Mr. G?" Shawn twisted his brows, surprised by the concept.

And Marvin jumped right into the Denial stage of the accusation. "No way... He cool as hell..."

Then it occurred to his shorter half, "But you *have* been hella close to his ol' lady lately..." Eyes examining Marvin's for hidden scandals— "You sure you ain't *hit* that in the back'a the parlor?"

Marvin just shook his head. "You trippin... *Both* you trippin'..."

"Don't be so quick to *dismiss*, young blood. You ain't heard what I got to say."

Marvin hardly had to. The idea was preposterous. Mr. Greggerson was a goddamned *school* teacher, for shit's sake. But he listened all the same.

"Now, I admit... I jus' took'a couple'a pulls off somebody else's spliff that night and the shit tasted like I smoked sommin' I ain't had no business smokin'... But I know what I heard."

"Whatchoo hear?" Shawn took the bait, hook, line, and reefer, sparking up the ignition on his robotic doobie with eyes thirsty for breaking news. Marvin just shook his head, already dismissing what had yet to be uttered.

"I was upstairs in'at porno crib we was hangin' at, 'fore you two niggas took off wit them lil honeys." Despite Marvin not wanting to hear, he found himself covertly listening in. "I made my way out back an' to the side of the crib to release some pressure from the firehose, and I see yo' boy's hat just on the other side'a the fence, airing hisself out on his celly on the driveway. I ain't notice at firs', seeing as how I could give two shits what this nigga's goin' on about, but, what caught my ear was his accent..."

With two lungs full of a hybrid strain, Shawn released his hit with a nod, partially choking. "That shit *thick*, right?"

Grandad tilted his head. "Not inna way you *think*, lil nigga… This dude di'n't sound like he at bat for Lady Liberty, if you know what'm sayin'. Sounded more like he hailed to Her Majesty the *Queen*…"

Neither of them were cultured enough to have any clue what the old drunken velveteer was implying.

"Whatchoo mean, 'the Queen'?" Marvin wondered, taking the pen from his friend, seeing the good it was doing him almost instantly.

"Niggas… Ain'tchoo ever seen a movie that di'n't star a rapper or wrestler in it?" Drooping mouth hanging befuddled lips, he stared for a minute before clarifying. "I mean he a limey – a *Brit*." He seemed to still be speaking in pre-internetese… "Y'all ain't know what a Brit is? As in, Great Britain? …A nigga who hails from the land of the Queen?"

"You mean like Sherlock Holmes? An English dude?" Shawn finally found his way into the "know" and Marvin almost laughed at the thought.

"Yeah, okay… Like Sherlock Holmes." Grandad leaned back and sighed. "Y'all know these folks don't jus' live in Hollywood movies, now, don't you—?"

Then, like God just put his palm on Shawn's forehead and burped the words, "let there be light!", it hit him—

"Hooooo…*shit!*" Mouth and eyes the size of baseballs, he couldn't even control his faculties enough to take back the pen Marvin was handing him for another hit.

Shrugging it off, Marv retracted his offering and took the puff himself, waiting for his boy to find the coherency to articulate.

Slowly, Shawn turned his gaping grill toward his friend who sat eyeing him curiously from behind the pipe. "Dooood…"

Marvin squinted, confused by his friend's sudden lack of vocal fortitude. He blew out a puff an asked, "You havin' a flashback'r somethin' right now, man?"

"The fuckin' movie, dude!"

"What?" Marvin was utterly lost, buried in smoky inarticulation.

"What movie?" Grandad asked, getting the feeling that this had to have been somehow related to what he was saying. It was either that or the boy's brains were jelly on toast.

" 'Member? I said he looked like that dude from the movie – the Shakespeare movie: Shakespeare Loves You, or some shit…"

"*Pfffff!!*" This time Marvin *did* laugh, blowing out his second hit. "Nigga, you was out'cho mind right then…"

"Nah, fool! I ate them brownies jus' before that class – shit was jus' startin' to kick in." —Marvin shook his head— "I'm tellin' you, that was him!"

"Whatchoo sayin, young blood?" Grandad still wasn't clear on Shawn's stoner-moment of clarity. "You sayin' yo' teacher was in the movie?"

"Yassss, man! He was in the fuckin' movie!" Frozen in anticipation of the weight of this revelation, he soon found himself astounded by the eruption of laughter to either side of him. "The *fuck*, man, I'm serious!"

"This shit even funnier the second time!"

"AAAHHahahaha!" Grandad spilled another belly laugh into the room while Marvin tried to contain it like he was sizzling bacon in a pan.

"Fuck this, I'ma prove it." Determined to be heard, Shawn dug his phone from his pocket and started searching the web for evidence he wasn't as mush-brained as his friends would have him believe. "Look…right here…watch…" Fingers scrolling with newfound purpose, he clicked on a picture to enlarge. "*This* nigga." He tilted the phone to show Marvin first, then stretched over to shove it in the face of Grandad. "Lord Jessex." It was a picture of the character in renaissance costume with a neckpiece rounding his throat that looked like it was crafted from coffee filters.

"That shit don't even look like him…" Marvin chuckled a little and dried the tears from his eyes.

"Grandad, c'mon, man… You see that shit, right?"

He squinted, then took the phone, squinted some more, then—

"Pull up a pic of him now."

"Yeah, shit, here, lemme see…" Typing in the name, he said the name out loud. "Rollin…Hearse…"

"Rollin Hearse…?" Marvin found himself somewhere between nausea and befuddlement at the audacity of the title. "Who the fuck names theyself Rollin Hearse?" He leaned over Shawn's shoulder to watch the truth come to light.

"A gotdamn nutcase *psycho* who thinks he slick," Grandad offered with befuddlement that rivaled the teen's.

"Ok, right here…" Shawn clicked on a link that brought up a biography, then scrolled until he found the most current picture – the resemblance was astounding… "Tell me that ain't him!"

Marvin fell silent at the sight until he uttered, "No fuckin' way…"

"Wiki don't lie, dude! Tha's that nigga!"

Marvin started scrolling, heart pounding, head buzzing, breaths getting shallow…

Shawn stood up in his excitement and sternly pointed at the phone. "Tha's that nigga! I *told* you!" His finger added vehemence to his howling. "Say it ain't him!"

Still numb to the thought, Marvin only had one concern on his mind, searching through the bio for some mention of Holly. "Wait…" When he found a photo of the actor and his better half, he exhaled a breath so heavy he almost melted off the couch. "That ain't her…"

"Her?" Shawn was confused… "Whatchoo mean 'her'?"

"It…it ain't Holly… His wife…"

"Lemme see the goddamn phone." Grandad decided it was time he was on the level. "Lemme get a look at this limey nigga."

Marvin eased back into the couch, immediate concern alleviated, but secondary one beginning to bubble.

Shawn leaned in with Grandad to set his eyes on the wife.

"Shit," Grandad muttered. "This him, alright…" He nodded. "Put a mustache on that razor wire he call a upper lip, throw a cowboy hat on a nigga and we got ourselves a suspec'."

"Yeah… An' that ain't Holly." Shawn put the pieces together in his mind that Marvin wouldn't allow himself to see. "…So she must be *in* on it, then—"

"You don't know that, man. …Maybe she think he is who he *say* he is…"

"Nigga…" He was almost embarrassed for his lost bud. "If she rollin' around with this fool, pretendin' to be his wife, then she *in* on it."

"Nah…"

It just didn't make *sense!* There was no *way* she could've been that conniving and manipulative. He'd seen through to her very soul; she was a good person… He *knew* she was…

138

"So, what we do now? Call the cops?" Shawn took his phone back and warily sat down next to Marvin, energy seeping out of him with the thought of what they might be facing.

"Not unless you two ready to fess up 'bout hidin' them bodies... Jus' cuz this creepy ass white dude actin' like he somebody he *ain't* don't mean he our man. These rich white folks is inta all *kindsa* silly shit."

"Yeah," Shawn agreed. "Maybe he jus' doin' research on a role or some shit. Actors do that shit, right? Live the life of they characters to get inna zone?"

"No tellin' what these cracka's get up to..." Grandad admitted.

"Oh, shit..." Still digging into the mystery, Shawn uncovered something more. "I typed in 'criminal history' and got nothin'—"

"So?" Marvin was a little on edge. "That shit ain't helpful."

"Nigga, let me finish, damn... Then I tried 'occult' an' got nothin'... So I googled 'Rollin Hearse' with 'Christmas' and look what this shit says..." He turned around an article with the headline, *10 Hollywood Celebrities Who Hate Christmas.*

Marvin sunk back into his daze and Grandad coughed up a thought-provoked, *huh.*

"Right here; he quoted, sayin': 'At this time of year, I am careful not to switch on the radio because those novelty jingles make me homicidal'."

"We gon' need to check this nigga out... He lookin' more an' more like our dude. You boys know where he live?"

Shawn shook his head and looked to Marvin. When Marvin didn't respond, he spoke up. "Marv... You know where they live?"

Distantly, he answered, "Nah."

So Shawn got back to work. He googled Rollin Hearse 's address first, but then realized that was the wrong name to investigate. If "Mr. Greggerson" had a job at a public school, he must've had a local identity lined up, citizenship and whatever other bullshit his money must've bought him.

"Oh, damn..." He uttered his subtle shock as the plot thickened, coaxing notice from Marvin who turned his head to look toward the bearer of all-kinds-of-fucked-up-news. "This shit jus' keep gettin' weirder and weirder..."

"This ain't yo' drama club, lil nigga... Spit it *out.*"

Shawn tilted the phone to Marvin first, then to Grandad, showing where Google Maps had pinpointed the homestead of a one, Mr. & Mrs. Clint Greggerson.

Marvin recognized the area right away and sat back once again to ponder. Grandad had to ask to be sure.

"Is that...?"

"Yeah," Shawn answered blankly. "The porno crib..."

"Hold up, man..." It was time, Marvin decided, he got back to stripping this mystery of its delusive layers. He reached for his phone and did some digging on the web of his own, looking into the name his possible, diabolical nemesis had picked for himself. What he found, he wasn't sure what to do with. "Shit..."

Shawn leaned over to try to shed some light on Marvin's find. He saw the profile he'd pulled up and the image that didn't fit the supposed host. "That shit don't even look like him."

"Like who?" Grandad would prefer the boys to be working on a screen he could see...

"This Clint Greggerson..." Marv turned his phone around to give Grandad a glance at a man who was much rounder in the face and smaller in the nose, then turned it back to dig a little deeper. "But his profile's private so I can't—" Then he saw it: *Married to Holly Greggerson*, with a link to her profile. He clicked the little underlined stalker-link with a stutter of his heart to be redirected to a page that *wasn't* private with the lovely Holly G decorating its icon.

Watching over Marvin's shoulder, Shawn pointed out, "Either she the real deal, or they seriously fucked up they cover story..." He watched as Marvin flipped through scores of photos of the real Clint Greggerson and his dashing, younger-by-a-decade bride, Holly.

"Do I gotta keep askin', niggas? Fill a brother in, shit..."

"It's her," Shawn announced. "It's Holly. She really this dude Greggerson's girl, but..."

"But" —Grandad took the liberty— "*that* Greggerson ain't the limey gunslinger we know he is..."

"Yeah..." Shawn didn't know what other conclusion he was supposed to draw, other than, "so she gotta be in on it..."

But Marvin could hardly comprehend it. Despite the evidence turning up, he couldn't believe it was possible. He kept seeing her smile in his mind, going over her every wink and laugh, her every movement, every touch… Was he so taken that he was completely blind to the truth of what she was?

Shawn found himself deathly silent, at a loss for how to break his best dude from the apathetic shock he was in, so Grandad made a reasonable observation:

"Still… Jus' cuz they in on some freaky shit together don't mean they killin' folk." He had to give Marvin some hope to hold onto, if for nothing else, just to snap him back into a functional role. "They could just be swingers; swappin' brides for the winter… We needa find out more 'fore we know what's what f'sho."

But the rusty wheels had been given a definitive shove and Marvin's mind was suddenly running on a full tank. "Nah. It's him. It's gotta be…" The pieces seemed to fit. Other than how or why any of this was happening, all roads pointed to that cowboy hat wearing mustache-monger formerly known as Mr. G.

"I got him right here:" Shawn relayed more intel from off his phone. "This *Greggerson* dude – the real one – really *do* own Tainted Studios. …So that big ass pad really his and not this Hearse fucker's." His mind was starting to spin, taking in all the possibilities of what might be going on. "Maybe this one'a them setups where the wife get some dude to take out her hubby and then run off with his dough."

"But they ain't run off," Grandad pointed out. "And Hearse got plenty'a dough of his own." He looked to the two boys – Shawn desperate for answers, Marvin growing cold and distant – and knew he needed to instill some direction. "We ain't gon' find them answers we need by sittin' here guessin' at 'em. We gon' have to go out there an' take 'em fo' our own." He stood up, lifted his double barrel chest-high and assured his underaged flock, "Jus' as soon as ol' Grandad handle some bidness on the commode. You boys hold it down out here; a nigga might be indisposed fo' a few shakes."

Twenty minutes of Shawn prying into the internet lives of those in question and Marvin flipping through photos of Holly and company brought no game-changing revelations to the table. Shawn discovered Hearse was a celebrated actor and a gentleman while Greggerson was believed to be alive and thriving just outside of Massena, IA, capitalizing on the abundance of barely legal dreamers in a state whose claim to fame was the world's largest truck stop and the future birthplace of Captain Kirk. Marvin simply found more confusion in the pure-of-heart smile that populated Holly's profile and the wholesome goodness of her posts dating back nearly a decade. She seemed to have met her husband through the business, but not as most teen guys (and plenty of grown men) would keep their fingers crossed for. She was an art major and a film student with aspirations of sensual romanticism in cinematography. She wrote freely of her appreciation for the act of love making and its display of primal passion, and how society has wrongly deemed sex and the discussion or expression of it socially inappropriate. She had the heart of an artist and the soul of a hippie. There was nothing dark, twisted, or sadistic about her… So, she was either a psychotic, criminal mastermind, keeping her darker urges hidden behind virtue or—

"Lil niggas!" Grandad strolled out of the backroom as chipper as a skunk in a garden. "I had a change'a heart…" He pulled a Remington 1911 R1 .45 from the back of his fuzzy waistline and tossed it sideways through the air, spinning it on a zero axis, satin-black barrel and walnut wood-grips chasing each other like a bulldog after its own tail.

Instinctively, being aware of the explosive nature of the fluttering firearm, Shawn jumped to dodge its descent in the hopes of evading a fatal mishap while Marvin, knowing his reaction time was *shit* on account of his sluggish temperament, turned his cheek and cringed, accepting his fate by bracing for the touch of the Death that pursued him. Shawn smashed his shin against the wooden knee-high table foiling his escape and simultaneously tried jumping over his own tumble, flailing without grace from the pain, somehow contorting his body to avoid the pistol in flight. If it had eyes, its lashes would have felt the brush of Shawn's long sleeve Rick and Morty tee twisting in midair just before it bounced off the sofa cushion and tumbled onto Marvin's lap, barrel snug to his nuts.

When it was over, the rumpus of Grandad's cachinnation slowly blended into perception while both teens waited paralyzed for the *bang* that never came. With Shawn floored between the table and the lazy boy, apparently not coming up until he knew nothing was going to explode, Marvin pealed open a lid from over his eye and frightfully peered at the chunk of stainless steel challenging his manhood. He wasn't sure if he should even touch it until he finally realized Grandad likely wouldn't be laughing his tits off it he was in any real danger. So he opened another eye and uncoiled from his cringe, reaching for the pistol's butt to experience the power of it at his command.

After several more seconds of listening to the old bruiser nearly laugh up a lung, Shawn's head found the buoyancy to float above dangerous waters and peek just over the table toward the gun in Marvin's mitts. "*Shit*, man…" His voice cracked a little while he dug up enough courage to slowly peel himself from the ground. "Grandad, what the hell?! You tryin'a kill us?!"

"That shit ain't loaded, you scury lil nigglets! How you think I'ma toss a loaded gun at a kid?" he gassed between laughs. "How high you think I am?!"

Marvin pulled back on the slide and saw the chamber was empty while Shawn got to his feet.

"Tha's fucked up, man… I almost shit my pants…damn…" He found a spot back on the sofa next to Marv who sat looking the weapon over. "Lemme see that shit."

"Oh, you all *about* it now, huh," Grandad teased. "I figure it can't hurt to have it on you in case you need to bluff yo' way outta gettin' killt. But don't go wavin' that shit aroun' like you some sorta thug robbin' the place. These white folk see a nigga wit a gun and shoot firs' and ax' for a reward later." He grabbed his lighter and blunt off the corner table between the sofa and lazy boy and adjusted his britches. "Now, let's get to gettin' on. Time to put the fear of *Christmas* up in these Santa-murderin' muthafuckuz!"

They decided on taking Grandad's wood-paneled station wagon so they'd have room to wriggle – a 1972 Ford County Squire the old bruiser decorated with fur-covered, faux antlers and a basketball-sized, foam red nose as a hood ornament. The spirit of Christmas was strong with this one, and the winter-chilled, six-pack of Pabst Blue Ribbon on the backseat seemed to fit the scene like an old pair of sneakers.

"Rudolph the Red-Nosed Hoopty?" Shawn observed.

"Bite yo' tongue, boy! This ain't no hoopty… This here a Christmas *classic*. She runs on weed smoke and good vibes so think happy thoughts, now, ya here?"

If that were true, they likely wouldn't make it past the driveway.

Marvin let Shawn ride shotgun, sliding into the shadows smothering the backseat to try to hide from his wretched thoughts. He wanted to stay focused on the fact his favorite teacher was a fraud and possibly a homicidal lunatic looking to frame him or worse, but his mind couldn't see passed Holly's face: that damn charismatic smile… He told himself to prepare for the worst. He knew it hardly made any sense that she wasn't somehow involved, but that fact made even *less* sense considering how well he'd gotten to know her.

He couldn't believe himself to be so easily lied to… If she had a part in this and managed to seamlessly play the role of his friend while working to set him up with a lifelong prison sentence, she would have to rank amongst the foulest of creatures on Earth… But how could that be? How could such a beautifully charming woman be a demon in disguise? Was the real world so perverse? Was this some sick joke orchestrated by the Devil himself? Marvin wasn't much for church, but he found himself willing to appeal to *anything* that might have the power to adjust the outcome of this night in his favor. And, ironically, approaching the outskirts of town and his sanity, a tall-standing beacon gleamed in white Christmas lights in the distance—

Glorifying the crown of a frosted hill that bordered the freeway stood a fifteen-foot, wooden, white cross lit up for all the town to see. Its serenity pulled him back from the brink… Locked in its gaze, he realized that regardless of what he'd learn this night, the strength he'd find to conquer those truths was what was important. The issue wasn't whether he'd been so gullible to be fooled, it was if he could find the courage to right the wrongs he'd been forced to turn a cheek to.

It didn't matter *who* did him wrong… What mattered now was how he'd set things right.

"Guess that answers our *firs'* question."

Pulling up to the ice-blue lights of the frosty, two-story party pad, Shawn quickly noticed there wasn't any security manning the door. The Christmas lights and snowflake laser show illuminating the trim of the home were precise, likely having been arranged by someone Hearse paid to decorate the place. And the lawn and beyond was caked with fresh powder, the walkway cleared by departing traffic.

"Probably sent 'em home, seeing how it's Christmas eve," Grandad guessed. He figured there was no sense in being cordial, so obtusely parked blocking the driveway. "Still music comin' from inside. And a lot of cars parked 'round here…"

"I'on't see any movement, though…" Shawn sized-up their objective from the front seat by gazing through the numerous windows; lights on within, illuminating the stillness behind them. "This shit just *feel* wrong."

"Could be they just cars peeps left behind, too fucked up to drive home," Marvin offered rationally. "Maybe the party's over."

"Then why they ain't turn off the tunes?" Grandad wasn't convinced, reaching for his shotgun resting on the dash. "Let's go shake some shit up; see what falls out." Snatching his Santa cap from between him and Shawn, he pulled it snug over his bald spot and stepped outside, seemingly not fazed by the chill.

Shawn looked back to Marvin, eyes desperate for a reason not to go on… But Marvin hardly blinked. He followed in Grandad's footsteps before overtaking him for the door – Shawn might've stayed behind if it weren't for fear of freezing to death while being left out in the cold.

A short whistle came from Grandad's lips to slow Marvin down, signaling that he wanted to peek through the window before barging in. The curtains were drawn, but if he could catch a glimpse of movement he'd at least know what to expect. After a solid thirty seconds of surveying the front room – eyes squinting to peer through the frost and cloth; Marvin's heartbeat escalating every second longer they took to crash the place – Grandad finally gave him a heads-up nod for him to make his move and go in. The mixed emotions – relief and frustration, both – tangled around the determination in his gut when the door wouldn't budge.

"It's *locked*."

Shawn wasn't conflicted at all. "Guess that mean the party's over…"

"*Sheeeit*, lil nigga," Grandad grinned, eight o'clock shadow collecting frost from the wind, "this party jus' gettin' started!" Gesturing with his head, he meant for his flock to follow him around back, turning to lead the way, the short hairs of his velvet getup showing impressions of the wind from behind.

The house was one of only six in the neighborhood: a community of elite private homes where each estate was a thousand feet apart from the next. A wooden fence bordered it twenty feet out from each side that closed in on a moderately sized backyard; gates stood on either side and one at the back that opened into several acres of land, a treeline holding off a small forest in the distance.

Braving the frosty buildup, the Lit Squad sallied forth along the yard's perimeter, planning to peek over it before intruding on any leftover partyers with a firearm. Their galoshes sunk into snow halfway up their shins while tromping awkwardly toward the rear of the estate, Marvin's head being just high enough to glimpse over the wooden pickets. Every window had vertical blinds shutting out prying eyes, only slivers of yellow light visible from the odd angle. Still no movement perturbed his notice. Grandad asked if he'd seen anything and Marvin shook his head with Shawn knee-deep in the holes he'd made before him.

The backyard – under the wooden canopy covering it – was a perverse, keg-cup-speckled smorgasbord of gluttony and sloth. The heated pool was littered with floating panties and bras, the waterfall-fountain in the corner likely half piss. Paper plates, liquor bottles, plastic wine glasses, defeated pool floaties trampled and flat... The only thing the afterparty scene was missing was the dudes who were too drunk to score, passed out in vomit, and several jumbo Greek letters painted with white shoe polish on the sliding glass door. When they were finally able to peer past the debauched battlefield and into the home they'd once so enjoyed, what looked like the casualties of a booze-war for the ages became apparent.

Marvin was the first to step inside, heading through the kitchen toward the still flesh in the distance. Grandad couldn't seem to slow him down even if he tried but figured it best not to be head-manning the operation with a loaded shotgun into another man's home. Despite the rational assumption that Hearse was up to no good, they still had no proof he was in any way hostile...other than there being bodies spread across the carpet in the next room like bones on the floor of the Abominable Snowman's cave... Accumulated past the dining area into what *was* the dance floor, the bodies had all seemingly been dragged there and situated so twenty or more could fit across the breadth of the room...but no visible blood haunted their conscience.

Shawn fought his instincts to run and hide in a hole for as long as he could, each step closer to the living room revealing more bodies until he finally lost his nerve and turned to make an escape. Hardly noticing the large black man in the Santa suit with a gun, he nearly ran the old man over if not for Grandad having more than a hundred pounds on the young buck and several inches to boot. The fleeing teenage gazelle had a bounce to his stride Grandad had never seen, and the old man was almost too slow to catch him before he flew the coop to dance amongst the trees. He swiped at the blur of Shawn's attire and clutched a handful of his fur-lined hood, but the struggle didn't end there. Shawn fought against his arrest with his feet going one way and body the other, as his Commander and Chief domineeringly pulled him back into line.

"Nigga…you gon' get yo'self *killt* runnin' 'round out there alone… Or you gon' *freeze*." He shook his head. "We goin' in. And so the hell is *you*." His eyes were those of a resolute parent's, and the child in Shawn seemed to respond. He squirmed a bit in a silent fit, then got back on track…after a slight nudge from his elder in the direction of his friend who was far enough ahead to be staring down at the body at his feet.

Marvin started leaning toward a limp wrist to feel for a pulse before several thumps against a wall caught his ear. His head whipped to his left to stare down a sparsely lit hall – the party lights and music not much help in making out details – and he threw one hand back to his companions to signal they approach with caution. Grandad stealthily moved with haste, passing by Shawn and getting to a corner that he bent his eyes around. The next few thumps they could make out under the beat of the Trap music seemed to suggest their source was moving downward…

"She alive?" Grandad's glance referred to the body at Marvin's feet.

Marvin, still squatted next to the slim figure face-down in scant Christmas rags, continued on his path for her wrist, doing his best to find a pulse. Not having a practiced hand while being distracted by the music, he had to close his eyes and focus, but after twenty long seconds, they shot back open with newfound hope as he nodded, confirming that she was.

The seasoned hard-ass hardly made it apparent, but a weight lifted from his chest when the young woman was found to still be breathing. Then he got back on the job, stepping over bodies on the floor and heading toward the next corner just before the hall, his ears trained on the slow, dull knocks heading further below. Eyes glimpsing around a new corner, he made out a doorway halfway down the hall. He looked back to Marvin, and now Shawn, who'd crept up to peak his head from around the far wall, and mouthed the word "basement", assuming that's where the sounds were coming from.

With a cool gesture, he signaled for the two of them to come beside him where they'd be out of sight, so they traversed the gauntlet of sleeping beauties that, Marvin noticed, all seemed to be in line to be dragged down the dark hall of Probable Christmas Doom next. They followed a path toward Grandad and made it to a spot standing beside the unmanned turntables still loudly spinning hip tunes.

Marvin looked toward the switchboard for the volume, aiming to knock it down a notch. Shawn got nervous the minute Marvin's hand stretched to make his attempt and, in a panic to stop him, reached out. In retrospect, he would've been better off still in the car, freezing his nads off where his bumbling haste couldn't screw over anyone's plans to not get killed.

Arm reacting faster than his brain could move his fingers, Shawn's hand shoved instead of grabbed, and pushed Marvin's into the table, skipping the record with a *screech* and knocking the needle entirely off the album. In a long, grueling human history of party fouls, there had never been one so egregious... But what the painfully fresh silence uncovered may have been worse—

One eye pinched shut in a deathly cringe, it took several seconds for Shawn and his rueful ilk's hearing to adjust and discover something impossible... Something...*inhuman*...

Then the clunking of rawhide attached to hard rubber quickly ascending several wooden stairs realigned their focus.

Grandad tightened his grip around his shotgun, positioning himself to face the wall and the approaching insurgent, gun barrel set tightly at the wall's edge. Marvin's heart finally reminded him he was alive by racing in its rhythm while Shawn slinked back around the DJ table to duck below the equipment...

...and the clunking of the boots slowed.

Only several stairs from the hallway, the sound became so soft it was hard to hear it over the blood pumping through their veins. When the boots finally made it to the carpet, all bets were off, and the sounds they'd heard before, resonating from the basement, now stood out over the absence of everything else.

A deep huffing, lapping, and primal grunting bellowed through the floor and walls. It was the sound of what might resemble the afore mentioned Abominable Snowman being *eaten* buy something much less snuggly and quaint… It was snack time for King Kong in a basement likely only big enough for Gorilla Grodd, and the sound was so surreal it faded into the white noise of obscurity while all ears strained to make out an approach…

But no steps were heard, so Grandad looked to the ground for a shadow, discovering the light was traveling the wrong way. If it weren't for the body partly jutting from the hallway, feet upright and apparently nudged, he couldn't have been sure anyone was there at all. But knowing his target was closing, the ex-war-vet centered his focus and zeroed in. And when the first strand of Hearse's brown hair slowly tilted around the edge to steal a glance, all he found was two barrels aiming back at his black, square-framed glasses.

Grandad Santa made no mistake and reached for a grip around several buttons on his hostage's shirt, being sure he couldn't recoil. "*Hands*, sick-o!" he demanded, needing to know he wouldn't get shot if he pulled him out into plain sight.

"Whoa, whoa, whoa!" Hearse lifted his hands to show them unarmed. "Hold on now, cowboy… I'm, I'm just tryin' ta get outta here…"

Seeing no weapon in his fists, Grandad pulled him out of the hallway, barrels still tight to his temple. "Yeah, you jus' happen to be the only mu'fuckuh awake… Makes perfect sense… Marvin, check this chump's waistline fo' weapons."

"Marvin?" Mustache straight out of a spaghetti western, Hearse put on his Shocked face and quickly melted it into feigned concern. "Marvin, you gotta get me out outta here! I don't know what happened… I-I-I just woke up in the cellar and—"

Marvin's glacial stare preceded Shawn popping up from behind the DJ table to get his licks in. "Knock that cowboy shit off, you Sherlock Homes motherfucker! We know who you are! We know you ain't Greggerson! You ain't even American!"

Hesitance turned to showmanship, his mouth wide with betrayal. "Shawn… What…?" He wasn't ready to give up the charade. Eyes pleading for mercy, he switched his glance back to Marvin who circled around him to pat him down. "Marvin… What *is* this? What's…" But being an expert in the craft, he knew when he'd lost his audience by the dull look in their eyes.

After a sigh, like kicking off your shoes succeeding a long day's work, his brow loosened and lips began to curl. A sleazy smirk found its way around his teeth and a sinister gloss gleamed over his eyes. It was like watching a puppy shed its skin to reveal the snake that had been hiding inside...

"Sodding hell..." He almost laughed. He took his glasses off and peeled off the fake 'stache as Marvin circled back around to face him, Grandad taking a step back. "It was the film in our last lesson, then, wasn't it..." He shook his head. "A bit rash, I know." Tossing his prickly disguise to the floor, he then rubbed circles over his lenses with his shirt and checked them for smudges before putting them back on. "Had to be sure, though, didn't I. And it was quite a rush, you can imagine." For a man with a gun aimed at his head, he hardly seemed at odds. He seemed more relieved, if anything, that he could finally stop pretending to be someone he wasn't. "Flaunting my true identity out in the open while living the life of another? Gave me quivers!" He shivered playfully. "Now then..." Palms up in a cordial gesture, he asked, "have you come to join the festivities?"

He wouldn't let it show, but Grandad felt the chill of being in front of a man who had a gun to his face that didn't flinch at the thought of it. "You dun lost yo' damn mind... Or it wuz never right inna first place; born wit wobbly marbles, or some shit. But that ain't gon' stop you from bleedin' to death if I pull this trigger, so you best start fearin' me and this here shottie I got aimin' at them fo' eyes."

"You're quite right, I'm sure..." He took a step over a body toward the center of the room. "But, you see...if you kill me," he threw his palms up again, this time as if at the mercy of the facts, "you'll never make it out of here alive."

"Fuck outta here, wit that Euro-villain *bullshit*. Where you think you goin'?" He pulled the shotgun tighter to his shoulder. "You run, I'll pop you right inna ass, boy."

"Run?" He grinned at the thought. "Oh, I won't be doing any running, no... Not unless I decide to have a little fun and *chase* the three of you." He chuckled, approaching a sofa. "Mind if I sit? I've been feeding that blasted thing since—" He looked at his watch while rolling a pair of sleeping legs off the couch and landing the torso attached to it on the floor. "By god, look at the time... It's nearly Christmas, lads! Ha!" He smacked his hands and rubbed them together while sitting down, crossing his legs. "Funny, isn't it? How a little premeditated mayhem can turn such a dreadful holiday into something I'm *actually* looking forward to?"

Marvin couldn't hold it in any longer; the thought wretched in his guts and squeezed bile into his throat... "W-where's Holly?"

Hearse was caught off guard, as if imagining someone had forgot to fill in the rabble that *he* was the star of this show. "*Holly*, dear boy? Are you daft?" He scoffed. "Here we all are, in the final moments of my most *brilliant* performance, on the verge of perverting this wretched pretender's holiday for *eternity* and the only thing on your mind is your knob?" Befuddled, it took him a moment to get back on track. When he thought about it, his head tilted in confusion. "...How is it that you're here?" Eyes narrowed, hatless head revealing disheveled hair, no one answered him, unsure of what he was asking. "I mean...I get that you may have...*Scooby Doo'ed* my real identity and perhaps wanted to, I suppose, *thwart* my evil plans... But what led you to believe there *was* an evil plan? Why come here with such," he inhaled the boiling hate and tension steaming from his captors, "*intoxicating* purpose? You two are hardly conscious half the time, pummeling your teenage brains with pot and god knows what... So, what's changed?" The heat in Marvin's eyes could have set fire to bone if Hearse wasn't so cool. "I can't imagine you've come here armed to confess your undying devotion to my lovely, pretend-bride..."

Shaking now, offended by Hearse's lack of taking responsibility, Marvin turned to Shawn and reached into the back of his waist to pull the unloaded gun from his pants and fiercely take aim—

"WHERE'S HOLLY?!!"

Shawn nearly dropped a log in his shorts at Marvin's haste and tone. If the gun had had any bullets, his boxers would have likely been equally as loaded.

Grandad decided to play along to make the threat more real. "Easy now, young'un... Ain't no need to catch a case over this whacko... Not when ol' Grandad can catch one *fo'* you."

Hearse wasn't moved. He never even flinched. He examined the palpability of Marvin's outburst and *tsked* at what he found. "No... no, no, no... This isn't about Holly..." Elbows mounting his knees, he leaned forward to show no fear of the threats hounding him. "Why are you here, Marvin?"

A tear escaped the young man's eyes when the truth of it was brought into the open.

"You…you killed my *friends*…"

Hearse leaned back, submersing himself in the accusation, searching for its basis. "*Did* I?" He seemed sincerely at a loss.

"The tree… The *wreath*… The fucking *snowman*, you sick fuck, you killed them all!!"

After absorbing the claim, something clicked. "Ahhh, I see… And these…*friends* of yours I killed… Their bodies were left for you? In these…snowmen…?"

"You *know* they were, you piece of shit…" Hand shaking, heart pounding, lungs quaking…he wiped another tear from his eye and took a breath to regain himself.

"Hm." Smirking the tiniest bit, he said softly under his breath with his eyes drifting into a corner, "She must really like you…" Focus back on his captors now, he addressed Marvin with sincerity. "I'm sorry, young man… But that wasn't me."

"No…" He wasn't about to believe it. "No… No, NO, you're FUCKING LYING!!"

"Hardly matters now, doesn't it."

"WHERE IS SHE?!!"

"Easy there, Keeper." He teased him with Holly's nickname for him. "She's…presently *indisposed*, I'm afraid…" He smiled like a wince. "…but close by…" A sigh preceded his bowed head. "Well… this is a bit of a cock-up, isn't it? I really hadn't intended on you lot being a part of this… I rather *like* you, Marvin."

"Yeah," Grandad chimed in, "You all kindsa considerate… Boys, keep an eye on this prim an' proper, tea an' crumpet mu'fuckuh… I'ma go pull some rope outta Rudolph's ass an' we gon' make sure this prick stays put. Shawn, call the po-po. Marvin…*shoot* this limey nigga if he so much as scratch his ass." He looked to Marvin to be sure he was still in the game. "Marv, you cool?"

His stare frothing with contempt, hiding a secret fear – not so much a fear of Hearse, but a fear of how and/or when he'd come across his ex-crush – he nodded to respond. "Yeah…I'm cool. He ain't goin' nowhere." His hands were starting to settle into his grip, now, the weight of the weapon providing him confidence despite it not being loaded.

Grandad nodded. "A'ight, sit tight, young blood. This almost over." Several steps over a bundle of bodies and Hearse's calm, obscenely polite tone froze him before he made it to the door.

"Good of you to dress for the occasion." He spoke before turning his head and setting his razor-sharp stare on course to knife at the armed Santa passing by. "You're not an entirely convincing version of the jolly old bloke, what with you missing the beard and no bag of goodies to speak of, but I don't think she'll mind." Another grin like a wince picked at Grandad's restraint so the old bruiser let the stock of his shottie do his retorting. The butt cracked Hearse in the cheekbone, splitting his flesh and forcing him forward; he clutched at the wound with a grunt.

"Tha's for skimpin' onna milk an' *cookies*, asshole." With a smirk, he glanced up at the boys to throw them a wink before strutting slowly out the front door.

Hearse reached into his mouth and worked lose a molar while Shawn nervously fidgeted with his phone. "Lovely old bean, that one." Examining his tooth, he tossed it aside after admiring its form. "Smells like the khazi in a Scottish pub, mind you, but right friendly!"

Marv kept his eyes on who he thought to be his nemesis, despite Hearse claiming otherwise, until Shawn started mumbling curses. He looked back at him pecking at his phone.

"You get through?"

"N-nah, man..." He lifted it into the air, searching for a signal when Hearse felt it a courtesy to speak up.

"Sorry to say, lads, but you won't be making any calls from here. Not for miles." Fingering another possible dental casualty, he stopped when the guys looked at him in disbelief. He returned it with some of his own. "You really believe I wouldn't't've thought of that? With all these *people*...?" He scoffed and shook his head. "There's only one cell-tower close enough to boost your signals. I paid it a visit before relieving these sleeping *prats* of their dreadfully overrated consciousness. ...Did them a favor, I think. A lonely lot, this bunch; the layabouts that Christmas *forgot*... That's why I started this bloody party five days prior the big event; needed to suss out those who wouldn't be missed." He sighed and leaned back. "This was all very well thought out, you see. And I would have gotten away with it 'if not for you meddling kids!' " He cheesed at his second Scooby Doo reference but didn't get so much as a snicker from his audience. "Oh, for heaven's sake, lighten up, won't you? It's nearly Christmas!"

And as if Tim Burrton had scripted the moment – surreal and ominous – the thumping of heavy footfalls creaked against the roof on queue with the digital clocks turning to midnight. Powder fell over the windows outside, making room for who or whatever touched down above, and Shawn and Marvin both whipped their heads around in a sudden, angsty fright, angling eyes up at drywall as if they might see through it and uncover the impossible threat looming above.

Hearse didn't hesitate. He jumped up for Marvin's gun, swiping it from his grasp and putting the butt to Marvin's head before he could finish yelping, "Shit!".

Shawn turned back at the commotion, caught between the fear of what was outside and in, and fell victim to the pretender-Texan's hold on his hoodie. Hearse warned him not to move, but knowing the gun wasn't loaded, Shawn ignored the threats and struggled to be free. Reluctantly, Hearse pulled the trigger…

"Cheeky little bugger," he mumbled, referring to Marvin holding him at bay with an unloaded weapon, then, just as Shawn began to call for help, he flipped the pistol around to whip him in the back of the melon with the walnut grips, delivering visions of tasty little weed plants dancing through his head.

"Nighty night, lads!" He let Shawn's body *clunk* against the floor. "…Be seeing you Christmas morn!"

DECEMBER 25TH

12:34 AM

Bing Crosby's winter classic, "White Christmas", on a 45-vinyl spinning at thirty-three revolutions per minute pulled Marvin from the anxious dream of trying to save Holly from a crazed Englishman on horseback, into a sluggish, harrowing nightmare. The slow, disfigured Christmas jingle paired with a probable concussion and all its debilitating symptoms melted reality into a hazy soup. Hands sunk into the floor, knees trudging through the muck of the swampy carpet, it took him several seconds to regain any bearing and recognize where he was.

He fought against his tar-pit consciousness to crawl toward Shawn laid out under the living room window. When he got there he began to take into account he was somehow still alive and wondered what hellish ending for him Hearse might still have in store.

"Shawn…" He pushed at his friend's shoulder, having trouble finding his voice. "*Shawn…*" The thought occurred his best bud might be caput. But he knew that wasn't Hearse's style. Then the snoozing lump of Christmas Regret began to stir, rolling over and pealing open his eyes.

"The fuck…?" He was as lost as Marvin had been at first, oozing his way back into the now— "Shit!"—which didn't take long. The top-half of his body popped up like Dracula bursting from a coffin and he scooted backward on his ass until he hit the wall below the window.

"*Chhh-chhhh-chhhh!* Chill, man!" Marvin hushed him with a strenuous whisper and his hand stretched out, suggesting he stay low.

"W-where is he?!"

Marvin crawled to his friend. He figured looking out front was a fair place to start. "I'on't know… I woke up and it was just us…"

Moving the curtains an inch to the left, the first thing he noticed was that Grandad's red nosed ride wasn't blocking the driveway.

"W-w-where's the bodies?!"

"The what?" It hadn't occurred to him yet, but the bodies that filled the room before they took they're trip to Carpet Kingdom were no longer there. He looked back, giving the room a onceover when the creaking and soft thumping on the roof reminded them there may be an even bigger threat nearby than a crazed British actor who despised Christmas.

"Fuck! W-w-what the fuck *is* that?!"

"Man...keep yo' damn *voice* down." They gazed up at the ceiling for all the good it did, until Marvin turned back around to look outside. "Shit... I see 'im."

"Who?!"

"Mr. G. ...Or, *Hearse*, I mean." Zeroing in on his life's antagonist, he squinted at the madman under the dim street light waving his arms around as if he were conducting a symphony. "...The fuck he doin'?"

"Man...we need to get the fuck *outta* here..."

"How we gon' do that? Grandad's ride's gone. An' if that fucker *has* 'im, then we ain't goin' nowhere."

Wearing Shawn's fuzzy-hooded bomber jacket, Hearse had an estranged focus carved into his brow, his arms whipping about with a stick for a wand in hand. Marvin tried seeing through the haze of the night and the frosted windows to make some sense out of what he was witnessing, but soon decided finding the last surviving St. Nick should be priority number one.

"M-maybe he got away, man... If his ride ain't there, then he gone!" Shawn's head whipped around, frantic, scanning his surroundings for an escape route. "All them cars outside... G prolly got they keys in the basement." He looked to Marvin, trying to convince him to see reason. "Maybe Grandad down there too. I mean, if he di'n't get away... And we gon' need a ride if Grandad's ain't here, no matter what."

Anger resurfacing, Marvin had a hard time not burning a hole through Hearse's skull with his stare, but Shawn was vaguely making sense. "Yeah...a'ight... We check the basement." The roof cringed with another foursome of thumps, a muffled, animalistic grunt perturbing their worries. "...Let's go."

Shawn put his feet to the floor and jackrabbited across the carpet, enthralled to be making a move toward freedom, grousing Christmas music still turning painfully slow under the needle. And Marvin moved to keep up, passing the turntables into the hall; an underlying itch concerning the other rooms in the house and who may be in them flared like a rash in his mind.

They approached the door to the cellar cautiously, recalling the strange sounds they'd heard before. But with all the commotion now outside, it didn't take Shawn long to gather the cojones to face the descending stairs. After a few, slowly measured steps and time to gage any pending reaction, he made haste and got to the bottom with Marvin dragging behind.

"I'll check this side!"

Shawn had never been more resolute. He darted straight for the far end and its rosewood desk and two chests of drawers while Marvin turned the corner to lay eyes on the sultry sex dungeon and erotic swings you'd expect to find in the home of a man who owned a porn studio. It was classy in the sense that everything looked chic and pristine, with artistic paintings of passionate orgies filled with caring, sexual embraces under soft lighting. The décor clearly had a woman's touch: walls painted in red and pink roses with floral bedding to match, the swings and restraints in the vein of comfort, as opposed to pain. It brought Marvin to a halt, jealous at the thought of another man having such grand, kinky adventures with his onetime crush. But when his eyes adjusted to the romantic ambiance they began to take in the giant, dark hole where a wall should be, leading into some dank, underground cavern.

He moved toward it. Its blackness was bewitching; its mysteriousness impossible not to question. It consumed the far corner entirely, from roof to floor, swallowing six feet to either side. The moist ground it was dug from was nearly as black as the void itself, mineral deposits throughout catching the artificial glow of the room and glitzing nearly imperceptibly like the most distant of stars in the sky. When he stepped closer, the breath of the void yawned and chilled him to the bone.

"I got 'em!" Shawn started filling his pockets with an assortment of keys on rings. "Let's go, man! C'mon!"

It was likely a wise decision not to wander too close to the mouth of the gaping, black grotto that looked like it housed an arachnid the size of Aragog... Feet kneading at the loose dirt that speckled the paisley, crimson carpet, he left the mystery where it lay and followed Shawn up the stairs.

"Hold up." When they reached the hallway, Marvin couldn't stow the thought that Holly may be unconscious in a room somewhere. Or worse.

"Nah, man... Don't say it..." Shawn knew by the shifty look in Marvin's eyes, roving up and down the hall, they weren't leaving yet.

"We need to check these rooms, man. Grandad could be in any one of 'em."

"Yeah...'*Grandad*'..."

"Or anybody *else*." Marvin focused his eyes on Shawn so he knew the score. "We ain't leavin' till we know."

Shoulders deflating with his hopes of escape, Shawn nodded. "Yeah, a'ight, man."

"Be quicker if we split up."

"Nigga...shit... Like we ain't seen enough horror movies to know tha's exactly what we *don't* do."

"This ain't no movie, man."

"Sure as fuck playin' *out* like one. Whatchoo think, they redoin' the roof in the middle of the night? Tha's a goddamn *monster* up there, man!"

"It ain't no monster, man..."

"Well it ain't no Mexican fixin' the shingles neither!"

"You wanna get the fuck outta here or not?"

"Nah." He wasn't about to cave. "I can wait. We gon' search this mu'fuckuh together. Straight up."

Marvin shook his head. "Fine, man, shit." He'd hate to admit it, but Shawn was right about one thing: whatever the hell was on the roof wasn't going to turn out to be a duo of underpaid hard laborers. "Follow me."

Quickly, knowing Hearse was out front, they darted from room to room, giving each one a onceover well enough to be sure the personable Mrs. Holly Greggerson wasn't stashed in a closet or bathroom or behind a bed somewhere. With eight rooms, upstairs and down, the hasty search took nearly ten minutes. The deranged, Bing Crosby Christmas mantra on repeat clung to their every step like gum on their shoe, suffusing with the thumps and guttural raucous traveling down through the ceiling. Then the thought occurred to Shawn that to get out of there they'd have to put themselves out in the open, and for all the good the keys jingling in his pocket would do them, they'd be for naught without managing to make it to a car unseen.

Once the rooms were clear, Marvin was ready to hold up his end of the bargain; eager, even, to get outside and make their next move. "A'ight, let's go—"

"Hold up, man…"

"Oh, what? Now you wanna stay?"

"*Nah…* But we can't just roll out there. I mean, you *hearin'* this shit, right?" He pointed to the ceiling, the sounds weighing on their nerves with disgusting heaves and growls.

"Yeah, I hear it…"

"Whatever the fuck that is, it's gon' see us creepin' out this bitch. We need, like…*camouflage* or some shit…"

The wheel churned in Marvin's mind. "…Or a way out where they can't see us leavin'."

"That's what I'm sayin'." Shawn wasn't sure if his "bruh" was having an early senior moment or… "Waiwaiwaiwait… Hold up, man. Whatchoo thinkin'?" Letting Marvin take the reins when he was in this don't-give-two-shits mood, Shawn surmised, wasn't in his best interest.

"C'mon."

Headed back toward the cellar, Shawn's slow-roasting suspicions *dinged* when Marvin started down the stairs. "Doood… No fuckin' way."

"You got a better idea?" Marvin didn't bother slowing his stride.

"Yeah. Stayin' the fuck out the *monster* hole, that's my better idea." His feet got heavier with every wooden stair, his progress coming to a dead stop three steps from the bottom.

"This *it*, man; it's our only way."

"You don't know that shit!"

"I know we gotta better chance of getting outta here unseen goin' *this* way than out the front or back." He stopped just in front of the hauntingly hollow cave, peering into its blackened depths. He couldn't see more than ten feet into it… "Yo, give me yo' lighter, man." Looking back, he scowled when Shawn still hadn't gotten off the staircase. "C'mon, fool! How much time you think we got?!"

Shawn took another step down, shaking his head. " 'This ain't no movie'…" He sucked at his teeth with another shuffle forward and a shake of his head. "Then why you actin' like that dude who gets everybody killt?! Talkin' 'bout goin' inna goddamn monster hole…"

"Man, hurry the fuck *up*." He held out his hand for Shawn's lighter.

Angerly digging through his pockets, he made it to just behind Marvin when he caught the chill from the yawning, dirt cavern. "Goddamn...fuckin' Hearse..." He handed Marv his lighter then rubbed at his arms. "...stole my damn jacket. That fool rich as fuck and he snakin' my gear..."

Marvin took another step closer, struck the lighter for its flame, and—

"Children!" Hearse's chillingly pleasant voice jumped out before either teen took another step. "Nipping out without telling daddy?" He tsked. "Naughty, naughty..." Head shaking slowly, he added, "I keep a *list*, you know," and smiled a frightfully pearly grin. Villainous.

The guys turned around to see what they were up against. Hearse had a gun in hand aiming for Shawn – it was the same gun Marvin had held to him less than an hour before. Hearse caught their eyes examining the weapon and thought to address it.

"Not terribly British of me, I know, but 'when in 'Murica!' " He slipped into an overly *hick* accent to land his punchline. "Read that on a meme somewhere... Haven't the foggiest of what it means..."

Marvin switched his intonation to Bravado. "What, you gonna hold us hostage with an empty gun?"

"Recognize it, do you?" He sighed and loosened his aim. "I was afraid of that. ...Can't blame a bloke for trying. Go on, then. Off you go!" He shooed them toward the hole, seemingly unconcerned.

Shawn peeled his eyes from Hearse to look back at Marvin, desperate to not have to make a decision. When Marv made one for him, slowly turning toward the dark, Shawn spoke up.

"Yo, man... He playin' us! If he know we down here, that thing do *too*."

Marvin stopped. He turned back toward Hearse. His eyes narrowed when he finally asked, "...What is it?"

Hearse grinned. "Funny of you to ask... Do you honestly trust me to give you a straight answer?"

Taking Hearse's point, he turned back toward the hole. After contemplation, deciding to make up his own damn mind, he moved toward it.

"C'mon, man..." Shawn *really* didn't want to go in there. His eyes pleaded, and his throat leaked a "...don't..."

But the nothingness of the void sung to Marvin... It was like his only option for answers was through the terrifyingly unknown. It made perfect sense that it was a trap; that Hearse was fluffing him up to walk right into the throat of the demon inside. But it almost didn't matter... The mystery was as potent as his instinct to stay alive.

Fingers rolling into nervous fists, heartrate escalating, breaths quickening...he stepped toward the dark.

Shawn could hardly believe it. Behind him, Hearse was just as surprised.

As his toes surpassed the plain of the basement, Marvin lifted the lighter in his hand. His thumb moved to illuminate his journey just as he caught the soft whisk of a breath...and felt the warmth of it against his cheeks...

He stopped again. And when the pad of his thumb rolled the gear to ignite the flint, two blue eyes the size of basketballs opened ten feet in front of him—

He didn't move.

The hum from the creature's lungs rolled like a purr, and its eyes bore the slender, elliptical pupils of a cat the size of a boxcar.

His thumb let loose its hold on the flame and he slowly – *ever* so slowly – moved his foot to retrace his steps.

"Having second thoughts, are we?" Hearse called out obnoxiously. He feigned curiousness, then replaced it with an open-mouthed smile. "Take your time, now. I'll be in the kitchen sorting some tea. Join me, won't you? ...At your convenience, of course." He turned to spritely jog up the stairs with an invigorated bounce in his step.

Shawn couldn't believe what either of them were seeing and whispered franticly, "*Nonononono...*" out the side of his mouth toward the back of Hearse as he fled; he never would've guessed he'd be eager to keep the gangly Englishman's company.

Then there was silence.

Shawn didn't want to breathe for fear of being prey, but knew his friend needed his help.

"Marv..." he whispered but didn't get a response. "*Marv...*" he tried again, then realized Marvin being nose-to-nose with...*whatever* the hell it was meant he wasn't likely to answer. "We gon' have to *run* for it," was his astute masterplan. He focused on his buddy for an accord and saw Marvin's head slowly moving side-to-side, rejecting Shawn's cunning strategy. "Well, *what*, then, fool?!" he strained.

Hearing no viciousness in its breath, Marvin thought his best option was a slow retreat. But the eyes were even more entrancing than the mystery before them. He found himself staring into their irises, marveling at their size and detail. They gleamed like they were made of ice with speckled blue and green dancing to what little light penetrated the dark. He couldn't make out the creature's shape until it shook its head at an itch and he imagined he could see catlike ears pointing from a six-foot cranium. Hardly able to believe it was real, he found himself chewing at the thought it was some kind of animatronic – something Hearse had gotten from a movie set and fancied himself its caretaker, out of his mind... But its movements were too fluid – too lifelike... Then he remembered he was likely to be its midnight snack along with the others Hearse had probably fed it, so decided it was time to act.

He bowed his head, lowering his eyes so to not impose dominance or threat, knowing not to make any sudden moves. He knew if he ran he'd be a meal, or a plaything, if he was lucky, but thought better of turning his back to it, so retreated the same way he came, every step painfully tempered.

"*Shitshitshitshit*," came the encouraging chant of Marvin's shorter half, still frozen in his boots and itchy to make a break for it.

As Marv backed out into the room, fifteen feet from the clutches of some unimaginable Christmas Killer Kitty, the creature's icy blues blinked once, then dissipated into the dark. Afterward, the sound of dirt rustling off the walls described its covert departure from the cavern.

When they could no longer see its stare, or hear its breath, Marvin met eyes with Shawn and they both sprung from their boots to dart up the staircase. Shawn tripped on his way but hardly missed a beat with Marvin hot on his heels.

Their hearts pounded faster than their feet. When they reached the hallway, they took advantage of the level ground and increased speed, full throttle or dead. Not even the inviting aroma of steaming Earl Grey slowed them down (to Hearse's aghast bewilderment), and upon seeing the middle-aged lady's man hosting a tea party with three severed heads on the kitchen counter, cup raised high with a was-it-something-I-said? look of puzzlement, they b-lined for the front door, Marvin crashing into the back of Shawn after he couldn't open it as fast as their panic demanded.

"There's plenty of tea for everyone, lads! No sense in letting it go to the dogs!" He watched them bounce off each other, trying to operate a door knob with four hands where only one was needed. "…Or should I say, to the cat?" he mumbled behind his cup with a grin as the boys finally managed to open the door and tear out the entryway.

The stinging cold pinched at their cheeks, but they hardly felt a thing. Shawn braved the weather in his long sleeve tee alone and couldn't tell you whether it was winter or spring, numb to anything but escape from the twisted Hell they ran from.

"Keys!" Marvin yelled, and received a set jingling through the air while Shawn rummaged through another, finding a Toyota emblem and then scanning the street for its match. When he spotted it, he scattered toward it—

"Fuck, man! Goddamn Toyotas an' Hondas all look the same!" he griped, making it halfway to a snow-frosted Civic that looked like it hadn't been moved in days.

"What's a goddamn Mitsubishi look like?!" Marven was likely even *less* informed concerning car models than his freshly licensed amigo.

"Shit!" Shawn gave the street another up-and-down. "There!" Finger pointing to a maroon sports car, he raved, "Tha's a Galant!"

So Marv made a run for it and Shawn followed suit. Slipping to a halt atop the frozen blacktop, Marvin stabbed at the Galant's driver-side lock while Shawn rounded the trunk for the passenger door.

"C'mon, man, c'mon!"

Hands already getting numb despite gloves to guard them from the chill, inserting a jagged sliver of steel into a miniscule vertical slot while terrified for one's life proved to be just as difficult as they made it out to be in horror movies. But the struggle was preferable to the view, as Shawn's eyes drifted back toward the house and its beast-infested shingles wrought with festive dead decorating the home from roof to lawn.

"Nononono…no fucking way," spilled from his lips, trembling now in the cold, but still unaware he was freezing.

"Got it!" Marvin opened the door and jumped inside, smashing at the button to unlock the other, pushing it repeatedly while Shawn stood paralyzed in befuddled terror. "Get *in*, man! GET THE FUCK IN!!" Shrieking, he found himself with a new dilemma just as Shawn snapped out of his daze to finally slip inside. When he reached to jab the key in its supposed slot he discovered there was no hole to fill. "The fuck?!" Then he read the Start/Stop label on the keyless ignition only to find out while pressing the button it somehow wasn't that simple. "It won't start, man, it won't start!!"

"It's real…" Shawn sat stuck in a stupor, looking back toward the corpse-covered porno pad—

Legless, headless torsos were placed with arms spread wide over every window, bare chests wrapped in Christmas lights and bedazzled with silver tinsel and gold glitter; their heads – with snowcaps, velvet chokers, and holiday earrings – hung along the eaves. Their legs made for eight meaty stockings above the garage, their frosted intestines drooping from head to dangling head. A familiar-looking wreath with mangled limbs, bloody bells and shrubbery adorned the highest point of the home. Giant candy canes of bones impaled nearly-nude cadavers along the yard's perimeter like a sickening white picket fence.

"Man, how the hell do you start this fuckin' space ride?!" Marvin pleaded, but the only answer he received was the thumping of padded feet touching down in snow, followed by the crunch of the vehicles the weight of them crushed on its approach.

"It's fucking real…" Shawn's skin turned to tapioca, gazing back in disbelief at what stalked them. "I can't believe…" He couldn't finish the thought.

"Man, would you fucking *help* me?!"

But Shawn could only stare, frozen…other than the pivot of his head that slowly turned his gaze toward Marvin, watching the fantastic blue beast of his craziest high creep through the middle of a suburban street until it's lowered head and shortened snout were right beside them.

When the heat of its breath steamed against the window he knew he shouldn't look… Instead – finger never getting far from the ignition, measured now in his attempts – he tried for their escape again, this time with his foot on the brake instead of the gas. The sound of the engine turning over was that of liberation. The proceeding decibels of blasting hair metal – possibly Bon Jovi or, even worse, White Snake – snapped him into action so fast he may have fractured his finger. He pushed at a plethora of buttons while the impossible creature with its curling lips revealing crystal incisors and glistening, icy-blue fur erect over its ears and spine, snarled in harrowing annoyance.

"Shiiiiiiiit!" Brain screaming *flee!*, Marvin's foot never felt so heavy.

He plowed through the gas and directed the wheel for a narrow escape, rubber slipping under the weight of the car. It felt like an eternity before the tracks caught ground and catapulted the vehicle toward salvation, clipping the corner of the Toyota (or was it a Civic?) parked in front of them. The *crunch* offended the beast more than the hair metal did and it leaped from its acerbated crouch onto an orange Caddy several cars up and on the left. As they fishtailed and kicked up ice, it wasn't a challenge for the beast to overtake them with but a leap ahead and into the street. And at seeing the astounding agility and prowess of the twenty-foot long, twisted snow tigress, Shawn reached for the wheel and pulled in any direction *but* toward its indomitable snarl…

The *bang* of the collision was so sudden, bringing them to a halt faster than thought, neither of them knew what had happened. The jarring of their melons at the impact from the exploding airbags put the entire concept of where they were and how they got there out of reach for several lengthy minutes. By the time Marvin's field of vision produced images he could understand, realizing he'd smashed headlong into a parked BMW, Hearse was perverting the glass beside his head with a frowny-face painted in blood. Two fingers drew two, vertical lines for eyes in a single stroke, and the same two squeezed together produced the wet and dripping, sorrowful upside-down smile.

Shawn caught onto the squeak of Hearse's fingers tainting their escape and turned to put a sight to the sound. Then the finger-painting maniac smeared a thin rectangle over the eyes where the brows should be and a flaccid triangle above it. But it wasn't until he added the finishing touch with a circle at the triangle's tip that they realized he'd drawn a Christmas cap.

Instantly the beast reacted. It snarled and growled like some monsterly mix between a lion and a bear and leapt at the crude image with fangs unsheathed. Biting into the metal roof, its teeth pushed through and busted the window, shattering glass with a shriek and pulling at the door's frame. Shawn panicked, opening his door to run, but Marvin thought better of it and grabbed his friend before he made himself out to be the mouse every cat loved to chase. He leaned into Shawn's seat to evade the steaming breath and fangs threatening to remove his head and held him still while the door was torn from its hinges. The creature clearly had an aversion to Christmas that rivaled that of its conniving puppet master's, Hearse waiting for the beast to do its work several paces from the vehicle with a severed head in his hands. When it tossed the door aside and went after it to be sure it no longer challenged its authority, a mustacheless, ex-Mr. G moseyed on up and leaned over to gaze at the two stiffly perched mishaps-on-legs *severely* "hugging it out".

He stared for a minute, unsure of how to approach his objective, then spoke up when the words came to him:

"Clever way to stay warm, that," he observed, referring to their embrace, "but it might've shown more tact to've not ran out in the blistering chill to start." He sighed when they didn't respond. "Ok... *out* you go." His hand gesturing back and forth showed them the way (in case they were at a loss as to how to go about it), and when they still didn't budge he reminded them, "Being *exuberantly* British, I do so despise raising my voice; it's just not civilized." He lifted his other arm that held the head of someone's favorite porn star and placed the dripping noggin on the roof. "But if you insist I devolve in order to coordinate our efforts, then—

"GET OUT OF THE SODDING *CAR*, YOU IMPISH LITTLE WANKSTAINS!! WE HAVEN'T THE *TIME* FOR YOUR PUBECENT, LEAF-BRAINED BUGGERY!!"

When that got a flinch out of them, he helped it along by grabbing at Marvin's hood and giving it two (ironic) yanks.

"*Out*...of the...*bloody*...car!"

Stuck between a Hearse and a hard place, it became apparent their options were limited to "cooperate or be food". Following the pull of the current (being the madman's indominable leverage), Marvin stepped out into the biting cold and hardly even looked the beast's way. He only had eyes, now, for Hearse.

"You too, Cheech— Ah-ah-ahh! Not that way..." He caught Shawn heading out the passenger door and felt it best not to give him the slightest notion of making a run for it. "This way, please. Thank you." Marginally agreeable, Shawn maneuvered out behind Marvin and lined up next to him. "There's a good lad." He looked at Shawn whose head was lowered but eyes darting from the side of his face toward the fantastic creature just now turning its attention back toward them. When Shawn finally caught the chill of the wind he shivered, and Hearse caressed the sleeves of the jacket he'd stolen. "Lovely coat, by the way." He stretched his arms out to show the sleeves were four inches short. "Little on the skimpish side, mind you. I suppose Mr. Jones' would have made a better fit…but these lines just seemed to be calling to me." They didn't look amused. "Right, then!" He turned back toward the house and its arrangement of corpses. "Behold! My boldest achievement! And first of many!"

Marvin, fire in his eyes hot enough to shield him from the winter, ignored Hearse's boasting and got straight down to business.

"Where's Grandad?"

Hearse turned with questioning eyes.

"Grandad Santa," Marvin clarified. "The dude we was with."

"Oh! Yes…" He *tsked*. "He abandoned you lot, I'm afraid. Hopped in his sleigh and flew off into the night!" He grinned against the chill, bits of frost on the frames of his glasses and the fur-lining of the hood pulled over his head. "Bit of a Christmas miracle he made it, I'd say. Quite lucky his cap blew off before *she* spotted him – and that you'd kept me preoccupied long enough not to instruct her to add him to the décor." He looked over them both – Marvin still locked into a stare-down and Shawn wildly distracted by the beast now only thirty feet away – and found it odd they hadn't yet inquired. "Go on, then… *Ask* me." When they didn't catch on: "Really, boys, are you not even curious?" His eyes blatantly pushed in the direction of the beast. "Ask me!" he cried with ecstatic enthusiasm, hands out and palms up, fingers curling dramatically.

Marvin wouldn't give him the pleasure, but Shawn couldn't help but need to know.

"W-w-what *is* it?" Shivering, he had his hands deep in his pockets, digging for warmth.

Hearse feigned ignorance. "What? …Oh, *this* lovely thing? Brilliant, isn't she?" He reached between them, stretching for the head on the roof of the car at their backs, grabbed it by its blond hair and tossed it into the air. The beautifully blue marvel took one short leap forward to pluck it from the path the winds had shown it, executing the move with terrifying precision. It swallowed nearly as quickly as it snapped and then shook its enormous head. *"Farðu!"* He barked an Icelandic command and it turned with power and grace to canter off toward the porno pad. "...*That*, my young friends, is what folklore in Iceland would call *Jólakötturinn*: The Yule Cat." When they didn't seem to melt in awe, he admitted, "Not a very well-known myth, to be sure. A rather silly and uninteresting one, as far as Hollywood films go... But that's largely because the myth had been contemporized and made to do man's bidding when the beast was no longer thought to be real." He turned to bask in its awing presence as it continued where it had left off, putrefying the front lawn with twisted Christmas shrines of rot and decay.

"You see," he went on while it positioned itself to do its work, crouched with its tail toward them as it heaved, regurgitating body parts into what looked to be the base of a pillar – the grotesque mass automatically taking shape by way of some demented magic. "Yon pillocks of old, who'd written its existence off as taking the piss, diminished its true nature into a dodgy tale of a snowy beast come Christmas that'd *swallow* you whole if you hadn't received new clothes."

He animated his tale with hands poised like claws. The boys looked lost, more taken by the sight of the mystical vomit, the beast spewing human flesh and bone into a twelve-foot high, rectangular post of death.

"In those days, a laborer was paid with clothing, you understand, so the tale was incentive to finish their work before— Am I *boring* you?" Offended, reminding them with his eyes that *he* was the star of the show, they both caught on to his tone and focused back on his account. He sighed. "I suppose it's not an adventure without a damsel in distress, isn't that right, Marvin."

The fire reignited in Marvin's stare.

"There you are... Thought I'd lost your favor, dear boy. Shall I continue?"

"I'on't give a shit how fuckin' clever you think you are, you twisted fuck. And..." He could hardly believe he was about to say it... "And if she *in* on this shit with you...I'on't give a shit about *her* neither." His tone was potent and had a finality to it. It seemed to all whose ears he had that he meant every word.

Hearse hmphed. "Well, then… That's where the story gets interesting, isn't it?" His smile turned as vile a thing as any Marvin had ever seen. "Our damsel wouldn't be in distress if she *was* in on it, now would she?" When Marvin's fists clinched, Hearse tsked. "Now, now… No sense in getting stroppy – there's no civility in it."

"Fuck yo' bullshit *civility*, asshole! Where the fuck is she?!"

The snaring roar of the Yule Cat at his tone brought him pause, realigning his stare for an instant. When the giant feline didn't approach, he turned his heated eyes back to his antagonist.

"Well, if you'd pay attention, I'll *tell* you, won't I." Marvin found patience in the promise of answers he actually cared for. When Hearse was convinced he had his ear, he went on.

"You see, lads, this marvelous beasty before you isn't exactly from *'round these parts*, as my counterpart, Mr. Greggerson, might say. You've heard tell of Jotunheim, no doubt." He looked for a semblance of recognition in either of their eyes. He was almost surprised to see Shawn was the one who caught on.

"Th-th-tha's where the F-Frost Giants in the Thor comics is f-f-from," he managed to get out, despite the tremors the cold afforded him.

"Spot on, young man!"

"You sayin' that thing from Yot-Yotden—"

"*Jotunheim*, yes." He recognized the look in Marvin's eyes. It was the look a skeptic smeared over his face when he figured the man doing the telling was likely off his meds. "You may find it hard to believe – as did I – but as you can see" —He gestured toward the beast who'd now puked up an upside-down crucifix made of bone and sinew, drenched in blood…and it wasn't finished— "the proof is in the…*vomit*, I suppose." When they still didn't look convinced, he added, "And there's more. …Come on."

Falling back, he shoved them in the general direction of the Christmas carcassing on Yule Terror Ave. In their previous escape attempt they had made it nearly a thousand feet away before colliding with the BMW someone parked in the path of their haste; it would take them several minutes to walk back against the wind.

"Loathing this hollow, commercial holiday as I do, I'd studied the tale of the man-eating Yule Cat in detail and found its roots traced back to Norse mythology. It seems the beast wasn't originally the pet of some terrible, Icelandic trolls, gobbling up workers who weren't awarded their new clothes for labors rendered, as man would have you believe, but were native to Jotunheim and trained to hunt the so-called "false gods" who would often claim sovereignty in a land that was not their own." He recited his account as though he were holding a seminar in an auditorium full of captivated historians as opposed to being in the middle of the street in twenty-degree weather, marching two teenagers toward a fantastic death sentence: punishment by consumption with regurgitation – the ultimate Screw You.

"Fascinated," he went on, "I eventually came across the supposed bones of one of the creature's victims found in the ancient lava fields of Iceland known as Dimmuborgir: The Dark Castles. I, of course, visited these blackened fields of Icelandic legend – of which are said to have been where Satan landed when he was cast from heaven, creating what was called the catacombs of Hell on impact – and tracked the bones to the cave they'd first—"

"Man…" Marvin couldn't handle any more of Hearse's braggadocios prattling. "…would you just tell us what the fuck is goin' on?"

He sighed. "So little appreciation for foreign culture… How oafishly American of you."

They'd made it about halfway back, every step a colder one, the stench of the fresh death-shrines adding to the sting of the wind. They could see, now, the mutilated corpse of the woman that adorned the inverted cross in the center of the lawn. She hung as a mockery of Christ in three pieces; her torso below her legs – arms spread out – and her head above her feet, right-side up. And surrounding the shrine, giant, people-sized candy canes with their festive, headless, cadaver-hosts impaled under them or propped beside them like plastic lawn ornaments. It seemed the beast was just making its finishing touches as they approached; intestines weaved with pine stringing from its throat and spiraling around the arms of the crucifix and the corpse it wore.

"Allow me to summarize, then, for the sake of your attention span." He grabbed them both by the shoulders and stopped them in their path, bringing them closer together to speak lowly into their ears. "What we have here, lads, is a creature from another realm; a minion of Giant Kings; devourer of Asgardian usurpers. …Without the will of a god to allow it passage here, it should not be *able*..." He pulled them in closer. "So, what, pray tell, might that make me?" He whispered with a grin they didn't have to see to know was there; they could *feel* it tightening near their ears...

After he left them there, on the precipice of dumfounded terror, he gave them a nudge to keep moving and went on.

"...Not a *god*, of course. That would be ludicrous!" He laughed wickedly. "Just a clever bloke, then, with an obscene amount of money and an unhealthy obsession with destroying Christmas. And what that money and obsession led me to discover was that a beast *could* be bound to another realm if it were attached to a native soul." Knowing he had their complete attention now, he teased, "This next bit is where our bony lass finds herself with a part to play... Enter our southern bell!" He stepped between them and made a grandiose gesture toward the predator in their midst.

They were so near the beast, now, they could feel the displacement of air from its whipping tail whenever it would thrash. At the tail's end stood a jet of hair that spiked upward, almost like a scorpion's stinger. The tail itself must've been fifteen feet long on its own, the coarse spike lifting from it and from the tips of its ears was likely three. The "glistening" that Shawn had remembered from the first night he'd first seen it he could now attribute to silky white hairs mixed throughout its icy blue that caught the light whenever it moved. Fur coat probably a foot deep, it wasn't so thick the muscles couldn't be seen in its legs. And its paws lightened to nearly as white as the snow, its claws transparent like ice, virtually invisible.

Marvin's heart drummed in his chest at Hearse's mention of Holly, hardly seeing anything but red. They were set on a path to be expelled as oral excrement from the Ralphing Cat of Jotunheim for a psychopath's pleasure and all he could think about was whether Holly was still alive and what the hell Hearse may have been getting at by alluding to the beast when mentioning her. He could hardly stand to listen to him for another picosecond...but knew his only hope was to hear him out, pick apart his maniacal tale-telling and try to salvage some sense from it.

"I'll save you the details of the ritual... Suffice it to say the *real* Clint Greggerson played a part as well. After all, I needed to get the beast's *attention*, didn't I. The ponce made better bait than he did a husband, I'll have you know. It was my chat with our bony lass –

before I decided she'd be the one – that made the decision for me quite clear. The poor bird was a tortured sort, barely clinging to a life she could hardly stomach. They were vacationing in Iceland and staying at the resort where I'd been, and after several glasses of Cabernet she bore her soul to me; cried her pretty eyes out. When I learned of her new, secluded home here on the outskirts of Winterset, everything just seemed to slip into place like a fat man sliding down a chimney and popping out of the fray to land exactly where he needed to be – a bloody Christmas miracle!"

"How you make her go through with it?" It still didn't make sense; her performance had been *flawless*. If she was distraught or being pressured he would have known… "If her husband *dead* then whatchoo got on her? A kid? A sister?"

"Nothing so messy, no… Hypnotism, dear boy!" He was as chipper as a tot spinning a top when confessing his plan. Rather fortunate, he thought, the boys ended up being a part of it. …Other than that now he'd have to do away with them, of course. "The silly tart truly *believes* I'm her husband and that our trip to Iceland rekindled our lover's flame!"

"You a h-hypnotist?" Shawn could hardly accept the claim. Just their luck they'd be up against a psychotic jack of all trades in command of a creature trained to kill gods by giants.

"Oh, heavens no. Don't be ridiculous. …I'm quite *rich*, you know. Also, a sociopath." He chuckled. "You wouldn't believe the list of professional 'associates' I have on my Dark Web retainer. Incidentally," he added, "if you lads ever need an organ removed from an acquaintance without killing them, do let me know." Hands back on both their shoulders, he guided them around the horrifically majestic creature up-chucking Christmas offerings and to the curbside at the foot of the entryway. "The trouble *now*, gents, is what on Earth to do with—"

And as if the three *honks* were asserting a very obnoxious and timely "Ho-ho-ho!", Grandad Santa in his wood-paneled, red-nose reindeer barreled back onto the scene with headlights glaring and a giant white cross strapped to the roof of his ride. Pedal to the metal and hand on the horn, he rounded the top of the hill with the wind at his back and Pabst in his belly, wide bloodshot orbs thirsty for redemption.

It took a few moments for the boys to make out the red hood

ornament and antlers protruding from the windows and realize who was making an entrance, and a few more, as the old boozer rapidly approached, for Marvin to recognize the giant wooden crucifix tied with twine to the roof as the very same he'd said a silent prayer to on the ride up.

"What in bloody h—"

"Holy…"

The pointed end of the uprooted symbol of Christianity hung over Rudolph's hood, jutting righteously into its path while its arms spread just behind the back windows. White, unlit Christmas lights still circled its form, and soil dirtied the stake-like tip. What Grandad planned on doing with it was a mystery to all until he was close enough for them to make out his arm reaching for the twine, a blade in hand to snip it loose—

"Heeeeere, pussy pussy pussy!"

Calling on the power of every horse harnessed in the badly neglected cylinders, he aimed the wheel for the impossible beast before him, eyes peeled with crazed ambition, a hint of a smile tugging at the corners of his mouth in mid rah.

It wasn't hard, now, for his onlookers to gather what he had in mind, and Hearse stepped forward from the walkway onto the sidewalk to his beast's defense.

"No…nonono…NOOOO!!"

When Grandad felt the twine snap he hit the brakes, hoping to catapult his beast-killing battering ram up the driveway for the ribs of the giant feline. He cackled some heinous war-cry with flaky knuckles bound to the wheel and eyes thirsty for Jotun blood. But the tires slipped on the wet asphalt and didn't provide the sudden thrust he'd imagined…

Plummeting for the snickering creature who easily sprung clear over the heads of Hearse and company, Grandad crashed through the four-car garage and into the porno pad's hallway, ceiling collapsing, front wheels breaking past the second wall and hanging over the cellar. Ultimately, his scrupulous stake of divine interception slid from the roof into the cellar's far wall, penetrating it as it might have the hide of a beast if unleashed by someone less boozed.

The home-crunching pandemonium was likely loud enough to stir the distant neighbors. If Hearse was hoping for a low-profile exit he'd have to wrap things up fast. But what was life without taking the time to laugh at the overwhelming fuck-ups of those who looked to best you? At witnessing such impractical heroics gone awry, gaping with rising glee at the back of Rudolph's smoking ass, he couldn't help but howl in utter amusement. He never would have scripted such an affront to his greatest work, but having gone from what looked to be defeat to indubitable victory with such a bang erupted him with near delirious relief. The rush was profound; the reward well worth the intrusion.

"Good show, Grandad!" he hollered while clapping in sarcastic admiration. "Bloody good sh—"

Thunk!

The sound the decorative Christmas laser-projector made after Shawn lifted it from the lawn and swung it at the back of Hearse's head cut short his applause. The numb-and-turning-purple young opportunist saw his chance and took a shot at saving the day, knocking Hearse out cold with the blow. And standing over the coldcocked villain, he almost looked as surprised that he did it as Marvin did, gawking at his shivering friend with eyes that had never shown so much white.

Seconds that felt like minutes ticked off as they stared at each other in shock until Shawn's gaze shifted to the encroaching threat stalkily perusing back into the scene. Marvin didn't turn his head right away... He thought not to make himself noticeable until he felt its warm breath around his hood start to defrost the tip of his nose...

As slow as a sloth covered in frosted molasses, after pinching his eyes shut and imagining the beast might go away, he gathered the courage to begin to pivot, his heart pounding so forcefully you could see his pulse in his temples. Marvin, even slightly hunched in fear, stood well over six feet tall, yet the Jólakötturinn lowered its snout to meet him nose-to-nose. The dimpled, giant sniffer that sampled his presence was a pale shade of cobalt blue, easily the size of a basketball, and its whiskers white and gray striped. Oddly enough, its breath didn't reek of the death or vomit it should have. It was somehow odorless (which would make it a more formidable predator). When Marvin finally allowed himself to breathe, relieved to not be heaving in moralistic agony, his mind quickly took a turn to optimism, likely as much to keep him from collapsing in terror as to follow any line of logic. But, being so close he could reach out and stroke its crystalline fangs, he recalled Hearse mumbling under his breath saying, "She must really like you", and now questioned if he had meant the *beast*, considering it was clearly what left the deathly gifts at his doorstep as an affectionate cat would its owner.

He began to wonder…

"D—" Swallowing hard, eyes finally lifting high enough to look into the beast's, Marvin took another shot at finding his voice. "D-do…you…know me?"

Hardly expecting an actual answer, he was surprised to see its mouth slightly open, letting out a soft breath as if to say, " 'know' is a strong word, tiny morsel".

Its brow tightened when he marveled at its gaze. A grumble that might pass for a purr (if a purr could make a grown man shit his spleen through his anus) resonated in his chest. Its eyes were so deeply intricate it was as if their consistency danced to the vibration of its hum around the elliptical sliver of mercury in their center. Caught in the moment, he dared to think…

When his hand lifted for its lip, Shawn's squeak of a whisper breathed to object, whisking something like, "*Nigga*…that thing gon' *eat* you!" through a clinched jaw and bluish lips. If his heartrate wasn't so through-the-roof he'd likely be near frozen stiff by now.

But with such closeness, trust became organic; intuitive… He could feel the connection between them so, hesitantly, reached to validate it; desperate, even, for a palpable experience – an experience he could fully ground. And with his hand close enough to feel the prickling of its coarse fur, it turned its head away, stepping forward, angling for just past him toward its caretaker.

Marvin backed off at its advance while Shawn leaked his petrified fright down his jeans and into his sock at its approach, the warmth a surprisingly pleasant bonus that was lost to mind-numbing angst.

"Don't move." Marv figured he'd better reiterate the obvious considering Shawn's previous "genius plan" in the basement to run.

"No *shit,* don't move!" he strained through ventriloquist lips, eyes following the beast's enormous head as it lowered to take a whiff of the bleeding and unconscious maniac on the concrete.

And after what seemed to be indifferent curiosity, inspecting the body for consciousness and then sniffing at Shawn, it left Hearse where he'd collapsed and pivoted back toward the street…until the rousing of Grandad from his busted mechanical reindeer caught its ear and it whipped its snout toward the stir, unsheathing its fangs in a peeved hiss.

The beast's indifference, it seemed, had expired.

DECEMBER 25TH
1:43 AM

He couldn't hear a thing at first. He thought for a moment his ears were full of blood… He wasn't sure what'd happened, other than that he woke up on a half-frozen sidewalk.

It occurred to him he'd been struck in the head, so reached for his brain case hoping it'd done its job and still housed all the pertinent meats securely inside. Propping up to his elbows, salt from his fingers stinging the contusion at the side of his head, his predicament came back into focus when he heard Marvin's distant cry toward the hairy, puckering asshole of the highly agitated Jólakötturinn nose-deep in the garage.

He grumbled while getting to his feet, disorientated by its swishing tail and the blur of Marvin streaking for the front door. One of them had conked him on the noggin when he'd been distracted by the chaos of Clause: the drunken heroics of a has-been for hire… But those heroics had perturbed his beast and would soon make an offering out of the hero to adorn the highest peak of the home-turned-deathshrine like a horrid Christmas angel atop a lit tree.

This so-called "Grandad Santa" would turn out to be the crumpet to his cup of bloody tea, he realized with a wincing smirk, with one lump, or, even better, two—

Thunk!

"M-m-merry Christmas, you l-limey asshole."

Shawn may have come up with a better one-liner if he wasn't seventy-five percent human popsicle and soaking in his own piss, but with blue lips and socks that squished, a sarcastic holiday tiding would have to do.

"Grandad!" Marvin was frantic, darting through the front door into the living room to try to get between the beast and his personal redemption. He'd thought that if he could save Grandad from being another body he'd have to clean up then he'd be on his way to atoning for what he'd done. He never stopped to think about how he'd redeem himself if he failed, and he didn't have the time to do that now.

The Yule Cat was stark raving pissed, tearing into station-wagon-reindeer ass for its metallic meat without a care for a second course. Dust clouds from the shattered drywall huffed away from its every breath and whorled into the living room. The hall it dug through was hardly a corridor anymore, the floor fracturing over the basement.

Marvin slowed his charge to a crawl, trying to maneuver around the fragmented path enough to see if Grandad was able to make it clear of the wreck before the Jotun god-eater made him into a side salad. Not that anyone would consider the boozed-up bruiser to be a healthy snack, but the shreds he'd be torn to may more closely resemble lettuce than beef.

Strategically, Marvin fought the urge to call out and instead weaved through the rubble while the scream of tearing metal and the growl of lungs the size of people rattled his focus. The beast pulled at the Christmas Classic (as Grandad had christened it) to dislodge it from the hall so to crack open its shell for the oyster of a man at the wheel. But the old wood-paneled eyesore was nearly as big as its aggressor and its tires wedged over the basement, the home's foundation beginning to give away...

When he was close enough to see Grandad still inside, unconscious and dripping blood, he realized no amount of stealth would save the bulky drunkard if he couldn't get him to wake up.

"Grandad!" Squeezing through torn wall and collapsed wooden beams, he got to the driver's side but couldn't open the door. "Grandad, get the fuck up!" If he couldn't get through to him this way he'd have to make it across the hood, which was twelve feet above the basement floor and being tugged at by a very frisky kitty...

But he hardly hesitated. There wasn't any time to think it through. The crunch of his weight against the hood was dwarfed by the snarl of the beast, and when he made it to the other side, he dropped five feet into the stairwell, surprising himself and stilling his heart. When his feet hit wood, knees weak and everything shaking, he stomped up to the passenger door and swung it wide—

Grandad was out cold.

Hands clutching fabric and flesh, Marvin pulled at the old man from under his arms, making very little progress, fast.

"The fuck up, man! C'mon!!"

With a jolt, the Jólakötturinn finally broke the wagon's tires free from the ledge, taking some of it with it and slamming Marvin into the dash. But the jolt knocked Grandad around hard enough to drag him from his inebriated slumber – Boozy the Bear had been aroused...

"Th'fug'sgoin'on—?"

"GET THE FUCK UP!!"

The eyes of the shrieking teen were blaring sirens that could only be accompanying death, and having seen eyes like these before, no more questions were asked.

With Rudolph shrinking from the hall and into the garage, Marvin fell from the passenger door while Grandad dove from *his* like escaping an exploding transport. They both rolled clumsily but got to their feet (mostly) and scrambled back into the broken hall. At the sight of the wagon being removed like a cat pulls a mouse from under a dresser, Grandad suddenly remember what fresh Hell he'd wrought and didn't waste time waiting for it to come back and find him.

"C'mone!"

He yelled for Marvin to get back to his feet after both had stumbled to their asses in the torn-apart corridor and they made haste in the only direction clear of debris. Halfway down the stairs Grandad's higher cognitive functions kicked in, telling him he was headed for an impasse.

"Shit! Back up! We sittin' *ducks* down here!"

"No, we ain't! Go, go, go!"

He wasn't sure if he should trust a terrified teen to make life or death decisions, but the kid had proven his head was on straight when he made a conscious effort to save his chaffed old ass from becoming African catnip...

So they descended.

Grandad looked back, questioning his decision immediately, but the young man was of a singular mind, streaking past him toward a possibly very, *very* bad idea...

Up above, the creature roared at its meatless reward and dove back into the garage, pushing through the rubble to poke its head past the hall and over the basement's staircase. This thing was huge by Earth standards – likely rivaling an elephant in size – but far more agile and narrow, long and nimble. It didn't come as a surprise to the old bruiser that, when it continued forward, it looked to be making steady progress through the broken wall with one giant paw on the stairs and the other reaching for paisley carpet.

"God damnit, Marvin, I hope you know—" Turning in mid-grouse, he caught the odd sight of the back of the lengthy teen disappearing into a blackened void consuming the far corner. "*Shit...*" He didn't like the looks of it...but liked the looks of the snarling Jólakötturinn a bit less.

Its agitated yowl sent O.G. Grandad hastily on his way just before it swiped with extended hooks at the velvet pants of him, missing its mark and losing its balance. It crashed downward onto its head leaving it temporarily caught with its hips still wedged in the hall and its nose in a wall. After it regained its jarred focus, its previous "agitated yowl" sounded like a flustered grumble compared to the beastly shriek escaping its throat.

It thrashed like a fish on a hook, infuriated by such an ungainly quagmire, more floorboards and wall coming undone with its struggle. It wouldn't be long before it broke free and looked to quench its thirst with blood.

The cavern was as cold and dark a thing as any Marvin had ever known. Grandad sporting only his long underwear for a top without his Santa coat would be a debilitating predicament if his leathery old hide wasn't as thick as a rhino's...

It was.

But neither of them could claim to see in the dark.

"Marvin!" Ol' St. Smokes-A-Lot pulled a gold-plated Zippo from his pocket engraved with his 173 Airborne Brigade symbol – a wing with a sword cradled below it in its hook – and shed some half-assed light on a dominantly dark and dank situation. He was surprised the kid hadn't sparked some light of his own, but realized he was in too much of a hurry, diving into the unknown with hopes of discovering salvation somewhere up ahead.

The dirt-black tunnel glistened with bits of minerals and ice against his flame and he got a feel for its size, it hardly seeming big enough for the beast but getting larger, and angling left and downhill. "Marv! Where you at, man?!" he strained, not wanting to rouse any other beasts that may be lying in wait. It'd be just his luck they'd be heading straight for a litter of Yule Cat cubs, and here he was without his hunting rifle and case of shells… He'd even settle for a crossbow or a goddamn African spear with a pointy rock for a head if he could get his digits around one. Jogging into a hole big enough to march the Iowa State Hawkeyes though with a fucking kittenosaurus on his ass and who-knows-what waiting ahead just seemed like an appropriate time to be pertinently armed. But pertinence didn't appear to be in the cards. Ominously dark, on the other hand, he had plenty of to spare.

"Marv, you alive?!" He figured he might as well get to the heart of his concerns since being evasive wasn't getting him a response.

"Y-yeah…" he heard in the near-distance, in a not so reassuring tone with a touch of an echo; then, *"Oof!"* and, "ShiiiiIIIIIiiittt…!" sung out afterward, oddly resembling in its pitch what it might sound like if the teen had just jumped down a water slide.

Two hundred feet downhill, a tiny flame from Marvin's hand met Grandad's prying eyes and uncovered Marvin flat on his ass looking up at the enormity of the deathly grotto he'd slid into. His flame likely cast thirty feet in every direction but hardly even touched the walls.

"Nigga, this shit ain't Cool Runnings! What the hell you dooooOhhhshiiiiIIIIiiiittt!" His scolding fell short when his feet slipped out from under him and his rump met an icy slope that dropped him fifteen feet down and sent him bobsledding into a wide-eyed teen trying his damnedest to get out of the way…

…and failing miserably.

"Oof!"

Santa-boots, say hello to Marvin's shins.

The impact kicked Marv's recently reestablished footing right back out from under him and landed him on top of the bulbous St. Nick who – after shielding his jewels – hastily pushed the fallen teen off him.

"We cool, lil nigga…but we ain't *that* cool."

"Shit." Marvin maneuvered his way back to his feet while Grandad struggled to do the same. "I…" He looked around at the walls and gazed up at fifty feet of frozen earth that shifted to an icy blue at the top. "…I think we under the lake…"

"Man…" Fighting the slippery floor, Grandad got to his feet. "…*what* lake?"

"On the map – there was a lake behind dude's pad… I think we under it."

Grandad followed his upward gaze to see the light of the flame bouncing off what looked like dark, frozen water overhead. "Better hope that shit as frozen as it look…"

"This whole cave is. Prolly that cat-thing… It must be able to freeze shit too – made itself a home down here."

"And you went an' took us right up *in* it? …*That* was yo' damn plan?"

Marvin started looking around for what he figured had to be there. "I know there's a way out. That thing got out of here earlier…"

"Yeah… It twenty feet long… It *jumped* out." He shook his head. "Can you jump outta god damn fifty-foot hole?"

He realized the old man had a point. "Didn't really think about that…"

"Well it ain't too late to start thinkin' now. *There*." His head lifted toward a dark corner of the cave that could *possibly* be— "Maybe tha's the tunnel out. We can't go back the same way; we'd need *cleats* to climb up that frozen shit – it's too steep." He took the initiative and passed Marvin, heading for the darkest corner, finding it was indeed a tunnel angling upward. Upward likely meant *outward*… "C'mone… That thing ain't gon' be stuck in that basement fo'ever." Eager to get his ass clear of the impending death that hunted them, he focused on his footing and made haste. But only ten feet in and the angle steepened, the tread of their boots losing traction. "Shit…"

It wasn't long before both were on all fours, trying to toe-and-paw their way up a slick passage with their lighters still in-hand. A *swish*, *thump* and *fwoosh* followed Grandad's slide into Marvin that took them both back to nearly where they'd started. When their momentum gave out and their trip came to a standstill, Grandad had a thought—

"Oh, we fucked…" —and then thought it prudent to clarify: "Christmas-*Kitty*-fucked… 'Bout to be Meow Mix fo' a bitch if we'on't grow some claws and scrape our way outta here…" Both their flames had blown out on their slide, both sliders losing their lighters to swiping hands clutching for a hold. "Lost my damn Zippo… You got yo's?"

After a second or two: "Nah…"

"Well they prolly slid down wit us…" So, they started patting ice-hard ground with gloved hands in search of the only bit of control they might be able to find: Sight. "Goddamn giant snow pussy… The fuck that thing come from, Russia?"

"Jotunheim."

"Huh?"

He wasn't about to explain. "N…never mind…" But it may have helped to pass the time if he *did*. It took several minutes they didn't have to sift through frozen shavings to finally come up with something useful. "Got it!" He sparked the flint immediately, igniting their path, then looked back to be sure Grandad was where he'd left him—

The newly enlightened view produced much more than he'd bargained for.

"Don't…fucking…move…"

The old man hardly had to ask – the breath of the Jólakötturinn became audible without the sounds of their hands sifting through frozen earth – and despite Marvin's words, and the rational judgment to know better, he slowly began to turn, *needing* to lay eyes on what stalked them, if for no other reason than to alleviate the suspense of when it might strike.

It was uncanny how close it'd gotten. Its cobalt snout with gray and white-striped whiskers weren't more than fifteen feet away. Its head low and shoulders cocked to pounce, if it were possible for an animal to smirk under a snarl, this thing looked to be enjoying the helpless countenance of the lubed-up velveteer.

When it took a step closer, clearing half the distance between them, Marvin decided to put his earlier theory back on the drawing board and move himself between his friend and the beast he clearly had some connection with.

Grandad put his arm out to try to stop him but Marvin pushed passed.

"If it wanted to eat me…it woulda already…"

But Grandad had a whole other line of logic picking at his process, and he whispered, "Or it jus' needed time to work up an *appetite*."

The thought almost caused Marvin pause, but he knew it was more than that. It *had* to be…

He slowly raised a hand, inching toward a mouth the size of a beach umbrella. "Hearse said…he bound its soul to Holly's…tha's how it's here…"

"An' you believe that fruitcake?! He nuttier'n'a bag full'a

squirrels!" His inflections were high-strung, but his voice hardly louder than a breath…and Marvin's hand continued on its path.

"M…maybe…they *connected* – it an' Holly. …I mean—" The beast huffed, and Marvin drew back his hand, but only a few inches, still several feet from its icy fangs. "I mean, I think…it knows…who I am…"

"An' how the hell is *pettin'* it gon' stop it from eating me?!"

"Just…don't…move…"

The old guy wasn't as up-to-speed, but remembered Hearse earnestly claiming he wasn't the one who left those heinous death-concoctions at Marvin's home, so started to piece together what the gropy teen was getting at. It made some kind of twisted sense that the bodies may have been left as a show of affection, and some other kind of sense that it was *Holly's* affection that might have shone through. But if that were the case, would it be enough to tame the vengeful Christmas Pussy and save him from becoming Hearse's bloody crumpet?

When Marvin's hand was stretched as far as he could get it, he was still two feet away – giant blue and white lip snarling, crystalline fangs salivating with anticipation – so he swallowed hard and lifted a boot to make his move…only to be swatted from its path like a hamster in a winter coat.

The beast's hooks sliced through several layers of his heavy fabrics, sending him tumbling awkwardly through frigid air until he landed and slid into a wall. But with claws the size of sickles, he was lucky he hadn't been ripped in two.

"Shit-shit-shit…" Shocked eyes followed Marvin's flight until his flame went out in mid-air and once again the cave was swallowed by dark. After Marv met the wall there was only cold blackness and the grumble of the beast – for all Grandad knew, the kid was dead. "Marv, you still wit me?!" He didn't bother keeping his voice down. He got the distinct feeling the beast had no trouble seeing in the dark… But his call was for naught. The only answer he received was a deafening roar that echoed through the cavern and rattled him to the bones…

He didn't move.

As his eyes adjusted, he thought he could make out the silver, elliptical pupils that now consumed the beast's irises whole. They reflected the twinkling minerals and ice in the walls like stars in the slate universe of its eyes, undulating with its slow, forward motion.

"Oh, I know whatchoo want, you big blue-haired Christmas snatch... You want this ol' vet to tuck tail an' run so you could stab me inna back like the evil bitch you are." It growled at his words, still getting closer while he instinctively back-peddled. "But I ain't goin' nowhere, big momma... You jus' gon' have to look me inna *eyes* an' kill me."

From the snarl of the thing, it wasn't likely to have a problem playing by Grandad's rules. Even as dark as it was it was close enough now for him to make out the silhouette of its enormous head mere feet from his. Knowing he couldn't run, and being too damn old to give a shit less about dying today, he reached into his pocket for the wooden cigar case he always kept a freshly rolled blunt in. He knew if he was careful he could manage to finger around inside it for the book of matches he kept and maybe, if time permitted, get a solid puff or two in before the flagrant feline from Jotun-wherever-the-fuck turned him into Christmas mulch.

"Mind if I toke?" He dropped the case on the frozen earth with blunt in-mouth and matchbook in-hand. "Ain't gon' lie..." He struck a phosphorus head to ignite the sulfur and sucked on the blunt's end, fueling the cherry. "...a puff or two could do you as good as it'd do me."

The matchlight illuminated its glasslike fangs, now hardly a foot from his face, and they absorbed the yellow-orange to fill its incisors with the color of fire...until it huffed at his nonchalance and its breath blew out the flame.

"Mmm..." A few more puffs and his cherry crackled and burned with his first pull.

Truth be told, he was surprised he'd made it as far as he had. But why *shouldn't* he die with a blunt in his mouth? He'd handled whatever pasty excrement the world had gone and smeared on his existence gracefully up until now and figured he disserved a moment of tranquility in the end.

"F'real, though..." Red from the glow of his cherry, he exhaled a serene cloud into the salivating pallet menacing him and watched it swirl down its throat. He chuckled lightly when it coughed a little from the burn. "...this that *Cali* crop – shit that Ice Cube an' them be chiefin' on." He shook his head, looking down at his roll, admiring its form. "Them boys got it good, though."

He went for another puff, wondering if he'd get it in-and-out before he'd lose his head, and his eyes wandered into the smoky maw of the death that craved him. Its blue tongue looked purple in the cherry's light, its drooling pallet opening wide as if to taunt him with his ensuing end. He wouldn't allow himself to show fear…but the inimical sight of its teethed throat churning in slow circles, shuffling corpses and ornaments like someone threw a Christmas fiesta inside a giant garbage disposal, wrenched at his composure—

There was an arm with red and green fingernails tangled in a wire of led lights. There was the head of a young woman he'd mingled with on the dancefloor a few nights back; her glitter-pasted cheeks made her gruesome death-cringe twinkle as it turned. There were bloodied, velvet hats and tassels and tinsel and pine. There were meaty stumps with bone fillings, more hands, feet, and Christmas stockings mixing into a chunky stew. He saw a tattered King James bible making its rounds, thorn-like teeth on fleshy conveyer belts in its throat gripping the contents in three circular layers of stirring hellish ingredients…

Its morbidity was hypnotic.

Entranced, he hardly noticed his head was nearly inside its mouth before he caught the soft glow of a distant, jittery light illuminating the ground at his feet.

His eyes squinted, snapping out of his fixation just as the Jólakötturinn turned to investigate. When it saw the silhouette of its master in front of a flashlight, it pivoted so that Grandad could take in a view of Hearse being escorted down the tunnel by Shawn and a loaded shotgun, Hearse's hands bound behind him, hair frazzled and clumped with blood, glasses gone.

"S-*say* it, asshole!" Shawn stabbed the ice-cold barrel into the small of Hearse's back. "Say it!" His grit was commanding, the white cotton ball of a Christmas hat hanging from his coat pocket (a coat that he had reclaimed for himself, leaving Hearse braving the ice-cavern in his tussled, long sleeve, black button-up shirt.).

Hearse weighed his options in his head one last time. It was apparent by his defeated stare the two had already came to an arrangement – Shawn seemingly had him by the "bollocks".

10 Minutes Earlier

With Rudolph broken, maimed, and defeated, picked clean and tossed into a parked SUV like the discarded bones of a very large chicken, its mutilator snarled unappeased and lunged back in through the busted garage door, sniffing and clawing for a more fulfilling *hors d'eouvres*.

Shawn flinched at the *crunch!* of the collision and the shriek of the disemboweled wagon, shivering overtop the twice-laid-out British Grinch at his feet. At a loss for how else to help, fearful that if he did nothing both Marvin and Grandad were as good as regurgitated goo, a plan began to form—

He wasn't sure if he'd find it, or if he could even get that far, but he ran for the upturned Christmas Classic all the same. His knees hit the frozen asphalt when he ducked down to pry inside the wagon's back window (the roof nearer the front being too smashed to squeeze past). Sifting through nudie mags and empty Pabst cans that decorated the ceiling, it wasn't until it was staring right at him, wondering when he'd come to his senses and grab it, that he began questioning if he had the balls to carry out his plan...

His greedy hands swallowed Grandad's indifferent double-barrel and he hugged it close, but stayed on course, knowing now his next step was to tie his soon-to-be bargaining chip up for easier management.

Maneuvering awkwardly – as only a twig-of-kid could – he squeezed back out the way he came and marched forth, eyeballing a segment of Christmas lights he decided he could use for rope. Then the ensuing roar of a very large and irritated feline a dozen yards away, caught in a frustrated bind, rattled his insides so fiercely he nearly vomited a death-shrine of his own...but held in his guts and yanked free a twenty-foot strand, disrupting those bulbs bordering the walkway to the front door.

He didn't have time to mourn the decorum's loss of feng shui. The last time he'd knocked Hearse out cold it only took him half this long to rouse to his feet, so he was somewhat surprised the rangy old lunatic was still clumped in a slumber; and only the tip of the Jólakötturinn's whipping tail was still visible through the garage when he glanced up to check. He got the feeling he didn't have much time to thrice-save-the-day but could hardly stand to incapacitate Hearse before reclaiming what was his.

Shotgun set down beside the propped-up cadaver of a shirtless, frosted stud in velvet boots and boxers with one arm on a giant, makeshift candy cane of human bones, Shawn took to disrobing the dozing villain before binding him, snappily tugging his jacket off his arms and body.

"S-s-steal my g-gear, g-goddamn *Hearse*..." Progress was difficult to come by, and he uttered his enemy's name as if it were a curse to say it aloud. "G-g-*gimme* that shit... F-fuck you think y-you are? P-pickin' onna lil nigga... You kn-knew damn *well* that sh-shit ain't gon' fit..."

When he finally managed to retrieve his stolen threads and had free range to slide on in, he almost lost himself to the warmth already accrued there. He groaned at the sensation, eyes rolling back, and silently hoped he could still feel his hands well enough to pick the shotgun back up off the cement.

And Hearse stirred...

Quickly, Shawn grabbed the strand of lights and started at Hearse's wrists, pulling his arms behind his back and circling them tight. Hearse's skin pinched under the wire and he grunted at the pain. Shawn ignored his complaints and tied a knot, still jittery and shivering but reclaiming control of his faculties. When he had Hearse as secure as he could get him, he stepped back and recovered the weapon, finding the trigger with a thick finger covered in knitted cloth.

Before his captive could regain his bearings, Shawn reached over to the icicle cadaver closest to him and confiscated his Christmas cap. If he was going to get the leverage he planned to, he'd have to have the proper tools to do it.

Cap extended outward like threatening a cooperate saboteur with documented evidence, he waited for Hearse to rustle his way into a seated position, watching him struggle to figure out what was happening with his non-responsive hands. And after mumbling an appropriately British swear, Hearse looked up through sideways eyes at Shawn shivering beside him, fidgety as ever with two barrels bouncing like Mexican jumping beans.

"You see this?!" Shawn waggled the cap in his outstretched grip at his hostage to clarify.

Hearse, groggy and wincing, had a hard time making sense of anything to start. He grunted at the pain in his head and squinted his eyes to focus. "*Hardly*... I've seemed to've misplace my specs—"

"It's a g-goddamn S-S-*Santa* hat, you asshole!"

He tried zeroing in on it again. "So it is… Bravo, young man. You've found a cap. Now be a good lad and untie me, won't you?"

"Sh-sh-shut up, you prick! This shit g-goin' on yo' *head* if Marvin' or Grandad hurt, y-you f-f-feel me? You gon' be d-desert fo' that thing!"

Hearse hesitated…but brushed it off. "Don't be daft. She's my *wife*, for god's sake." He scoffed. "You really haven't thought this through, have you…"

"You wanna take that risk?" His eyes told Hearse he wasn't going to be shook from his place of empowerment. "You either gon' get sh-shot or *ate* if shit don't g-go my way so it's all the s-s-same t-to me."

"If you shoot me, there won't be anything to stop her—"

"Ain't nothin' stoppin' it now!"

Hearse took a second to think it over, then smirked. "And what if I tell you even *I* can't stop her – your only chance is to run?"

"I'd s-say I'ma shoot you inna leg and t-tie yo' ass to a ch-chair with this *hat* strapped to yo' head." Hearse's eyes were still digging around in Shawn's, trying to sniff out a bluff. "That h-how you wannit to go down? 'C-cause one way or another, you gon' get yours. So, you goin' to jail? Or you gon' get shot inna leg an' ate?"

After a long pause, and a sudden lack of ruckus from inside the garage, Hearse's eyes finally broke his stare and he sighed. "Bloody hero now, are we?" He shook his head. "Alright, lad, I'll call her off. I'll stop her from devouring Marvin and this Grandad chap, and you three will be on your merry way. But quickly, whilst I'm still *swooning* over your bravado."

"Nuh-uh. This shit ends here. *Now*."

"And how do you purpose to pull that one off, you sniveling little bleeder?" His tone turned sour – the pressure was getting to him. He was frustrated, tied-up and growing colder by the second. "You must've smoked yourself witless! You really believe you can out smart me? …*Me?!* Rollin-Fucking-Hearse?! …You *do* understand I'm British, don't you?"

"I understand you gon' be *cat* puke or you gon' tell me how to get rid of it."

"Rid of it?" He almost laughed. "You mean send it back to Jotunheim?"

"Nah, I mean buy it a ticket to the Bahamas, asshole…"

"It's bound to her soul, you twit! She's *branded*. Her heart bears the mark of their union – quite *literally*, I'm afraid." Shawn looked lost, so Hearse went on, likely just to bask in the genius of his efforts. "Do you recall that Black Market retainer I spoke of?" Shawn's eyes shifted at the thought. "I had a 'professional associate' put her under to perform the surgery – he split her open and carved the binding sigil into her right atrium. It's positively permanent!" He grew villainous with a confident smirk. "The only way to separate them is to *kill* them. And, quite frankly, as beastly as my lovely wife is feeling at the moment… that's beyond either of us."

"Then h-how you control her?"

"She *adores* me. …Who doesn't?"

"You…you *hypnotized* her…" He was starting to put the pieces together, remembering Hearse's boasting. Hearse didn't validate his statement with a response. "Then you gotta be able to s-snap her out of it – some kinda key word or phrase. Tha-tha's how they do it."

He was noticeably impressed. The boy's brain wasn't entirely baked beyond reasoning. "You really are quite clever, young man. *Stupid*… and likely going to get us all killed…but clever." He decided to recap before they reached an agreement and maneuvered to his feet to do it, towering a good six inches over his captor when he got there. "So, you want me to release the lovely Mrs. Fake Me from her hypnosis so that she's no longer under my spell, and…you think that's going to stop the beast from killing everyone?"

Shawn's eyes turned cold and righteous. "Maybe not *everyone*…"

Hearse mulled it over for a moment, hardly taking notice to Shawn's not-so subtle threat.

"It's a bit of a crap-shoot, I'd say… She may or may not remember anything that's happened over the last several months, including meeting your best chum. She may or may not kill me or save *him*…"

"Move." Shawn was done talking it out. He knew they wouldn't have much time if they still had any at all.

"Easy now, lad… I'm cooperating. I like my chances, really. This is shaping up to be a very stimulating turn of events. How would your generation put it…?" He slipped into his best American internet-nerd accent to cheer, "Best Christmas EVAR!" then laughed while Shawn jabbed him in the back with the shottie.

Now

Carefully navigating the slope, not quite at its steepest grade, Hearse's cowboy boots weren't much help on the freezing cavern floor. Shawn had jabbed him with the double barrel for the fourth or fifth time since he'd agreed to do his part and that last one nearly turned the pretend-Texan to a toboggan. The middle-aged Brit Who Killed Christmas found a touch of surprise at his own hesitation to carry out the command that would snap Holly out of her hypnosis – who's to say what affect it'd have on the beast…?

He slightly tilted his head back toward his captor while eyeing the giant blue blur being illuminated by the soft glow of a flashlight – it had pivoted fully now to face them, leaving Grandad time and space to check on Marvin.

"Are you quite sure about this plan of yours?" Murmuring out the side of his mouth, he thought it only prudent to give the vengeful teen one last shot at thinking it through.

"You could still choose the bullet an' the dunce cap…"

"I'd doubt she'd fancy such a loud bang in her cubby – you?" Eyes slyly surveying the path, he stopped just short of the sudden declivity that sent the two before them on their way into the heart of the monster's cave.

"You don't fess up, we 'bout to find out."

Baiting the young do-gooder, he whined, "This really *is* a terrible id—"

"Fucking Hearse…SAY IT—!"

Thrusting for his sixth jab, Shawn let his impatience get the best of him and Hearse planned to capitalize. He'd gotten a feel for the rhythm Shawn succumbed to when he'd shout the words then jab, so turned just in time to pull the proverbial chair out from under the shotgun causing the teen to fall forward, his footing compromised as Hearse used his back to push the weapon toward the wall. Losing his own footing with the spin, and being on the cusp of the decline, Hearse's feet were taken out from under him and both snow-goers found their asses made for decent sleds over frozen earth.

"SsshhhhhiiilIIIiiiiitt…!"

…And the beast roared.

To the side of the commotion, Grandad made it to Marv and checked for fatal breaks but figured the kid was alright when he started coming to, groggily sitting up. By the time the light of the flashlight described a familiar, panicked descent, Grandad nearly had Marvin to his feet, Marv's arm draped around the old man's shoulders as a crutch.

And on the slope – a clump-of-a-mishap speeding toward crystalline fangs – Shawn topped off a not-so-hot strategy with a shit-I-suck-at-this improvisation by finding the trigger on the shotie and attempting to aim for the mouth waiting to consume it—

KRAKOW!!

He let one loose with hardly an inkling to where it would land and had about as much of a chance of hitting the beast as he did the moon. And with the ear-shattering clamor, Hearse did his damnedest to contort in mid-slide and struggle for control of the weapon, but Shawn's already half-way-firm grip gave him the upper hand.

The next round he let loose blasted into the top of the tunnel and he suffered a shower of bits of ice and frozen mud for the effort. It wasn't until they slammed into the hind leg of the beast in the center of its cavern that a third shot rang out —*KRAKOW!!*— with a robust echo bouncing off the walls and high ceiling.

The beast roared again – an excitable yelp – and bounced off the walls putting some distant between itself and the gratuitous boomstick before it quickly regained its composure and lowered its snout to a crouch that looked eager to spring.

And like a pretzel fighting its own tangled parts, Shawn and Hearse continued to tussle for control, legs kicking, arms and torsos intertwined, jerking while grunting... The flashlight was lost in the struggle but found a spot to settle where it still enlightened the onlookers enough to make out the brawl; their shadows long and deep, stretched up the opposite tunnel.

Grandad made haste to help Marvin scuttle for the exit, but stopped dead in his tracks when his ears caught a sound that was new to their shit-show...

He cocked his head then shifted his eyes toward the cracking and splintering of ice above and quickly realized where that third buckshot had gone...

"Oh, hell nah..." He couldn't see the cavern ceiling with the flashlight laying flat on the ground, but when the sound of lake-water spraying through deepening cracks confirmed they were up shit's creek—

"SHAWN, GETCH'YO ASS UP, NOW!!"

Head snapping at the cry, taking heed to the old man's tone, Shawn let go of the shotgun and climbed over Hearse with a knee in his ribs and foot on his stomach. And with Hearse not making much of a stable path to tromp on, Shawn tripped up and likely jabbed his shell-toe into the villain's groin by the guttural groan of him. Then, shuffling on all fours till he found ground under his treads, he sprang for the uphill climb Grandad was already scrambling toward.

Hearse felt the spray and heard the shattering block of ice but still found time for requite. Hair flattened by the drizzle, eyes thirsty for blood, he barked, *"Drepa!"* toward the frenzied beast – the Icelandic command to kill.

The Jólakötturinn snarled…but found more concern in the sounds of several million gallons of water weighing on an ice cube not more than two feet thick.

When the creature had first burrowed there and turned the earth to its icy cave, it froze the bottom portion of the lake directly above it, but seemingly not all the way through. And Hearse wasn't enough of a nut to risk waiting around to see his enemies die, so darted for the opposite tunnel. But the Yule Cat looked to be more confused than decisive, pacing back and forth, agitated by the falling spray.

Grandad and Marv had already reached the pinnacle of their progress – both on hands and knees, clawing at frosted floor – when Shawn caught up and added his empty efforts to their own. When a chunk of ice the size of a car door broke off and water rushed into the cave by the cubic meters, they hardly even noticed the feisty Christmas Murder-Kitten leap over them and climb out from their predicament. Then another violent *crack!* – like the sound of a tree snapping in two – turned cubic meters to megaliters and the roar of water as thick as slushies drowned their world in frigid dread.

The cavern would be filled in seconds and the pressure-wave overtook them almost instantly. It lifted them from their bellies and spun them on every axis imaginable, flushing them upward like a reverse toilet giving back the turds it'd been forced to swallow; the chill might have stopped their hearts if their adrenaline wasn't already through the roof. Spaghetti limbs flailing helplessly, each took turns bouncing off the tunnel walls without any hope of defending themselves. Ten thrashing seconds of getting firsthand experience of what being human excrement was like, and suddenly they went from shit to projectile vomit when they reached the tunnel's end. They shot out on the far side of the lake through a passage that was slightly downhill of it so enjoyed the full benefits of the laws of physics, flying several dozen feet through the air before they tasted snow and rolled clear of the stream.

Lungs burning, heads swirling, throats gasping... All three men squirmed in fits of coughs and gags, spouting lake water while pressing disfigured snow angels into the ground; they were so damned cold the winter air felt like a blanket over their skin.

Just outside the tree line, Marvin finally settled on his back, gulping at fresh air, staring up into the cloud-covered sky as a crescent moon defeated the gloom and cast its light through the trees. The sound of the lake emptying beside him, thudding against the ground and rushing downhill into a shallow gully, was so loud he couldn't hear anything else. He tried calling Shawn's name; then Grandad's, but could hardly even hear *himself*... So he dug up the strength to roll onto his stomach to survey his surroundings, spotting Shawn collapsed on his side but breathing, then Grandad further up, flat on his back and draining a flask into his gullet that he somehow managed to hold on to through the thick of it all.

Finding the ease to roll back onto his ass, Marvin let out a relieved chuckle. How the mutilated *fuck* they made it out of that cavern alive was mind boggling enough to cause him to choke on his own exhausted bewilderment... Then the realization that somewhere close by stalked a man-devouring beast with a subconscious attachment to him slipped back into the scheme of things and he cautiously sat up, big eyes scanning the trees for those two, much *bigger* icy blues...

The unremitting *thud* of spouting lake water rendered staying quiet and listening a moot advantage, so he scrounged himself from the snow and stood tall enough to see over the spray. Light from the crescent moon cast more shadows than there were trees, and with his jaw chattering and breath steaming, even a ten-foot tall blue beast from Jotunheim was difficult to spot.

Eventually Shawn made his way toward Marvin – the two separated by the running stream between – and called out over the roar. It took him several tries before Marvin heard him; time enough for Grandad to make his way to Shawn, flask in jittery hand.

Marvin gave his two Christmas companions a glance, unwilling to take his eyes off the Uncooperative Unknown hindering his search efforts for too long, and saw Shawn shivering so hard he could hardly complete the gesture to wave him back toward the porno-pad. Feeling bad for the teen popsicle, Grandad paternally reached out to embrace him from behind, but the kid wouldn't have it, shaking the soggy boozer off him like shunning his mother for showing affection in front of the gamer homies.

Marvin seriously wanted to get out of the cold but couldn't bring himself to turn his back on the trees. He didn't know if it was out of fear of being attacked from behind or guilt from abandoning a friend, and the uncertainty brought him pause.

Growing impatient, Grandad and Shawn *both* were hollering over the water flow now – apparently the leathery hide of the old war vet had had its limitations – and they caught Marvin's eye with multiple waving limbs.

Instinctively his head moved in their direction, eyes shifting from shadows to shooting water, and somewhere in between, at the precipice of conscious awareness, a translucent image flickered under the moonlight at his peripheral, several yards past the point where the water slapped at the ground…

And he froze.

Shawn's face had twisted into a dramatically disgusted sneer at Marv's lack of response while Grandad could spell out, "this lil nigga takin' his sweet ass time!" with his eyes. But Marvin only had enough worry to consider what he thought he saw.

Slowly, he turned his trembling jaw downstream to cast his sight toward the dark trees, this time with eyes fixed closer than before, focusing on the empty space fifteen yards from his feet. The image he thought he caught sight of was more like an outline of the beast than the creature itself, as if it were made of ice – like its fangs – and only could be seen when light passed through it.

He strained to focus on nothing, looking for light bending awkwardly or drips falling where they shouldn't and found some…but thought, looking up, that they could be coming from the trees…

He almost hated himself for needing to know… If what he thought he saw was really there, wouldn't he be better off leaving well enough alone and getting his frosted ass back in doors before he started losing irreplaceable extremities? Fingers and toes weren't hard to come by if it came down to it, but losing the Mamba was hardly worth the risk…

Yet…

Knees creaking through the cold, hands reaching for snow, he lowered himself anyway to clutch at a pile by his feet. He collected a baseball-size handful, then straightened back up, ready to throw. His onlookers had gone still, picking up on his intuition. They found themselves gazing in the direction that held Marvin's stare, throats closing at the thought that this freakshow wasn't over.

Blue lips mumbling through tremors, Marvin chanted in a whisper, "Pleasedon'teatme, pleasedon'teatme, pleasedon'teatme…", then cocked back and let loose.

The snow ball sailed mightily with purposeful intent. Bits of itself were lost to its velocity and spin, but its path stayed true. Flying down the mild slope and sailing over the rushing stream, when it got far enough to clear the water's path and then hit ground, Marvin nearly collapsed in relief. It seemed Nothing, in fact, was right where it was supposed to be…

He looked back over to his motley crew, eyes oozing with mitigation—

But his crew's eyes didn't respond in kind.

Grandad's glossy peepers spoke of fear and Shawn's: enervating terror. They seemed fixated on the fallen snow slightly downhill of him, which…hardly made sense… Such fear saturating their eyes could only come from that of the beast, but the beast was a towering threat: ten feet *tall*…

He followed their downward stares to what took him a moment to realize were tracks the size of manholes in the snow. They led from the trees up to mere yards from his toes, and, as they watched, another pressed into the frosty buildup a step closer. Then another, with droplets falling from the thick coat of an unseen giant.

Marvin's eyes found the form of the beast only by the water that laced it and the distortion of the moon's glow when it moved, stepping so slow it seemed to drag the passing of time along with it, bringing everything to a near standstill. When it bled its appearance back into visible light, starting with its slate eyes and cobalt nose, it no longer appeared to harbor the same curiosity it once had – now it just looked *incensed*...

He was out of tricks – a friendly human/monster petting-zoo-moment was off the table. There was nothing up his sleeves but freezing lake water and depleted hopes. Then the beast gnarled with aggravation in its curling lip and murder on its hungry breath...

And Marvin closed his eyes.

His heartbeat seemed to slow to one thunderous percussion per second...

Then it sopped.

What he heard next was so foreign to his ears it was almost angelic. Strange to think such a thing since it was brought to him in the form of Shawn's voice – and even *stranger* that it sounded familiar...

Shawn had somehow mustered the courage to be standing right beside him. It was as if he floated over the turbulence of it all to miraculously appear by his side. When he spoke, the words rolled elegantly off his tongue without being chopped into a half-frozen stutter. And he said them with articulation, and conviction, as if he truly believed they carried the secrets of the universe within—

" 'Love denied...blights the soul we owe to God'."

Marvin felt the warmth of the ballad in his heart when it kick-started it back into rhythm. He didn't know why the words sounded familiar, and he didn't know why they'd come from Shawn's generally bumbling yap... But when he opened his eyes, all ire was drained from the Jólakötturinn's stare and replaced by uncertainty.

Its brow faltered in confusion and it even staggered back, its mountainous shoulders temporarily losing the will to hold it up. Head whipping to-and-fro to rattle away a storm of dismay, it thought to try Pissed on again for size but quickly found it didn't fit.

Its ears folded back, and eyes glazed over, staring at its prey with what almost resembled fear... Then it turned, tail whipping over their heads, and trounced into the trees, seeking solace in reclusion.

Marvin felt its departure like it dragged a piece of him with it, and he reached out as if to stop it before it was gone…

Then he realized what he was doing and lowered his quivering hand.

Shawn – understanding it all now – gave him a moment to adjust before tugging on his jacket to politely suggest retreating to shelter as an alternative to frozen genitals.

Marvin silently agreed.

CHRISTMAS DAY

They couldn't find his body.

Ironic that in a predicament as wrought with corpses as theirs the one they needed to see to believe was nowhere to be found.

The porno-pad sat higher than the lake behind it so the surge of water that pushed through the tunnels barely reached the basement floor. It turned an artistically tasteful sex dungeon into chilly marshlands with less than a foot of water soaking into the carpet, but no cadaver washed ashore. Hearse had either been caught in the cavern, thrown against a wall, or shoved into some crook and drowned, still down below, pruning in ice cold waters, or the wily ol' Brit simply floated to safety and made haste while he still could.

Being two-thirds frozen, drenched, and exhausted beyond imagining, the only other thing on the minds of the Three Amigos after searching for the infamous shit-head was warmth. With their homes nearly a forty-minute drive away, they took advantage of the porno-pad's three full bathrooms, each defrosting under lukewarm waters to slowly regain a body temperature that resembled a living being.

Afterward, the topic of Official Police Involvement inevitably surfaced and each agreed that the last thing they wanted to do was sit in a jail cell for a week while the Law decided if they bought their story. Without Hearse (or his body) to hand over to the authorities, who's to say what conclusion they'd reach? They'd never believe the tale of the Yule Cat and the Limey without undeniable evidence, so it was more likely all fingers would point to them.

No… They weren't about to spend what was left of Christmas in cuffs, trying to convince a squad of regular Joes that a mythical beast that vomits death-shrines decorated the house they were squatting in with the cadavers of the state's most popular porn stars. Or, better yet, that that rascally middle-aged womanizer, Rollin-Fucking-Hearse was behind it all. The only way they'd all agree to testify was if Hearse's body turned up in the aftermath and/or the Yule Cat made a public appearance in all its stealthy winter glory.

Shawn filled Marvin in on what he'd learned about Holly: that she was irreparably bound to the beast against her will and consciously unaware of any of it… But Marvin wasn't sure if that made him feel better or worse. Now, knowing she was innocent, his mind dwelled on what would happen next: Where would she go? What would become of her? Would he ever see her again? Would the killings stop without Hearse demanding his offerings? …Did she even remember…*any* of it? Any of *them*?

The drive home was mostly a quiet one. It was around five in the morning when the boys finally got back to Marvin's. They hijacked a random victim's vehicle to get Grandad home, left the car in the mall lot afterwards (planning ahead to be careful not to leave any prints), then made their way to basecamp where Shawn planned to crash for the remainder of the holiday. If Hearse had accomplished anything, he'd permanently turned the boys off the concept of Christmas. Shawn knew his mom would be peeved that he'd miss their family dinner, but there wasn't a chance in Hell he could be around anyone but his best bruh so soon after what they'd suffered.

Marvin's mom woke them around supper time with marginal Christmas cheer, baby bro in arms, but neither of them could eat. He told her they were sick – and it wasn't a stretch to believe by the looks of them – so they both went back to bed without much hassle.

When midnight reared its sordid head they shuffled around a bit. Two or three b-loads from Marvin the Martian led to microwaved leftover ham with chestnut dressing, coleslaw with bacon bits, about a gallon of water each, and three rounds of Black Ops 4.

Eventually they discovered the need to turn on the news and see what, if anything, was being said about the Corpse Castle they left freezing on the outskirts of Massena. But, as of yet, no report was televised. They figured that, even if the scene had been discovered – and it was likely it had – the local stations decided it to be in bad taste to air the telling of it on Christmas day.

Worry festered like a bad smell in a corner of their minds, but they'd already agreed there were too many people at the house to pinpoint anyone's involvement in the murders – the evidence would just be too superficial. Sure, they could find signs that Marvin and Shawn had been there, but the same could be said for several hundred other people over the past week.

In the end they were too exhausted to dwell, so soon found themselves dragged back into a shallow and angsty unconsciousness.

The longest Christmas in the history of man, they found, would not go quietly into the morn.

DECEMBER 26TH
7:22 PM

It wasn't easy for Grandad to convince the boys to get out of the house. Stipulations were made and, after haggling over specifics, an arrangement agreed upon. Food, inherently, was implied, since they all found it in their best interests to sleep through Christmas and miss out on the traditional feast. But when the question arose, it wasn't a chore for the gang to decide where they wanted to start a reboot of their lives:

Zombie Burger + Drink Lab.

Thirty minutes northeast in downtown Des Moines.

It being horror themed and gore-inspired, Grandad was somewhat surprised the venue was an option. A lesser pair of teens may've entirely lost their taste for comedic morbidity, but Marvin and Shawn didn't blink at the concept of grotesquely sloppy meals and corpse-riddled decor. And having been there himself on a stoned and drunken bender, Grandad could think of no better burger joint to begin making up for what they'd lost.

"Good *lawd*, have mercy on my insides!"

Atop its obsidian gleam, the black dinner plate Grandad slid in front of Shawn harbored an affront to all meals decent. Three, greasy beef patties dripping with white cheddar cheese under a fried egg and bacon merely set the stage for the maple icing and bacon-topped croissant-donut that held it together. No burger had ever been so blatantly ominous... Except for maybe the seasonally-appropriate Krampus burger that Grandad sat down with. Just as many patties under twice as much bacon, fried onion strings, pepper jack cheese, red Chile sauce, and housemade goat Chorizo smothered it all between a pair of buns. Only a meal beyond the confines of mortality could possibly survive such an impetuous and irresponsible design.

Marvin, being a sucker for the classics, couldn't help but go with the Army of Darkness. A horrid mess of Coney chili and cheese whiz topped with a gratuitous spillage of crispy Fritos, this thing was every pot-head's grub-filled dream come true...

"Befo' we get to ruinin' our apatite..." Grandad smushed his Krampus burger into a reasonable *facsimile* of a reasonable meal and skillfully maneuvered it from plate to maw. He knew they'd have to get a few things off their chest and exchange what they'd learned, but it was only human to prioritize, and zombie burgers most definitely came first.

The boys followed his lead, finding their own creative ways to conquer the challenges that lay before them. Marvin discovered his pile of edibles was far too sloppy to eat by hand so took to forking off bites thrice the size of normal ones and shoveling them home.

"Hard to say if this wouldn't be easier to eat with a spoon," he admitted, chili with Fritos plopping off his utensil and back onto the plate.

Shawn had made a civilized attempt at surgical precision and diced his meal into fours. A quarter-slice at a time was nearly manageable, the savory mixture of maple and moist beef fluttering his eyes upon meeting his tongue.

Moaning, smacking, slurping, and groaning was the edacious rhythm of their celebration song. It seemed odd to think it but making it out of last night alive and dropping a deuce in the maniacal workings of a crazed lunatic was a hell of an accomplishment. Despite not feeling up for laughs, they'd agreed they indeed had plenty to be thankful for.

Grandad took a pull from the straw of his spiked Zombie Joe, a coffee inspired ice cream shake with a double-shot of scotch, then muttered, "Now I remember why I'on't come here no mo'..." He belched and raised his half-eaten burger back to his eager lips. "...This place jus' downright deadly!"

A pair of agreeable *Mmhmm*'s hummed through mouthfuls of meaty depravity. None could disagree with the gluttonous bliss they'd immersed themselves in...

But, when it came down to it, everyone knew what topic they wanted to avoid:

Where had Holly ended up in all this?

So Shawn started off on a lighter note.

"My moms said she ain't mad." He wiped his face with his napkin and took a slip of his Tallahassee, referring to him ditching his fam on the big day. "Said I didn't miss nothin' but my sis and her hubby screamin' at they kids."

"You goin' home tonight, then?" Marvin wondered through a bite of meat and chili.

"Fuck nah... They ain't leavin' till tomorrow. I can't be 'round that shit right now – can't be all 'catchin' up' an' shit... My head's still too fulla goddamn Christmas corpses."

Marvin nodded and Grandad chimed in, clearing his throat and taking another pull off his shake:

"You get any calls from work today, Marv?" He was cautious when he asked, knowing what the question entailed.

"I called *them*," he assured him, then drifted into the distance with his heavy-lidded stare. (You could bet your sour taint they all chiefed a robust, mammoth of a blunt on the drive over. No stoner in their easy-baked mind would be caught anywhere *near* sober after what they'd been through.)

"Anybody heard from her?" Grandad noticed Marvin drifting into silence. Apparently he needed a push to continue on the topic.

"Nah... They said she ain't called... But she had the day off. Me an' her *both* did. ...We were 'posed to work together tomorrow night."

"You goin' in?" Shawn asked.

It took him a minute to answer. He could hardly stand the thought of working there without her if she never showed. But if she *did*, after what she'd been through, after her home had been turned into a Christmas cadaver-collage, and she needed a friend...?

"Yeah... I *gotta*. What if she comes in?"

"Like nothin' even happened?" Shawn added.

"They pad already made the news. Seventeen dead so far, and still countin'. I doubt she'd bother tryin' to play that off."

"Hearse said she might not even remember anythin' after the hypnosis broke..."

"If that was the case," Marv surmised, "then she woulda gone home by now an' been held for questioning. News said both her and her hubby are missin'." He shook his head. "Nah... She remembers... That's why she ain't go home."

"What *was* that shit you was sayin' back there, anyhow?" Grandad directed his question to Shawn, remembering the words he spoke that saved all their asses. "Somethin' 'bout 'love denied bites the soul'?" He'd never heard the ballad before, but Marvin had since remembered why it sounded so familiar.

"*Blight's* the soul," Marvin corrected. "It's Shakespeare."

And Shawn added, "From that movie Hearse was in he made us watch, the cocky asshole... I fuckin' *knew* that shit was him! But ain't nobody believe me..."

"That was some powerful shit," Grandad admitted. "I felt them words an' I ain't even *like* poetry."

Marvin poked at his two-thirds of a meal but had already lost the will to attempt to put any more away. It went without saying he'd tried calling Holly's cell and texting her at least a dozen times. Weed and crazy-good grub helped to distract him for a bit, but Distraught once again settled in like a cloud-filled sky. Grandad decided it was time for some good news.

"Seen Kevin at the mall when we was pickin' up our last checks today. Lil' dude was buggin' about the whole shit; askin' if I heard anythin' from the rest'a them peeps that went missin'."

They both were relieved to hear Kevin wasn't one of the stragglers-turned-decorum, but him asking questions made Shawn a little nervous.

"Whatchoo tell 'im?" His eyes tried not to give away his blatant worry.

"That you two buried they bodies inna woods," he offered casually.

Shawn froze at his reply; Marvin hardly even noticed he'd said anything.

A chortle burst from Grandad's saucy lips at the look in Shawn's wide eyes. The poor kid's neck-tendons were so tense they looked ready to snap. "You should see yo' damn face right now, boy..."

Shawn slumped when he realized the old prankster was pulling his leg. "That ain't some shit you fuck *around* about, man!" He kept his voice low, leaning over his two-fourths of a burger like getting closer would cause Grandad to take him more seriously.

The old man snickered instead. "Jus sayin'... Whatchoo think I'ma tell him? I said I ain't heard from *nobody*." He took another bite then eyed Shawn with a hint of authority. "You do like we talked about? ... Call yo' friends an' get them talkin' 'bout Hearse?"

They decided that if they could slyly plant the idea of Hearse being the history-teaching imposter, having people comparing the two faces, they could covertly place some heat on the British movie star.

"Yeah," Shawn nodded. "Hit up three dudes about how the fake Mr. G looked like the dude inna movie we watched. Got 'em buggin' on it. And I made a post on Snapchat, Insta, an' Tumblr with dude's picture sayin' he look like my teacher that's gone missin'. People's talkin'."

It had been all over the news that the missing Clint Greggerson was not, in fact, the local high school teacher, but the owner of Tainted Studios, and that the *teacher* Mr. Greggerson was also missing and was seemingly posing as the local. He'd given the school Greggerson's address but when the connection was made, he obviously wasn't the one whose picture the police had on file. ...It seemed *no* one had a picture of the imposter while in Winterset. His involvement in it all was the very definition of premeditated.

"You look up them anonymous tips, like I said?"

"Yeah." Shawn leaned back in his seat, officially giving up on his meal. "Uploaded that pic of Hearse from the 'Celebs who hate Christmas' article and said he look like the teacher they lookin' fo'." He sighed. "Set my phone to alert me 'bout any news on 'im... Got nothin' so far."

"We on the right track, then. People start talkin' 'bout him, they lookin *out* for him. If he show up anywhere *near* here, he a top suspect. Po-po'll prolly be hittin' up all the usual spots, lookin' fo' a dude who's try'n'a get the fuck outta Dodge." He nodded in confidence. "He gon' get his. They gon' find him and he gon' get what's commin'."

"Unless he dead in them tunnels," Shawn reminded them. "They said they can't troll the lake till after winter. If he down there, we won't know till spring..."

"He ain't down there." Marvin's certainty was disconcerting. "Them basement stairs were *wet* when we came back lookin' for him—"

"Yeah, but," Shawn countered, "like we said: it coulda been melted snow from the busted open pad. That shit was everywhere when we got back."

"Yeah," Marvin agreed, "and none of it was melted."

His rationale caused them all to dwell on the pertinence of it. The wind had kicked up enough powder that night that, by the time they thawed out and went looking, it would have covered any evidence that proved Hearse had walked out of there. He'd had his pick of a dozen cars to escape with; and the boys, regrettably, didn't get a chance to take note of which were there when they were running for their lives. There was no way to know if one was missing. The police would undoubtedly be accounting for the cars of the victims, but they had only just begun to identify anyone and likely wouldn't have a list of names for a week or more. Especially considering the shape some of the bodies were in and what they'd been through. Who's to say what being regurgitated by a beast from another realm into a deathly offering did to a corpse?

Shawn didn't want to bring it up, but the sudden silence was irking him, and the thought on his mind was swelling like a zit on his nose he needed to squeeze.

"You think there gon' be more...offerings?" He figured it was slicker to ask about the possible *outcome* than it was to bring Holly's name into the conversation.

Marvin had already thought it through.

"Christmas is over; ain't nobody dressed up to worship false idols. Hearse said she was trained to kill pretenders: peeps claiming to be someone they ain't. At least tha's what I *think* he was sayin'..."

Shawn almost found some hope in the concept. "So maybe she – *it* – will jus' stay asleep, and Holly will be cool."

"What," Grandad cut in, "till next Christmas?" He put the last few bites of his Krampus burger back on its plate and pushed it away. "You said that thing ain't goin' nowhere until one'a them dies, right? It's bound to her soul? Carved into her heart, or some shit..."

"That...that's what Hearse said... But how *he* know what's gonna happen? Maybe without him pullin' its strings it won't attack *no*-body..."

"Or maybe we got till Halloween befo' bodies start turnin' up dead." Marvin's voice trembled with near anger. "People start dressin' up like who they ain't and maybe she can't control the beast inside."

"Well," Shawn guessed optimistically, "maybe she don't even remember us – or *you* – and she drops the bodies off inna woods or on someone *else's* porch."

Grandad decided to stop them right there. "Ain't no sense in worrying 'bout it till she shows up... Or the *bodies* do..." Taking his own advice, he reached for his Zombie Joe and got back to enjoying the meal. "And now you boys got good ol' Grandad to help out, so you *insurmountably* better off, lil niggas... *Know* that shit."

Shawn *hmphed* in appreciation of Grandad's wry smile, then went on. "One thing I can't figure out, though: Why he pose as our teacher? Why di'n't he just lay low, outta sight till he did his thing?"

"Timing," Marvin offered with a familiar, distant stare. "He got with Holly when he *got* with her... He couldn't choose when the perfect opportunity came 'round. And once he had her he needed her to go about her business like nothin' changed. She thought he was her *husband*, not her master. He couldn't just keep her locked up or some shit. He needed a life to live while he waited for the chance to...I'on't know...kill Christmas."

"An'a married man teaching high school is 'bout as inconspicuous as it get," Grandad added when the thought occurred. "Not like he could work at the Studio where folks knew him. He had to be livin' a life where no one suspected he could be the mass-murdering, Limey Anti-Santa Clause."

"Damn..." Shawn took it all in, letting it writhe around in his mind. "Tha's some twisted, supervillain, *Moriarty* type shit, right there... This fucker had it all planned out."

"Except for love..." Marvin muttered.

"Whatchoo mean?"

He almost felt stupid saying it out loud, but... "Or affection, I guess..." He looked up to Grandad, then over to Shawn next to him. "Tha's what fucked his shit up: he didn't expect her feelin's for me to – I'on't know – *influence* the Jólakö—" he stumbled in its pronunciation. "The *cat* thing..." The guys were starting to take his point. "If me an' her didn't click like we did, it never woulda showed up at my pad, droppin' off them...them bodies..."

"Shit... Yeah... And then we never woulda even found out about Hearse..." Shawn shook his head. "Fuckin' Hearse... That motherfucker jus' put me off Sherlock fo' *good*. I fuckin' *like* Sherlock, man... He a funny ass...like, human unicorn, or some shit. Now'm jus' gon' see Hearse's fuckin' face every time I here that tight-wad English accent..."

Silence again consumed them. Eyes drifted into emptiness.

Children and their families sat quietly at tables nearby, the restaurant environment eerily sedated. It was as if everyone was carefully trying to go about their vacation without mentioning what the season had brought: The festively, mutilated corpses of dozens mere minutes from their homes… So fresh after the big day, it was odd to see the holiday spirit entirely drained from them all. No one wore their fuzzy red hats or ugly Christmas sweaters. No one was smiling and chirping about the gifts they'd received. Not a soul dared to go on celebrating for fear that it might offend the dead.

"I'on't know about you, lil niggas…" Grandad felt it was time to shake things up. "But this *ol'* ass nigga is soberin' up. How 'bout we swing by the Trot, grab us some drinks and some ass, on me."

Oddly enough, the offer wasn't even tempting. Not to either of them.

Shawn spoke up for them both.

"I ain't up for that kinda good time right now, Grandad. Give me a blunt an' a PS4 an' I'm cool."

The old stoner had a hunch that would be the case but felt the need to offer. He looked to Marvin to be sure he felt the same way; Marvin only had eyes for what wasn't there. "New Years, then. Ya'll gon' come out with me if I gotta hogtie yo' skinny asses and po' beers through funnels down yo' throats."

Shawn smiled, *hmphed,* then nodded. "I'on't think it's gon' be that hard to get us inna mood to stare at some ass. But do what you gotta do."

"You know I will, young blood. C'mone, then. I got one rolled for the ride home. Ya'll look like you need it even worse than *I* do."

Ah, the medicinal and temporarily therapeutic qualities of getting baked…

Once home safely and immersed in the stoned roving of Nuketown, firing insurmountable deposits of lead into zombie Nazi ass, the boys were distracted enough at times to chuckle and bait each other, nudge and mock. Momma Jones, Marvin's mother, tried getting her son's attention from the top of the stairs so he'd take out the garbage, but the kid was sucked in deep, all eyes on virtual assault.

Just as well, she figured. Any other day she'd have stomped down there and smacked him in the back of the fade. But she wasn't entirely oblivious to his dejected mood since Christmas. It was likely over some teen tail, she guessed, shaking her head with a partial smile, and decided to let him slide for the night. Once Shawn made his way home in the morning (or what would pass for morning in the eyes of her stoner child) the gloves were coming off. But for now, she'd let them have their "guy time" killing video game zombies.

Baby Chris was properly contained, wrangled within the confines of his play pin, chewing on the plastic lid of a container that had once been home to cottage cheese. The kid loved to chew on soft plastic and was especially fascinated with disk-shaped objects. He had the soul of a UFO enthusiast, this one, and the saucer eyes to match.

It being colder than a penguin's pecker outside, Momma Jones readied herself for the stroll with purple galoshes and a heavy winter coat over her mismatch, flannel pjs. She figured she could make it to the side of the house and back without freezing to death if she didn't trip, fall, and break a hip. It was either that or let the smell of aging ham and baby shit fester in the kitchen until morning...

Bundled up tightly, drooping white bag in hand, she reached for the cold metal door knob and turned. The wind rushing into her home caught her by surprise—

"Whoooo, *lawdy*, tha's chilly!"

Particles of snow swirled into the kitchen and she made haste through the door, yanking it shut behind her. If it weren't for the frigid breeze that whistled through the house and into the basement, nipping at Marvin's neck, he likely wouldn't have been cognizant enough in the seconds that followed to hear his mother scream.

DECEMBER 26TH
10:43 PM

He didn't think to call out when he jumped up, or to arm himself with a bat or golf club on his way. He didn't wonder if Shawn was following behind or if he'd heard the scream too.

He didn't feel the pounding of his feet against the stairs or the pinch of cold on his face when he made it to the back-porch. The only definable thing going through his mind was the words, *please don't be dead, please don't be dead, please don't be dead* in hellish repetition, burrowing into his soul.

He had found a way to cope with what he'd suffered through so far...

He didn't think he could cope with this.

The porch light cast enough of its lackluster glow to illuminate fifty-feet from his home, just past the shed and leading into the trees before the night conquered the manmade photons and swallowed any distant details. Tiny pupils absorbing all the help they could get discovered his mother wasn't anywhere his eyes could see.

"MAAA!!" Voice horsed and panicked, he bolted down the stairs for the open woods wearing only a long sleeve thermal and a pair of joggers to cover his bones – he didn't even have on his boots...

"Mrs. Jones!"

Shawn's voice called out from behind him, but Marvin didn't falter in his tromp through the snow...until—

"Here! M...Marvin, I'm here!"

It came from behind him; to the right of Shawn, on the side of the house – his mother's voice.

Shawn snapped his head toward her call, face smothered by the rush of wind that stung his eyes, and Marvin skidded to a stop in wet socks over cold snow and ran back the way he came. He could see her silhouette in the shadow of their home – standing – moving toward them…

Immediately, relief filled the hole in his heart. If she was walking and talking, then she couldn't be dead. But in an instant his brain flooded with the possibilities of what might've made her scream; what she might have found…

Was it a fresh shrine of mangled corpses left to taunt his complacency? Organs still steaming in the cold and dripping a syrupy, mockery of his life into the snow – Christmas leftovers waiting to be served? Or maybe they dropped a piece of someone when they were hauling away the bodies; a lost organ or limb left to freeze out in the open on the side of their home. That tiny bit of evidence the police needed to connect the whole damn thing to them. The careless mistake that would cost them their freedom and possibly their lives…

"Ey…Eyes…" She finally uttered one word with a blank stare, just now coming into the light.

And Marvin's heartrate once again soared, his temples visibly convulsing.

Shit! … We left someone's eyes! She's gon' call the cops!

"Momma, what?" He tried playing the part of utterly baffled – genuinely confused – and stepped close enough to take her hands in his.

"W-what eyes, Mrs. Jones?" Shawn's throat was closing up on him just as he suspected Marvin's would be, and he swallowed hard, trying not to give anything away in his voice. The same life-ending scenarios ran through his mind as his friend's, with the added detriment of never again *doing it* with a girl…

"…Eyes…g…giant eyes…in them trees…"

Fuck! It's Holly! …She's here!!

His head whipped back around faster than any sane man's would.

What was he going to do? Try to talk the beast down again? Convince his mom to give this giant, otherworldly, man-eating creature a place to stay? Nourish her back to a healthy emotional state and then confess his undying love with a diamond-studded collar?

"Momma, where—?" Quickly he remembered he wasn't supposed to believe in any such things as what his mother was raving about and tried adjusting his demeanor. "What…what do you mean, eyes?"

A trembling hand lifted from his grips and pointed into the shadows of the rustling pines. He strained to find something...but knew she – the beast – could easily hide from their sight if she chose, so the effort would be in vein.

Shawn – heart in his *nasal* passage – cleared his throat and played his part. "It's jus' shadows, Mrs. Jones. Ain't nothin' out there—"

"I know what I *saw*, goddamn it, don't you tell me what I ain't see!"

Gazing hard, examining every branch that moved with the wind, scanning over the snow for evidence of her presence (and finding none), Marvin turned to his mother and backed Shawn's position as best he could.

"Ma... There ain't nothin' out there." He gave the woods another look, hoping to find her, but planning to claim he didn't, regardless. He had to get his mom somewhere where he could deal with Holly without her shrieking in terror. "C'mon inside – it's cold as shit out here."

Her breaths were short and head fidgety, eyes bouncing all over the open wilderness. "I seen eyes, goddamn it! Eyes like you wouldn't believe! As big as...as big as pumpkins! They seen me and they blinked!"

"Ma, c'mon..." Gently, he pulled at her arms; Shawn stood on her left, guiding her homeward by her elbows.

"Damn near fell on my ass when they blinked... They...they was real! As real as the two'a you!"

"It's jus' the wind in them trees, Mrs. Jones. Ain't no monsters out in this cold ass weather."

"Call yo' uncle Ty! Tell 'im, bring his gun!"

"Ma, you need to chill – it's past midnight... Ain't nobody comin' over right now to shoot at monsters—"

"Don't you patronize me, boy! I'll slap the smart right outta you!"

"Okay, ma, jus'...jus' come inside, a'ight?"

They'd made it back to the stairs, helping her climb each step, her knees weak and gait unsteady. Shawn looked back more than once, expecting to see a ten-foot tall, twenty-foot long, salivating monstrosity snarling right behind him, threatening to finish the job it had meant to...

But nothing but the snow on the breeze, catching the sickly light of the porch passed them by.

As soon as they got Momma Jones inside, Marvin quickly geared up for the weather, not bothering to find dry socks, and headed back out despite his mother hollering at him not to. He had to have Shawn stay with her to keep her from coming after him or looking out the door. Shawn was at a loss for how to gracefully go about it, but with her heart speeding and breaths short, she could hardly get up once she'd sat down. And when baby Chris started bawling, Shawn did his part by rescuing the little plastic eater and using him as a distraction, filling his mother's arms with him to ground her in her chair at the kitchen table.

Marvin shut the door behind him and the night seemed to come alive. When before he was too numb to notice, now he felt, heard, and saw everything around him. Every hollow whistle of the wind, every rake of the hickory tree branches against the shed. An owl hooted despite the cold, and the fast-moving clouds spilled pale moonlight between the shadows that moved across the snow.

He tightened his hood around his face and headed for the trees. Being more prepared this time – and more appropriately dressed – he switched on the flashlight he'd grabbed and shone the beam outward, roaming it from right to left. To the right a few hundred feet were the backs of neighboring homes. They made a semicircle around the edge of the woods, fifty feet or so between each, the farthest porch light he could see about a quarter-mile distant.

To his left the woods thickened, pines protruding from a shallow canyon that extended for several miles. He knew damn well he wasn't prepared to hike very far in... He'd hoped he wouldn't have to.

Just past the first pine he saw the prints in the snow: giant tracks made by padded feet that sunk into the soil. He knew he shouldn't... but being as loud as the wind was and as distant as the houses were, he figured it was somewhat safe to try... So he called out:

"Holly!"

He froze to listen for movement but couldn't differentiate the sounds of the woods from what may have been running through them.

"Holly! ...It's...it's okay! You...you can trust me! I wanna help!"

Her tracks were prominent and easy to follow, even in the dark, but the further he went the shallower they became.

He called out again.

Then again…

Calves-deep in fresh powder, nose runny and numb, when the tracks became so faint he could hardly tell if he was still following her trail at all, he looked behind him and realized he'd been walking for so long *his* tracks would be disappearing as well. He grew up in these woods, he knew them well. But it was dark and overgrown, and he couldn't feel his feet or his hands, and his vision was blurred.

Why?

Why come back just to run away? Why wouldn't she let him help her? What…?

What the hell am I supposed to do?

Forty minutes passed, and Shawn was running out of options. Momma Jones had fallen asleep with baby Chris on the couch and Marvin still hadn't come home. Shawn knew that Best Friend Etiquette suggested he go after him but didn't know if that was a reasonable thing to do. What if he was walking right into the same death that took his friend? Marching through frosted Hell only to offer himself as a snack to a Norse god-eating cat from Jotunheim? …*Jotunheim*, for fuck's sake! Beasts from other realms were so far above his paygrade he'd need Loki on retainer just to scoop its shit!

So when the backdoor swung open and his best friend stepped in, dragging only the cold behind, he leapt from the chair he'd slouched in and threw his arms around him.

Other than the cordial embrace they'd normally share as a greeting, with one hand in the other's and a quick arm wrapped around the upper back, this two-handed bearhug was likely their first real *bromantic* entanglement. Out of respect for the moment, Marvin returned the embrace halfheartedly, but, if nothing else, welcomed the gratuitous warmth.

As soon as Shawn realized he was hanging on to his stoner buddy like a five-year-old hugs his dad's leg, he broke the hold and took a step back.

"*Shit*, man!" He tried keeping his voice down, not wanting to wake Momma Jones before they had a chance to talk. "I thought you…" he shook his head. "You—" His eyes snatched a glance over his shoulder to be sure they still had privacy from waking ears. "…You *find* her?"

Marvin's head hung in defeat, body trembling from the residual cold. "Nah, man…" Posture drained of vitality, he shuffled past his friend and into the living room, stopping to appreciate the sight of his mother and baby bro. "She…she gone. …She…" He turned toward the basement, on course for sullen darkness. "…She don't want my help."

EPILOGUE

On December 27th Marvin showed up to work twenty minutes early for the nightshift, tired eyes wide with hope, pink polo tucked into khakis, matching visor embroidered with melting triple-scoop logo tight around head. He didn't think twice about showing up, even after he *did* and found the store closed down. Hand pressed against glass to dull the reflection, he peered hopefully inside, looking for movement – a hidden face in the shadows signaling him around back…

But the parlor was empty.

Desolate.

Dark.

He went back home shortly after.

On New Year's Eve Grandad did his damnedest to raise spirits byway of exploiting teen hormones and managed to get a few laughs out of Shawn at the Fox Trot. Marvin tagged along for appearances but was hardly there in heart.

As was with most "emotionally unavailable" guys, Big Bry's salacious ex couldn't seem to get enough of him, and he enjoyed the thrill of her shadowy figure and catlike prowess. He played his role so well she took him home with her – the chance of a lifetime – but under the guise of it being "awkward" because of his friendship with Bry, he talked his way out of getting laid, crashed on her couch, and soulfully regretted it clear through morning. She politely tempted him the next day by letting him know she was getting in the shower, but, knowing if he'd gone through with it there would be strings he-wasn't-in-a-position-to-strum attached, he just choked down his coffee (when his face *wasn't* buried in his palms) and patiently waited for a ride home. She wore her disappointment with playfully sad eyes but knew not to take it personally.

With all the chatter Shawn had roused about Hearse, an investigation was quietly launched. On January 3rd the local PD made inquiries into his whereabouts and found him alive and well, his alibi unshakeable. He had been in "Morocco" over Christmas Day hosting a charity that raised awareness for rural inequity. The photos were made public online through the CARE foundation – photos of which were questionable at best but coupled with reservations and donations with his signature on them, couldn't be refuted. The wily "limey" villain remained irrepressibly at large and as gut-wrenchingly charming as ever.

Shawn stewed over it, as did Marvin for a time, but Hearse's apprehension was not what plagued him, and Shawn wasn't going to dwell much beyond a third blunt.

On January 7th school resumed, and aside for a week of gossip concerning the missing Shandra and Yvonne, things slowly returned to normal, with the exception of the boys having seemingly aged a decade in maturity over the break. Both having had a dose of fucked-beyond-belief, in appreciation of making it out alive, they pursued the oncoming challenges of life with inspiration and ease.

On January 12th Marvin aspired for utter sobriety, looking to raise the stakes on his newfound, personal growth.

On January 17th he got baked beyond recognition.

Shawn refused to endure any of the responsibility for his friend's "relapse". He did, however, bake the brownies and supply the dabs.

February 14th was a day to remember, but altogether uneventful in comparison to the previous holiday the "bruhs" had endured. They could only hope that their next shared V-day would be as commercially typical.

And on April 20th, the night before Easter, the absurd once again perturbed the lives of Winterset's most high.

Bodies falling in their wake, the boys reluctantly discovered that the Easter Bunny, contrary to popular belief, was not one to be fucked with.

FINIS

AFTERWORD

Congrats on making it out of that mess alive! How about that twist, huh? With the (SPOILER ALERT) Yule Cat? (If you say you saw that coming you're a lying sack of dirty weed stems and seeds: nobody's buying that shit.) When I came across the myth of the thing I figured someone had to be the one to try to make something of it. I took some liberties, of course, and threw in the whole "Norse" angle with it being from Jotunheim; that was entirely fabricated. And, yes, I took some liberties with the city of Winterset, as well. I've never been there so don't know how far from the reality of it I swayed, but the details of its locale were in no way detrimental to the story. I doubt the little city has an indoor mall – shit… It might not even have a strip club – but, with any luck, if this story gets the attention I believe it deserves, maybe it will inspire the small town to live up to its newfound popularity. -insert overly enthused emoji here-

So it occurred to me, about halfway through this misadventure when discovering I was having a blast living through my boys, Shawn and Marv, that, if my imagination serves, I can cook up a string of kooky holiday plights of a similar like and try to bang out a goofy new horror tale a year. As you can probably guess from the ending, my sights are on a deliciously morbid Easter next, so keep your glossy peepers marginally open for more of these two dudes to come. There's no telling if my hopes for an annual release is a feasible timetable – I'm still very much new at all this. But, with any luck, Easter 2020 will be an especially gory one indeed.

Look for my author name on all your favorite social media hangouts to get in the know and stay updated. And thanks again for supporting an independent creator and his outlandish scribblings. You could likely inscribe "He did it for the lulz" on my tombstone and not be far off, but the cheddar doesn't hurt either.

-CM

www.ingramcontent.com/pod-product-compliance
Lightning Source LLC
Chambersburg PA
CBHW031948170626
46807CB00006B/2403